Monkie Business

Debbie Thomas

Illustrated by Stella Macdonald

MERCIER PRESS

IRISH PUBLISHER – IRISH STORY

MERCIER PRESS
Cork
www.mercierpress.ie

ISBN: 978 1 78117 170 7

10 9 8 7 6 5 4 3 2 1

Printed and bound in the EU.

Praise for the first two books in the series:

Dead Hairy

'We love *Dead Hairy*!' *Woman's Way* – recommended as part of their 'Bring Back Books' campaign

'… extremely well written – immediate, clever, smartalecky … immensely enjoyable.' *The Irish Catholic*

'… romps … with exuberance and sparkling dialogue …' Mary Arrigan, *Irish Examiner*

… great fun, loaded with laughs … this one is a pure delight.' *Fallen Star Stories*

'I can't recommend it highly enough. I think it's a brilliant book. I was roaring laughing at the first couple of pages.' Brendan Nolan, radio presenter and author of *Telling Tales*

Jungle Tangle

'Hysterical … fantastic characters … utterly delightful, laugh-out-loud funny and leaves the reader wanting more.' *Inis* magazine

'Bonkers humour, a plethora of quirky characters and snappy dialogue. Terrific fun.' *Recommended Reads*, Children's Book Festival 2013

'Weird and wonderful …' *Evening Echo*

For Stevie and Jobe,
my walking generosities

'For where your treasure is, there your heart will be also.'

Jesus (yes, that one)

MEET THE CREW

The Hartleys

Abbie

Grumpy
(ex-Squashy)
Grandma

Little bro Ollie

Dad Graham,
history nerd

Mum Sadie,
ex-fusspot

The Platts

Perdita

Mum Coriander,
hairdresser & world explorer

Dad Matt, Very Odd
Job man & inventor

The Camping Companions

Mr Dabbings,
teacher and
nature-lover

Marcus

Terrifica

Ursula

Chester, a shy
patch of chest hair

The Crook

Henry

Dr Hubris Klench,
burger-on-legs
& super-baddie

Prologue

Is there anywhere left to hide these days? You can dive the oceans on YouTube. You can Google-Earth Guyana. You can Skype your mum in Mumbai, text your Trini-dad and email Aunt Arctica.

The hidey-holes are vanishing. The world is baring its knickers.

But one place remains tucked away. A place where creepers trail and phone lines fail. Where jaguars prowl and Simon doesn't Cowell. The Amazon jungle, deep and dark, still hides a secret or two.

Both of those secrets were sitting in the ruins of an ancient palace. The first, on a throne of crumbling stone, was poking a snake that lay coiled in his lap. It whipped up and bit his arm. He rubbed in the deadly venom.

The second, at the foot of the throne, shook his head. 'It won't work, O Mighty Radiance.' (A rough translation of the ancient Quechua language he spoke.)

The Mighty Radiance sighed. Flakes of dandruff fell from his head like exhausted moths. 'Gotta keep trying, Bacpac.' (Another rough translation.)

'But you know the deal, O Orb of Awesomeness.

Remember the potion you drank on your father's death, and the prophecy spoken by Wiseman Wonco, all those years ago?'

The Orb of Awesomeness frowned. 'Run it by me again. My reading's not what it used to be.'

Bacpac nodded sympathetically. 'Hardly surprising, O Ruler of the Known World and Pencil Case of the Unknown. You're an old man.' He didn't point out that his master had never been able to read the quipu, the knotted ropes used by the Inca people more than four centuries ago to record events. That, in truth, Chunca Inca wasn't the smartest emperor on the block.

Bacpac stood up and crossed the ancient flagstones of the throne room. A curtain hung in the doorway, made of dangling knotted vines. His fingers ran down each vine, pausing at the knots.

He took a deep breath. Titles were a big deal in Inca poetry. 'The Prophecy of Wonco the Wise at the Deathbed of Tupac Inca, Son of the Sun God, Lord of the Heavens, Master of the Mountains, King of the Rainforest and All-Round Super-Inca, on His Defeat by Spanish Conquistadores.' His fingers felt more knots.

'O Mighty Tupac, you've been thrashed,
Your people killed, your Empire smashed.
But don't despair: those rotten Spanish
Cannot make your kingdom vanish.

Get your son to drink this brew
And he'll outlive the whole damn crew.
Hidden under jungle sky
Chunca here need never die.'

'Yeah, yeah.' Chunca waved a hand dismissively. 'It's the last bit I'm interested in.'

Sighing, Bacpac continued:

'Only if the stoutest crook
Who ever trod this jungle nook
Takes his hand and holds it fast
Will your Chunca breathe his last.'

Bacpac stopped. That wasn't actually the end of the prophecy. Out of love and loyalty he'd never read out the last few knots, which weren't the most flattering.

P.S. Just a tip for you:
Get a slave to drink it too.
Chunca's not exactly clever –
He'll need help to live forever.

Chunca sank back. 'I don't get it.' He stroked the snake who'd nodded off in his lap. 'I thought these guys were supposed to be the biggest crooks in the jungle – all that hissing and slithering. So why doesn't their poison work on me?'

'Due respect, your Superbness, but the prophecy says "*stoutest*". Snakes tend to be pretty skinny. Plus, they might take your hand in their mouth, but only for a nip. That's hardly holding it fast.'

'Alright, smarty-sandals. Who *is* the stoutest crook, then?' Chunca stamped his royal foot. 'I'm bored of this life. I want to go up to the Great Golden Palace in the sky.' He pointed through a hole in the roof, where a hazy sun was struggling through the trees. 'In a nutshell, Baccers, it's time to die. At my age, is that too much to ask?' He pulled off his headdress – a red turban with feathers stuck in the folds – and hurled it across the room. 'I've had enough, Bac me old Pac!' He smacked the arm of his throne. 'Let's go and find that stoutest crook so I can breathe my last.'

'But your Fantasticness–'

'No buts. That's an order.'

Bacpac bit his lip. He'd served his emperor for four hundred and fifty years in this once-magnificent city where the Incas had made their last stand against the Spanish. While temples and houses crumbled around them, Bacpac and Chunca had lived on in the ruined palace. Every day, while vines intruded and roots protruded, the servant had collected food, cooked Chunca's meals, polished his earrings and read him bedtime knots. And now the Emperor wanted out. What to do?

It was Bacpac's duty as a slave to grant his master's wish. But it was his duty as an Inca to preserve the royal line.

A tear trickled down his cheek. The Emp's happiness was the most important thing. He bowed in the doorway. 'Your wish is my command, O Sapa Inca, Unique One.'

Chunca leapt from the throne. Apart from his dandruff and a little stiffness in the joints, he was astonishingly well preserved. Thanks to the elixir and the humidity of the jungle he looked a sprightly seventy-five, a sixth of his age. And Bacpac's attentions had left him plump and soft-skinned, a stranger to hard work. 'Cheers, Baccy. Knew you'd understand.'

Considering how long they'd lived in the palace, it didn't take long to pack. Twenty minutes later they were stepping through the doorway for the very last time. Bacpac led the way. He wore sandals and a loincloth. Apart from a slight stoop, his small, wiry body was also in splendid shape. On his back he carried – you guessed it – a backpack. Inside were two brightly woven cloaks and Chunca's jewellery box containing a spare pair of golden earrings, a few golden brooches and a bracelet or two. In his hand he carried an axe.

Behind him came Chunca, looking more like a parrot than a pensioner with his orange tunic, bright red cloak and feathered headdress, not to mention the huge golden discs in his earlobes. On his back he carried – you guessed it – nothing. In his hand he carried a fan.

'Farewell, city of our forefathers,' said Bacpac as he stepped over the last crumbling wall of the city.

'Good riddance, you old ruin,' yelled Chunca.

For three hours they hacked their way through jungle along the edge of a narrow river. Well, Bacpac hacked while the Emperor stuck out his hand towards every stout creature he saw. 'Bite me,' he ordered a hairy pig. It waddled off in alarm. 'Dinner time,' he tried to convince a jaguar that yawned from a branch.

On they struggled until the servant stopped abruptly. 'Look.'

Chunca crashed into Bacpac's backpack. 'What?'

'Smoke. There's a village. Perhaps they can help us. But let me do the talking, O Son of the Son of the Sun.'

They entered a clearing where ten earthen huts with thatched roofs stood in a circle. Two naked children squealed and ran into a hut. A young man came out. He wore a shirt, frayed trousers and Nike trainers. His eyebrows rose at the sight of the odd couple.

'How dare you look me in the eye?' boomed Chunca. 'My granddad's the Sun, you know.'

Bacpac winced.

The young man looked unimpressed. 'What can I do

for you?' he said in modern Quechua, which had changed so little over four and a half centuries that even the Emp understood him.

'Kneel, for starters. I am Chunca Inca, last living ruler of the Inca Empire. This is Bacpac Snacpac, last living subject. We are both in our mid-four hundreds and wish to die. Arrange it.'

Bacpac sighed. 'I asked you to keep quiet, O Grandson of the Sun.' He smiled apologetically at the young man. 'My master doesn't get out much. He means no harm. Now he's spilled the beans, perhaps I should explain.'

The young man nodded. 'I've just put the pot on. Come and meet my uncle while I make some yuca tea.'

Half an hour later Chunca and Bacpac were sitting on a log in the clearing. The uncle sat cross-legged in front of them, his eyes closed. The whole village – men, women and children – crowded behind him, silent and wide-eyed.

At last the uncle opened an eye. 'Their story is true,' he said. 'I feel it in my kidneys. My father told me the legend of the lost Inca emperor. His father told him, whose father told him, whose father … you get the picture. The forest is full of magic. It is no harder to believe in this eternal elixir than it is in, say, anteaters. I mean those noses – have you ever seen anything so weird?' An anteater snuffling in the undergrowth burst into tears and ran off to look up plastic surgeons in the jungle *Yellow Pages*.

'Wow,' said the crowd, and got down on its eighty-six knees before the Emperor.

Chunca beamed. 'That's more like it. Now, here's the gig. We have to find the stoutest crook. Any suggestions?'

'Him,' squealed a little boy pointing at his brother.

The Emperor hooted. 'No seriously, guys.'

The young man looked at his uncle. 'Actually,' he said, 'we know the very man.'

The Emperor leaned forward. 'I'm all ears. Well mostly earrings with bits of ear round them.'

The young man cleared his throat. 'My name is Quempo. A few months ago I worked in a hotel near here. For a foreigner. The stoutest and crookedest ever.'

Quempo's uncle spat on the ground. 'He stole from the jungle. He nearly destroyed our village. He …' the old man jabbed an outraged finger, 'he ate a *bun* in front of our hungry children.'

'Wait.' Quempo ran into his hut. He ran out again clutching a book. 'Are you sitting comfortably? Then I'll begin.'

As the sun sank behind the trees, Quempo read the Quechua translation of *Jungle Tangle* (the prequel to this story. If you haven't read it, you'd better, so that you can answer the following exam question: *If Chunca, Bacpac and half the villagers listened enthralled, while the other half yawned and picked their noses, which half was correct?*).

When Quempo had finished, there was a long silence,

16

broken only by the rustle of a million soldier ants putting on six million bedsocks.

Finally Bacpac said, 'So now, you say, the stoutest crook is in England?'

Chunca leapt up from the log. 'Incaland? You mean there's a country where my kingdom lives on?'

Quempo laid a hand on his arm. 'No. *England* is far away, across a huge river called Ocean. To get there you must travel to a big city called Quito and climb into a huge metal parrot called Plane. But first you've got some work to do.'

Chunca frowned. 'I've never lifted a finger. It's one of the perks of dictatorship.'

Quempo grinned. 'No fingers needed. Just ears.' He ran into his hut and came out carrying a black box. 'This is called a radio,' he said. 'I brought it from the hotel when I left.' He pressed a button on the side. There was a sniffing sound. Chunca backed away.

'Relax,' laughed Quempo. 'It's just modern magic.' He twiddled a knob. The Incas squealed as the box cleared its throat. Quempo put a finger to his lips.

'BBC World Service,' said the box in English. 'And now our restaurant drama for language students: "Eat Your Words".'

The Incas sat back for their first English lesson.

1
~

The Call of Nature

'Remarkable,' said Mr Dabbings. 'Quite remarkable.' He patted the exercise books on his desk. 'An amazing effort all round, kids. But three poems especially impressed me.'

Mine, thought Abbie. *Please mine.*

The teacher looked round the class. 'Rukia, Marcus and Henry. Please come out and read your Nature poems.'

Mean, thought Abbie. *He's mean.* Dabbers never chose her. She never impressed. She was useless ... pointless ... an odd sock in the washing basket of life.

The chosen children strutted to the front. With a smile as neat as an envelope Rukia Zukia took her book. 'Walk in a Field,' she began.

'Dandelions sprinkle the air with soft down,
Cow pats sit everywhere, crusty and brown.
Brambles all tangle and mangle my dress.
Nature, I hate you, you make such a mess.'

Mr Dabbings nodded. 'Thanks Rukia. Marcus?'

Marcus Strodboil cleared his throat. 'Bee. A bee does nothing but trouble you. Unless it's a BMW.'

'Well read, Marcus. And finally, Henry.'

Henry Holler took a deep breath. 'Rock,' he shouted, 'you ROCK!'

'Good expression, Henry. Thanks kids, you can all sit down.' As they swaggered back to their desks, Mr Dabbings ran his fingers through his golden curls. 'Those poems spoke to me, boys and boyettes. And do you know what they said?'

'Ouch!' squealed Ursula Slightly, a tiny, pale girl, as Henry passed her desk and pulled her ponytail.

'No, Ursula. They said, "Oh dear. We are written by children who are blind to the beauty of Nature. Children who wouldn't feel the peace of a sunset if it punched them on the nose."'

Ursula ducked as Henry tried to punch *her* on the nose.

'Do stop fidgeting, Ursula. Now, where was I? Oh yes. In a nutshell, kids, those poems upset me.' Mr Dabbings sighed while Marcus scowled at the floor, Rukia sharpened an already sharp pencil and Abbie decided that not impressing had its plus side. 'But guess what.' The teacher winked. 'A little bird gave me an idea. A darling little bird, with hair like corn and eyes like chutney.'

Abbie looked at her best friend and rolled her eyes. After four months of marriage Mr Dabbings was still as soppy as soup over his wife Wendy. Her best friend giggled till her three plaits wiggled.

Abbie grinned. What would she do without Perdita Platt? With her crazy hairstyle and even crazier home life, Perdita was another odd sock in life's washing basket. The difference was that she didn't care. And being around her made Abbie care less too.

'A holiday!' Mr Dabbings clapped his hands. 'Yes folks – Mrs Dabbings suggested a field trip for the class.'

Gasps went round. 'Wow.'

'Cool!'

'Barbados?'

'Las Vegas!'

Mr Dabbings reached behind his desk. He brought out a tube, unrolled it and stuck it to the wall with Blu-Tack. It was a map of Northern Europe. He took a knitting needle from his desk and pointed. 'Where's that?'

'Ireland,' said Perdita.

'Correct.' The needle moved left. 'And that?'

'The Atlantic Ocean,' said Marcus.

'No, I mean that dot *in* the ocean.'

'America,' said Craig Nibbles, who wasn't the sharpest crisp in the packet.

'A squashed hff … ant,' said Barry (a.k.a. Snorty) Poff through his permanently blocked nose.

Mr Dabbings frowned. 'We don't squash ants, Snort–,

um, Barry. We hug them. No, this,' he tapped the dot, 'is Remote Ken.'

'Who?'

'Not who, Abigail, *what*. Remote Ken is a tiny island. Most people haven't even heard of it. Which makes it perfect.'

'For what?'

'Not what, Abigail, *who*. For us. To go there and make friends with Nature.'

Abbie pictured the teacher high-fiving a daffodil.

Questions flew. 'What's the hotel like?'

'Is there a jacuzzi?'

'Sky Plus?'

'Whoaa!' Mr Dabbings held up a hand like a policeman stopping traffic. 'Everything's explained here.' He waved a piece of paper. 'Give this to your parents tonight.' He strode round the room, throwing a letter on each desk and breathing deeply, as if already hiking over hill and dale.

Abbie read the note.

Dear Dads and Daddellas,

The class is invited on an Easter field trip to the island of Remote Ken. We'll be spending ten nights in self-catering cottages, enjoying the wonders of Nature. Parental volunteers are required to come and help supervise the children. Everyone must bring a sleeping bag and clothes that harmonise with the natural world.

Abbie imagined a T-shirt singing duets with a tree.

I give/do not give permission for _____
(name of child) to embrace the earth and rejoice
in rain.

I am happy/not happy to come along and lend a
hand because that's what hands are for.

Signed _____ (parent or guardian)

Abbie wrinkled her nose. *Earth plus rain equals mud*, she
thought. *And self-catering's just a sneaky way of saying
washing up.* She scrunched the letter into a ball.

Perdita frowned. 'What are you doing?'

'Cold, wet, miles from anywhere?' Abbie shuddered.
'No thanks.'

'But we trekked through the Amazon jungle last term.
You can't get more miles from anywhere than that.'

'Those were hot miles. Exciting miles.'

Perdita thumped her arm. 'Oh come on,' she laughed,
'don't be such a stick-in-the-mud.'

'That's what I'm worried about.' Abbie pictured her head
poking up from a bog.

'Hey, I thought you wanted to be a journalist.' Perdita
took the scrunched-up letter and smoothed it out. 'Where's
your sense of adventure?'

Curled up under the duvet eating Jaffa Cakes, thought

Abbie. But she couldn't admit that to Perdita. Sighing, she dropped the letter into her bag. There was only one thing wrong with brilliant friends who loved any adventure. They loved *any* adventure.

Mr Dabbings returned to his desk. 'Letters back tomorrow, please. We break up next week so I need to start organising.' He wrote a number on the board. 'If your parents have any questions they can ring me tonight. But not after nine. That's Buddleia's bedtime.'

A snigger went round. Mr Dabbings's baby wasn't due till October. But he'd told the children how, every night, he sang his wife's stomach to sleep while she played the triangle.

'Now, back to work everyone.' The teacher held up a ball of wool. 'Needles out. We're going to knit babygros.'

At lunchtime Abbie sat with Perdita and Claire.

Marcus came over to their table. 'Who's on for this trip, then?' He sat down next to Abbie.

'Not me.' She opened her lunch box. 'Sounds grim.' Which went for her lunch, too. Oil had leaked from the tuna wrap Mum had packed. Her apple was slimy, her biscuit mushy.

'Yeah,' said Marcus. 'I mean – of all the places to choose.' He held out his crisp bag to Abbie.

'Thanks.' She took five. It was amazing what they agreed on these days. You'd almost think they were friends. What a change from last term, when Marcus had done everything he could to ruin her life. But after she'd stood up to his bullying dad, Marcus had begun to treat her with respect. He'd even kicked the football to her three and a half times this term.

Which was three and a half times more than to Perdita. Marcus still couldn't stand her. Or rather he couldn't stand the way she beat him in maths tests.

Not that Perdita needed his friendship. Her kindness and sense of fun, and the amazing zoo where she lived, had made her top of the pops with the rest of the class. 'Well I'm definitely going,' she said. 'How about you Claire?'

Claire Bristles nodded so hard her fringe bounced. 'I'd love to.'

'Yess!' Perdita smacked the table. 'Hey, do you want to share a cottage?'

'I'd *love* to.'

A needle twisted in Abbie's chest: a tiny wire of pain.

'Done.' Perdita grabbed Claire's hand and pumped it up and down.

The pain sank to an ache in Abbie's stomach.

'Let's seal the deal.' Perdita took a pot from her lunch box. 'Dad's latest invention – blackcurrant hair gelly. Fizzes the tongue and whizzes the fringe.' Unscrewing the lid, she passed it to Claire who dipped in her finger and licked it.

'Wahay!' Claire's fringe flew in all directions.

Abbie scowled. 'I thought I was the whacky snack taster.'

'Go ahead.' Perdita passed her the pot.

But Abbie didn't feel like whizzing. Didn't Perdita care that she wasn't going? *Maybe I should go,* she thought, biting into soggy wrap, *just to remind her who's her best friend.* But what if it didn't? What if there were only two people per cottage and Perdita still wanted to share with Claire? What if they ignored Abbie all holiday? What if, when they got back, Perdita wanted to go and sit by Claire, and they never spoke to Abbie again, and no one else did either, and she grew up alone and misunderstood and ended up living in a lighthouse with only seagulls for company, and even they ignored her, and she died of loneliness and an overdose of herring?

Abbie put her head in her hands. There was only one thing wrong with brilliant friends who liked everyone.

They liked *everyone.*

***

The bus wheezed into Quito. Pulling into the city's central station, it burped to a halt. Passengers stumbled off, yawning and stretching after the six-hour journey that had shunted them up from the Amazon jungle to the capital of Ecuador, perched high in the Andes mountains.

Last to climb off were three men. You'd never guess that the two older ones, who looked in their spry mid-seventies, were actually in their *incredibly* spry mid-four hundreds. They wore flowery shirts, jeans and baseball caps. Behind them came a much younger man, who'd insisted on buying these modern clothes to avoid attracting attention. Imagine the fuss if the papers got wind of an ancient emperor and his sidekick turning up alive and well in Quito.

Chunca Inca blinked in the sunlight. 'Blimey. Can't see a thing.' Shielding his eyes he looked up at the sky. 'Hey, Granddad, turn it down.'

The sun blazed even brighter, as if annoyed by his cheek.

The young man took off his sunglasses. 'Here, try these. The light's much stronger in the mountains.'

'Cheers, Quempo me lad.' The Emperor hooked the shades over his ears. Well, they were more holes than ears, thanks to the whopping golden discs which had filled them till yesterday. 'How about you, Bacpac?'

The old servant bowed. 'My eyes are used to your radiance, O Dazzling One. A little extra sunlight makes no difference.' (Which was a noble lie. When the Emperor turned away, Bacpac pulled down the rim of his baseball cap.)

The Incas gazed in wonder at the bustling streets: the shouting people, the strange signs and, above all, the shiny boxes on circular legs, rushing along and honking like a herd of hairless llamas.

Chunca whistled. 'Quite a kingdom you've got here.' He slapped Quempo on the back. 'Where to, laddie?'

'A gold dealer's. You need to sell some of your jewellery before you go anywhere. I have a friend who can rustle up some passports and visas for a not-so-small fee. Then on to a travel agent to buy your tickets.'

Chunca frowned. 'Run it by me again, dude – what are they for?'

Quempo sighed. How many times did he have to explain to this right royal thicko? 'For catching the plane to England and finding that stoutest crook.'

***

28

Who, at that very moment, was parting his lemon hair with a comb. Dr Hubris Wildebeest Klench, super-baddie and flabster supreme, looked in the mirror. He sucked in his cheeks. *Not so bads*, he thought, *considerink I am in cell in Bradleigh Prison and haff vay little chances for exercice.*

'Don't fool yourself, kid,' hissed a voice in his brain. Oh no. Inner Mummy had woken up from her nap. 'Sucking ins von't hide your chins.'

Klench took a deep breath. He was slowly learning to stand up to the dead parent who lived on in his mind. 'Who cares, Mums?' he said quietly. 'I know a voman who likes my chins and forgives my sins.' He smiled at the thought of the old lady who, on her weekly prison visits, was teaching him to break free from Mummy's wicked influence. Funny really, considering that she was the grandmother of Abigail Hartley, the very girl who'd brought about his arrest in the Amazon jungle last Christmas.

As usual, Inner Mummy did her best to squash Klench's affection for Grandma. 'Don't be lummock,' she snapped. 'Who could stomach your vast stomach?'

Klench gasped. Mummy, who so loved to rhyme, had repeated a word! Was she finally losing her touch and loosening her grip on his brain? A spark of hope lit up in his heart.

2

History and Hogwash

'Course,' said Mum, washing up that evening, 'you know why Wendy suggested this trip.'

'Why?' Abbie was at the kitchen table, frowning over her maths homework.

Question 5: After 3 months, what fraction of Baby is formed?

'To get rid of Mr Dabbings. She needs a bit of space.'

'Jumpin' Jemimas,' said Grandma, 'they've only been married five minutes.' She was drying up. Well actually, she was holding a plate while Chester wriggled over it. The shy patch of chest hair worked very hard as her wig and home help. Now he flew over to Abbie, grabbed her pencil and wrote '⅓' next to Question 5.

'Thanks Chess.' Abbie tickled him. 'I wonder *which* third. Head and shoulders? Tum to bum?' Chester shrugged and flew back to Grandma.

Mum pulled off her rubber gloves. 'Well, I know how Wendy feels. She wants some time to get things ready for the baby, have a good polish, without Branston breathing all over the place.'

Grandma grunted. 'She should've married a spoon. No breathin', and the silver comes up lovely.'

Mum laughed. 'Don't get me wrong. She loves him to bits. It's just that she wants everything to sparkle when the baby comes. And she says it's a chance for Branston to enjoy his precious Nature. He won't be doing much hiking after the birth.'

'But it's not due for six months.' Abbie shut her book. 'And just because Mr Dabbings wants to wade through mud, why do *we* have to?'

'You don't. No one's making you go. If you ask me, it's a no brainer.' Mum shuddered. 'Rejoice in rain, indeed. Get the note and we'll write a big No.'

Abbie nodded. She'd shown them Mr Dabbings's letter at dinner. Dad had taken it to his study, saying he wanted to check something.

She went into the hall. Running her fingers along the wall, she told herself she was glad. But her stomach was filling with cement. Scenes flashed across her mind. Claire and Perdita paddling in streams. Perdita and Claire singing round camp fires. Pillow fighting, midnight feasting. Fizzing and whizzing through a whole soggy week, without even mentioning her name.

Dad was sitting at his desk, thumbing through a book.

Mr Dabbings's letter lay on his lap. He turned and grinned at Abbie. 'Ha! The very girl. Wait till you hear this.'

Oh no. History moment. Rolling her eyes, Abbie went over to the desk. When would Dad realise she was his daughter, not his number-one-superkeen pupil?

His study was a shambles. Books were piled on the shelves and floor. Next to *Forts and Crosses and other Celtic Games* was *Smelling History.* On top of *Tudor Toilet Bags* lay the Viking joke book *Løeff Your Soeçks Üff.* In the far corner a spider had spun a theme park for her nine hundred and fifty-two children.

Beside the book on Dad's desk stood a family photo, three used teabags and, oh yes, a pair of shrunken heads. Fernando Feraldo, the topmost remains of a Spanish conquistador, and Carmen, the topmost remains of his wife, were yawning.

'Hi,' said Abbie, standing behind Dad's chair. 'Busy day?'

'Eight client,' said Fernando.

Carmen tossed her long black hair proudly. 'All happy ever after.'

In return for doing paperweight duties, Dad let them live in his office. During the day, while he taught history at Bradleigh Secondary School, they used it to run their new business. 'Head to Head' was a counselling service that offered advice to couples with marriage problems. Well, it was more of a show really. Estranged husbands and wives would sit in gobsmacked silence as the Feraldos told their four-hundred-and-thirty-four-year-old tale of shrinkage and separation in the Amazon jungle. The punch line of the story was, 'Eef we get back together, so can you.' After that the clients would be rudely dismissed. So far, every couple had gone home and patched things up. There was no charge. Clients simply had to sign a form saying they wouldn't tell any journalists about their unusual counsellors.

Fernando yawned again. 'Time for esleep. I tiredy boy.'

Dad patted his nose. 'Well, I've got a great bedtime story for you.'

The heads grunted their approval. They might be in their four hundred and sixties, but they still insisted on being read to every night.

Abbie perched on the edge of the desk. 'Go on then.'

'When I say *story*,' said Dad, 'there's definitely some truth in it. The question is, how much?' He picked up Mr Dabbings's letter. 'I knew Remote Ken rang a bell. I heard of it years ago, at university. In the Stuff 'n' Nonsense module.'

'The what?'

'Stuff 'n' Nonsense. Real historical facts that have been spiced up over the years.'

'You mean legends?'

Dad nodded. 'King Arthur, Atlantis – that sort of thing. I remembered there was some tale about Remote Ken but I'd forgotten the details. So I looked it up in *History and Hogwash*.' He patted the book on his desk and began to read.

'Like all legends, the story of Remote Ken is based on fact. It is known that three monks fled there when their monastery in Ireland was attacked by Vikings. Gentle Father Kenneth and two humble brothers set up home on the deserted island, building simple shelters and living off fish and seabirds. There they lived out their days, close to God and cut off from the world.'

It was Abbie's turn to yawn. 'Wow, Dad, amazing. Bye.' She turned to go.

'Hang on, itchy knickers. I haven't got to the good bit.'

Sighing, Abbie stopped at the door.

'The brothers' only visitor,' read Dad, 'was a fellow monk. Brother Donal rowed out to the island once a year with supplies: seeds, salt and chickens. He described these visits in the *Annals of Donal*, a record he kept of events.'

A snore interrupted him. Carmen had nodded off.

'And it's in these annals,' Dad continued loudly, 'that Donal wrote about … oh, never mind.' He shut the book. 'You're right. Boring. Forget it.'

Abbie frowned. Since when did history bore Dad? 'Forget what?'

'Oh.' Dad batted the air with his hand. 'Just some nonsense about treasure.'

Carmen's eyes popped open. Abbie rushed back to the desk. She snatched the book.

Chuckling, Dad grabbed it back. 'Where was I? Oh yes. Donal described an exquisite golden cup that the monks brought to the island: the Goblet of Dripping.'

Abbie snorted. 'Not a very exquisite name.'

'Until you hear what it dripped with.' Dad read on. 'The huge cup was encrusted with rubies and diamonds the size of grapes. When it wasn't being used for religious services, the monks kept it hidden.'

'Why,' said Abbie, 'if they were the only people on the island?'

'Because they lived in constant fear of attack. Not even Donal knew its hiding place.'

'But I thought monks were all holy and stuff. Surely they could trust him?'

'It wasn't a matter of trust,' said Dad, 'but protection. The Vikings were always finding new raiding routes from Scandinavia. The monks knew that Donal could be nabbed any time he rowed out. If he didn't know where the goblet was hidden, then even if the Vikings caught and tortured him, he couldn't spill the beans and rouse the wrath of God.'

Abbie sort of understood. It was like Mum not telling her little brother Ollie where treats were hidden. Even if

Abbie caught and tickled him, he couldn't spill the jelly beans and rouse the wrath of Mum.

Dad looked up from the book. 'You can guess what happened next.'

'The Vikeeng they come.' Carmen was wide awake now. 'Always in heestory, the men they want treasure. Vikeeng, Roman, Conquistador …' she glared at Fernando, 'all men same.'

'Er, exactly,' said Dad, before she could shout at Fernando for the quillionth time about his raid on an Amazon jungle tribe which had led to their beheading and shrinkage. 'Brother Donal rowed out one summer to find the island deserted. He realised the monks must have been captured and either killed and thrown into the sea or taken as slaves by the Vikings.'

'How terrible.' Abbie pictured three kindly granddads being herded onto longboats. She heard their sobs, smelt the smoke that curled from their burning homes, felt the crack of whips on their backs. She shuddered. Never mind maths, never mind friend worries: modern life was peachy compared to the brutal olden days.

'Terrible, yes.' Dad shut the book. 'And wonderful too. Because no one knew if the Vikings found the goblet.'

Abbie gasped. A huge golden cup glittered into her mind. 'You mean it could still be there? So why aren't people looking for it? Why isn't Remote Ken famous?'

Dad put his hands behind his head. He was enjoying this. 'It was, at first. Donal looked for the goblet of course. And when he couldn't find it, he wondered if perhaps the Vikings hadn't either.'

'Why? They must've done if it was no longer there.'

'Aha! Who says it wasn't?' Dad rubbed his hands. 'The goblet never turned up in Scandinavia, or anywhere else. So Donal thought of another possibility. The monks would have seen the Viking boats approaching. Even if the goblet happened to be out – and it's a big if, as it was hidden most of the time – they would've had time to hide it again before the Vikings landed.' He waited for Abbie to try, and fail, to pick holes in the logic. 'When Donal returned to Ireland, word got out, and hundreds of treasure seekers tried their luck. After his death the story lived on in the *Annals*, until thousands were visiting Remote Ken every year. But nothing was ever found. By the nineteenth century interest had faded. The *Annals of Donal* were chucked into a library archive and the legend was forgotten. Since then, few people have bothered visiting Remote Ken.' He waved Mr Dabbings's letter. 'No wonder Branston wants to go. His precious Nature must be running riot.'

He can't know about the legend, thought Abbie. *Surely he'd have told us.* Her heart did a hop. 'Do you – do you think the goblet might still be there?'

Dad's eyebrows did press-ups. 'Well *that*, my sweet, is

the question.'

'And *this*, you twit, is the answer.' Grandma was standing in the doorway. Abbie hadn't heard her approach in her soft slippers. 'Of course not.'

Dad took a deep breath. 'Hello, Mother.' He turned his chair round and smiled patiently. 'How can you be so sure?'

Grandma slurped a cup of steaming something. 'The story stinks.' As if to prove it, she scrunched her nose. 'It's obvious what really 'appened.'

Dad sighed. 'Do tell.'

'Donal nicked the treasure.'

Dad rubbed his forehead. 'No, Mother. He wouldn't have returned to Ireland if he'd taken the goblet; it was far too famous and precious for him to sell without raising suspicion. Besides, he'd never steal a sacred object – or indeed anything. He was a holy man of God, remember.'

Grandma snorted. 'Says 'oo? The blinkin' *Annals*, of course, written by the man 'imself. Course 'e's goin' to show 'is best side.' She shook her head at Dad. 'You 'istorians – so blinded by your books, you can't see the truth when it's starin' down the centuries. If you could send me back in time, I'd prove it.'

'With pleasure,' muttered Dad not quite softly enough. Grandma shook her cup at him. Steaming something spilled onto the carpet.

'What Dad means,' said Abbie hurriedly, 'is that *he'd*

love to go back in time too. Wouldn't you Dad?'

He nodded gratefully. 'Er, yes, that's exactly what I mean.' Clearing his throat, he pretended to study the letter in his lap.

You owe me one, thought Abbie as he frowned over the note. He blinked. Then sniffed. Then tapped his foot and bit his cheek. 'Hmm.' He looked up. 'Was there, um, something you wanted, Mother?' A strange little smile twitched under his beard.

'Thought you'd never ask.' Grandma folded her arms. 'A word with the Shrunkens. In private.'

'Hmm?' Dad was staring at the letter again. 'Oh. Right.' He got up. 'I'll, ah, leave you to it. Night all.' He wandered out the door with the letter in his hand and the grin in his beard.

'What's got into 'im?' asked Grandma. Shrugging, Abbie opened a drawer in the desk. She took out two tiny frilly nightcaps and popped them on the Feraldos. They looked like pots of homemade jam.

'Imagine' she murmured, 'if the treasure *was* still there.'

'Bad news,' sighed Fernando. 'Treasure breeng trouble.'

'No news,' said Grandma. 'Because it isn't. Now 'op off so I can ask me pals a favour.'

Abbie wandered into the hall. Never mind their carping: no amount of cold water could douse the spark that had lit in her mind and was glinting like – ooh, like gold.

Nah. Slowly she climbed the stairs. *Grandma's right.* If the Vikings hadn't taken the goblet, someone else would've found it on the island yonks ago. She stopped on the landing. *Probably.* She spread her palm over the cool banister. There was still a teeny chance – a chance that only she in the class knew about. A whiff of mystery, a sniff of a story … a journalist's gift. *And a secret.*

She smiled. Because there's nothing like a secret to win back a friend.

***

'What's this for?' Chunca Inca lifted the lid and peered inside.

Behind him Quempo coughed. 'Well.' He could hardly say 'Doodoo' to an emperor. 'Your – um – business.'

The Emp looked blank.

Quempo tried again. 'Your offering. Contribution.'

The Emp shook his head.

'Your gift?'

'A prezzie? Cool!' Chunca bent over the toilet bowl again. 'But there's just a puddle of water down there. Hey Bacpac, have a poke around. The present must be stuck underneath.'

The old servant got on his knees and shoved a loyal arm down the loo.

There was a rushing sound.

'Aaaah!' Bacpac leapt back.

'What did I do?' said Chunca.

Quempo sighed. 'Pulled the flush.'

'Wow.' The Emp grinned. 'Even water obeys me now.'

Bacpac wiped his dripping face.

'Don't cry, Baccers.' Chunca squeezed his arm. 'You have a go. I'll command it to obey you too.'

Bacpac pulled. The Emp commanded. The empty cistern gasped.

'Sorry, Bacs.' Chunca patted his shoulder. I guess we can't all have superpowers.' Linking arms, he led his servant out of the bathroom.

'Hey,' came his voice from the bedroom. 'You gotta try this!' There was a boing of bedsprings.

Quempo leaned his forehead against the cool bathroom wall. One more night, thank goodness, then this imperial idiot would be on the plane to England and out of his hair for good.

***

Sitting on his prison bed, Klench looked at his watch. Eight fifty-two and nineteen seconds. He yawned loudly. 'Time for sleepinks.'

'Vy so early?' snapped Inner Mummy. She scoured his brain in search of trickery, just as she used to scour his bedroom in search of doughnuts. 'You can't hide, I know your mind. All your secrets I vill find.'

'No secrets, Mums,' he said as lightly as he could, while she rifled through his inner wardrobe. 'I am just tired bloke. Vy not you sleeps too? You are not as young as look.'

Inner Mummy's suspicions were calmed by the compliment. 'Zat iss true, my toffee pie. Sleepink keeps me smart and spry.'

When she was snoring away in her inner granny flat, Klench stood up. He grabbed the mint-green sponge bag on his bed. He skipped out the door and along the prison corridor to the bathroom. He cleaned his teeth, flossed, gargled and cleaned them again. Then he returned to his cell, changed into his mint-green pyjamas and bedtime tie, put on his hairnet and got into bed. Glancing at the calendar on his wall, he chuckled. 'Not as spry as you think.' Mummy had been so busy searching his brain she'd forgotten to look and see he had a meeting tomorrow. A meeting she'd be very unhappy about indeed.

3

Holy Father

Abbie raced into the classroom next morning. 'Guess what?' She plonked her bag on her desk. 'I'm coming!'

Perdita was perched on the neighbouring desk talking to Claire. She grinned like a radiator. 'Brill.' Then she groaned like a fridge. 'But can you believe it? Claire isn't.'

'I've got to go to my cousins' for Easter.' Claire stuck out her bottom lip. 'Pig.'

'Oh, pig,' agreed Abbie. *Oh, prancing white horse with a whinny like bells,* she thought. 'We'll really miss you.' *Like a verruca.* 'Are you sure you can't come?' *Be sure, be sure.*

'I'm sure.' Claire sniffed.

'You poor thing. That's just …' Abbie shook her head. *Brilliant.* 'I mean what a complete …' she sighed. *Whoopee.*

She sat down, party popping inside. As soon as Claire was out of the way she'd tell Perdita about the legend. Not that there was any problem with Claire. In fact, in the last eight seconds, Abbie had realised what a lovely person she was. But hidden treasure was for a best friend's ears alone.

Before she could nab Perdita's ear, though, Mr Dabbings burst in. 'Twinkly Friday!' he cried, bounding up to the front. 'I can't wait to hear which of you lucky lentils are coming on the trip. But first I've got a surprise. Settle down, everyone.'

All the children sat on their chairs except Henry Holler who sat on Ursula Slightly. She burst into silent tears.

'Didn't see her, Sir. Honest.'

Mr Dabbings nodded sympathetically. 'Easily done, Henry. Now, back to your seat. We've got a very special visitor.'

Abbie rolled her eyes. Their last very special visitor had been a salad farmer who'd taught them how to dress winter lettuce, not in oil and vinegar but cardigans.

'Please welcome,' cried Mr Dabbings, 'all the way from the tenth century …' he threw out his arms, 'Father Holybald!' Everyone turned to the door.

A figure came through. He wore a dark brown robe that reached the floor. A rope was tied round his waist. A grey cloak fell from his shoulders. A pointy hood covered his head. He glided to the front, his hands clasped in prayer.

'A monk,' murmured Claire.

'A ghost,' whispered Jeremy Boing, clutching his huge knees.

'A *choo*,' said Snorty, whose nose didn't cope well with stress.

Ursula gasped so loudly that a fly on her shoulder almost heard.

'Don't be daft,' said Marcus nervously. 'It's an actor.'

The figure stopped at the front. He turned to face the class. He threw back his hood. 'The Lord be with you.' He made the sign of the cross.

Abbie squeaked. The Lord must be having a day off. Because the clown in the gown was Dad. On his head was a pink swimming cap. Circling the cap was a ring of grey hair. Her cheeks burned. She slid down in her chair. *If I pretend not to recognise him, perhaps no one else will.*

'Hey, it's Abigail's dad,' said large and loud Terrifica Batts. Abbie's stomach leaked into her toes.

'Indeed it is.' Dad grinned. 'And yours, too.'

Terrifica blinked in alarm.

Dad chuckled in a deep, medieval way. 'I mean that, as a monk, I'm the *spiritual* father of you all.' He raised his arms. 'Bless you my children.'

Abbie stuffed her chin into her neck. *How dare he? In front of my friends. In front of my un-friends. How could he? Why would he?*

The silence was unbearable. She had to look up. Dad winked. And suddenly she knew. It was all her fault. Last night – what had she said to Grandma? That he'd love to go back in time. And that's exactly what he was doing.

'A special thank you to Abbie,' he said, 'for inviting me on this trip as your historical advisor.'

Before Abbie could shout, 'Over my dead body!' Mr Dabbings had thrown a matey arm round Dad. 'When Mr Hartley phoned last night, I jumped at his offer to step into the shoes of yesteryear.' Dad pulled up his robe, baring leather sandals and hairy legs. 'But you won't be coming along to model clothes, will you, Father H?'

'Indeed not.' Dad clapped his hands. 'I'll be your medieval advisor, teaching you about the monks and how they eked out a living.'

'What's eking?' asked Craig Nibbles.

'This.' Henry pulled Ursula's ponytail.

'Eek!' she cried obligingly.

'Not quite,' said Mr Dabbings. 'Eking is living off the land, making do with what Nature provides. But that ponytail brings us to a fascinating – or should I say *fashion*ating? – fact from the tenth century, doesn't it Father H?'

Dad pointed to his head. 'Anyone know what you call this hairstyle?'

Hands went up. 'Prince Charles?'

'Egg in a skirt?'

'Bonkers?'

'Correct,' said Dad encouragingly, if inaccurately. 'A *tonsure*. Now, in those days, monks had different kinds. This was the traditional Roman tonsure, arranged in a ring like Christ's crown of thorns. But *this* –' he stuck his hand in the pocket of his robe. A gasp went round as the tonsure reshaped into a vertical arch over his crown, like a hairband – 'is the style worn by Irish monks.'

'Wow!' said Claire whose own fringe looked a bit jealous of the hairy gymnastics.

'Aweslicks!' shouted Henry.

'How did you do that?' gasped Jeremy.

Abbie caught her breath. She and Perdita had introduced the class to lots of remarkable creatures last term: an elephant who could paint, a superstrong orang-utan, a poetic parrot. But they'd always hidden Chester. Whenever Ollie asked to take him to school for Show and Tell, the shy patch of chest hair trembled on Grandma's head. The Hartleys and Platts had agreed he should never be put on show. And now here he was in front of a crowd. Chester would die of stage fright if Dad introduced him.

'Batteries,' Dad lied.

Phew. Abbie breathed out.

'The remote control's in my pocket,' Dad continued smoothly. 'It flips the tonsure between the two styles.' Chester moved back and forth from Roman ring to Irish arch.

The children applauded. Dad bowed. Chester danced for dear life.

Mr Dabbings slapped Dad on the back. 'A wonderful preview, Father H. We'll be honoured to have you on our trip, won't we kids? Let's all put our hands together in a grateful way.'

Abbie kept her hands apart in a very ungrateful way.

When Dad had glided out, Mr Dabbings looked round. 'Now then. Who's decided to come?'

Perdita waved her hand. 'Me. And my parents would love to. But they can't leave the zoo.'

Mr Dabbings sighed. 'What a shame. Their skills would come in very useful.'

Abbie pictured Coriander singing to seals until they ate from the children's hands and Matt inventing a food processor that turned mud into chocolate.

'I'm game,' said Terrifica. 'I worked out that I can earn at least three badges for Girl Guides. Finding Your Way, Cooking Outdoors and Making Do for Loo Roll.'

Marcus's hand slunk up. 'I've got to go. My dad wants me to develop leadership skills.'

Winnership, you mean. Abbie could just see Dr Strodboil wagging his finger and telling his son to 'Be best at everything, boy!'

'Me too.' Everyone turned to Ursula. Her eyelids fluttered like moth wings. 'My parents are going away for Easter. They said the trip will build my character.' She gulped.

'Awekicks!' yelled Henry. 'I'll come too and un-build it.'

'Henry, please!' Mr Dabbings looked shocked. 'That's not proper English. The word you're looking for is "demolish". Now, who else? What about you, Snor– Barry?'

'Can't,' said Snorty quickly. 'It's my ffhhay ffever.'

'Too bad. Rukia?'

'Not on your ... I mean, I have to cut my fingernails, Sir.'

'For ten days?'

'It's the angles.'

'How about you, Jeremy?'

'You must be ... I've got pole-vaulting camp.'

'Craig?'

'Cake-icing classes.'

'Oh, please. Greg?'

'Window-shopping.'

The teacher tutted. 'Well, I'm sorry to see such a small turnout. You Stay-at-Home Stans and Stanettes are missing a wonderful opportunity.'

'To find treasure.'

Heads turned. Chairs scraped. All eyes fixed on Abbie.

She bit her lip. *Why the poop did I say that?* But blinking round at the startled faces, she knew exactly why. After the Dad disaster, what better way to save her reputation? 'There's this legend,' she mumbled, 'that the monks hid a golden goblet on Remote Ken.'

'Awebricks!' Henry leapt from his seat. 'A treasure hunt.'

'I'll get my Gold Digger's badge!' cried Terrifica.

'Not if I find it first,' said Marcus.

Hands shot up. The room filled with volunteers.

'My ffhhay ffever's better.'

'I'll bring my nail scissors.'

'I'll cancel pole vaulting.'

'Now hang on!' Mr Dabbings rapped his desk with a knitting needle. 'Hold your horseradishes. I'm sensing here that some motives aren't pure. That the gold you seek isn't sunlight on water, the silver not moonlight on sand. Well, let me remind you,' he wiggled the needle, 'the whole point of this trip is to enjoy the riches of Nature, not Man. There will be NO treasure hunting.' He glared round as sternly as a man with

Wendo
Tremendo

on his jumper can glare. 'And only those who volunteered *before* Abigail's rather unhelpful contribution will be coming.'

Hands fell. Faces fell. Silence fell. Abbie could taste the disappointment in the room.

'Hey!' Perdita jumped onto her desk. 'Here's an idea.'

Mr Dabbings pointed his needle. 'Desks aren't for standing on, Perdita. Desks are for covering with kind graffiti.'

'Sorry.' She jumped down. 'It's just … maybe the people who don't go on the trip could help out at the zoo. Then my parents can come with us.'

Mr Dabbings smacked the desk. 'Top turnip, Perdita! Wendy could do with a hand running the café. You kids can make her dandelion tea and sing to Buddleia.'

'I didn't mean the café,' said Perdita, 'I meant the animals. Feeding the penguins, skateboarding with the gibbons, playing Parrot Scrabble.'

The cheer was so loud that Miss Bellicorn, who taught Musical Expression, burst in and told them to pipe down please, her class couldn't hear their inner trumpets.

When she'd gone Mr Dabbings rummaged in the drawer

of his desk. He brought out a woolly brown hat with a silver star on the front. 'Perdita Platt. I hereby award you the Beanie of Brilliance for Outstanding Cheering Up of Class.' Everyone clapped as she took the hat for the fourth time that term.

OK, not everyone. Marcus, who'd only worn it once all year, looked at the floor.

And Abbie? Obviously she was thrilled for Perdita. Praise, popularity – what more could you want for your best friend? Especially when your own father had just embarrassed the living daylights out of you. Of course she clapped … on the outside.

On the inside she had a little puke.

***

Chunca had a little puke. Bacpac held out the sick bag just in time.

'Ooh,' giggled the Emperor. 'I haven't felt this nervous since the day those Spaniards stabbed my old man. When was that again?'

Sitting on his left, Bacpac did a quick sum. 'Four hundred and forty-one years, two months, three weeks and five days ago, your Terrificness.' The old servant wiped his forehead. Nervous was the word. At the airport check-in he'd nearly been loaded onto the luggage belt. That was because, when the lady behind the counter had asked

52

how many backpacks they were taking, the Emp had said, 'Three. Mine, his – and him.' Not that Bacpac blamed him, of course: his master was far too important to understand such lowly things as luggage.

'Pwah!' Chunca spat something out of his mouth. 'Call that a snack? It's tougher than tapir teeth.'

Bacpac looked at the packet of peanuts on the Emp's lap. 'I think, your Fabbiness, you're supposed to open it first. Allow me.' He tore the packet open.

Chunca looked inside. 'Nuts! Now we're talking. Let's play Gob-Lob.'

Bacpac glanced at the lady on his left. 'I'm not sure this is quite the place.'

'I'll be the judge of that, me old cocoa bean.' The Emp threw a nut in the air. The lady on Bacpac's left gasped. The nut landed in her mouth.

'Shot!' Chunca clapped himself on the back.

'My turn,' said a boy in the seat behind. Chunca threw a peanut backwards over his head. The boy caught it in his mouth.

Two minutes later the cabin air was thick with peanuts.

***

'Peanuts?' Grandma held out the packet she'd just bought from the vending machine in the visiting room. The prison guard took one.

Grandma pushed the packet across the table to Klench. 'So. 'Ow's it goin' with 'Er Upstairs?' She pointed to his head.

'Most vell.' Klench explained excitedly how Inner Mummy had repeated a rhyme *and* forgotten about their meeting. 'I think she is losink her hold over me. Every time you come, her voice goes quiet. You are only voman can shut her ups. Oh Grandma, vy you not believe me ven I tell you she is brains behind my bads? Zat beneath her vicked ideas, I am good man?'

Grandma tutted. 'Ideas are one thing, *actions* quite another. I don't care 'ow many crimes she's thought up in your 'ead. You're the one 'oo carried them out, so *you're* the one to blame.'

Klench folded his arms. 'Zat is *so* not fairs. Ven vill you understand?'

'I'll tell you when.' Grandma tapped a rhythm on the table with her finger. 'When the sun turns blue. When the moon does a poo. When ... the legend of treasure turns out to be true.'

Inner Mummy's ears pricked up. Her voice may be softer when Grandma was around, but her hearing was as sharp as ever. 'Ask her vot treasure,' she hissed in Klench's brain.

'No.' He pursed his inner lips.

'Go ons.'

'Vill nots. I am becomink good man. I am no lonker

54

interested in vord "treasure", vich is first cousin of vord "stealink".'

'Don't make me laughs,' said Inner Mummy – which he hadn't.

Klench chewed his inner fingernails. 'I am turnink my back on crime.'

'You? Ha!'

Klench swallowed. 'Honest.'

'Oh pull ze uzzer vuns.'

Klench scratched his chin. He bit his lip. His face went pink like a guilty marshmallow. At last he gave in. 'Vot treasure, Grandma?'

'Oh.' She waved a hand dismissively. 'Just some nonsense I 'eard.' She told him the legend of Remote Ken and how Abbie's class was going there on a field trip. 'Daft as daffodils. Sounds like the grimmest spot on earth.' She yawned. 'Anyway.' She looked at her watch. 'Me time's up. Enjoy the peanuts.' With a little wave, she got up and shuffled towards the door.

Sighing, Klench reached into the packet. His fingers closed round a bumpy stick. Glancing down, he gasped. A hairclip! A weapon that could open locks, stab prison guards …

'Set us frees,' whispered Inner Mummy.

Klench squeezed the clip in his fist. He frowned. He fidgeted. He sucked in his cheeks. He sucked in his other cheeks. He took a deep breath. 'Grandma,' he called, 'you forgot somethink.'

She spun round and punched the air. 'Yess! Well done that man.' Shuffling back to the table, she clapped the prison guard on the arm. 'What did I tell you, Bob? 'E's reformin'.'

Klench stared at her.

'Me and Bob,' she chuckled, 'we're old Bingo pals.'

The guard nodded. 'She asked me to have a word with the prison governor. He agreed we'd turn a blind eye while she smuggled in a clip.'

'We 'ad a little bet,' said Grandma. 'I told 'em that you're on the road to reform and that you'd give it straight back. Congratulations.' She patted Klench's shoulder. 'You've just passed the Trust Test. And *you*,' she thumped the guard in the chest, 'owe me five Galaxy bars.'

4

Honking Muckstems

At ten o'clock on Saturday Dad dropped Abbie at the zoo. She waved him off from the entrance gate and breathed in the stinky air. Closing her eyes, she played her regular game of pin the pong on the animal. 'Gina,' she murmured as musty ellie lumbered up her nostrils and 'Silvio' as raw tiger padded behind. 'Ooh.' She scrunched her nose at the reek of fish. 'Penguins.'

The gate was open. Inside, a handful of her classmates were huddling round Perdita. In their bright puffy anoraks they looked like boiled sweets.

Perdita waved at Abbie then spoke into a walkie-talkie. 'That's everyone.' They waited by the entrance pond, chattering excitedly.

All except Abbie. Catching sight of Claire, she frowned. 'What are you doing here? I thought you were going away for Easter.'

Claire sniffed. 'Nice to see you too. I was invited anyway.'

Perdita patted Claire's arm. 'To make up for not coming on the trip. It won't be half as good without you. Will it Abbie?'

'Nope.' *It'll be twelve point three times better.*

Coriander and Matt came down the path by the pond, followed by the zookeeper Charlie Chumb.

'Helloo!' Coriander threw out her arms. The sleeves of her pink poncho flapped like flamingo wings. 'A big thank you for volunteering to help.'

Matt smiled shyly. 'Yes. I'm really looking forward to a break.'

Me too, thought Abbie, watching Perdita's bottom lip jut sadly at Claire.

Coriander turned to the zookeeper. 'Charlie here will explain your jobs,' she said.

He cleared his throat. 'Well, I thought we could start by, um ...' he pointed down the path by the pond. 'Then you can all, er ...' he tugged his huge earlobes. 'And everyone will be ... you know.'

Oh but they didn't. Everyone stared at Charlie. In the pond a duck ducked. On the right a gibbon gibbered. To the left a tapir taped.

'What Charlie means,' said Perdita, 'is that we'll walk round the zoo. Then everyone can choose what job they want.' Excited murmurs went round.

An hour later the children were sitting at a table in the café.

'I've got the biggest job,' said Greg Fnigg, who'd chosen water work. That meant feeding the seals, penguins, ducks, flamingos, Angelica the fish eagle and Hepzibah the hippo.

Moody Jack Doody had chosen birds with attitude.

'Don't take any beak from Mackenzie the parrot,' Perdita said. 'And ignore the ostriches. They're always in a huff.' Jack grinned – or was it grimaced? You could never tell.

'I'veff got the slimiest jobhff.' No one could argue with Snorty. Reptile care involved throwing rotten meat to Edie the crocodile and making hot water bottles for the zoo's most recent arrival. Mamelodi, an African python, had escaped from a local pet shop and glided to the zoo so many times that the owner had donated her.

'Dunno why she prefers it here,' he'd mumbled glumly. Coriander didn't have the heart to tell him that poor Mamelodi hadn't been getting enough hugs.

'Well my job's the scariest,' crowed Robbie Rudge. He'd picked snarling practice with Silvio to prevent tiger tonsillitis.

'And mine's the tickliest.' Craig Nibbles had volunteered to clean the nostrils of Alphonse the giraffe with Matt's latest invention, the Nosehole Pole.

But the best job had gone to Jeremy Boing. The bouncy boy had begged to help Ollie with the orang-utans. That meant cutting Winnie's hair, which grew megafast; taking lazy Vinnie for walks, and playing Kiss Chase with little Minnie.

Rukia came over to the table. She was carrying a tray with a jug and glasses. 'Mrs Dabbings says I can help in the café. And I can call her Wendy. *And* I get to fold serviettes.'

'But leave the polishing to me.' Wendy was behind her with a tray of Kit Kats and chocolate buttons. 'And don't tell Bran– er, Mr Dabbings, that I carried this.' She put it on the table. 'He'll say it's bad for Bud.'

'Hey,' said Jeremy. 'Bran, Bud – your family's a breakfast cereal.'

'Shhh!' Wendy's hands flew to her stomach. 'Don't listen, poppet.' She glared at Jeremy. 'Budney accepts your apology,' she said, though there hadn't been one. 'He may be only three months old but he understands everything.'

'He?' said Rukia. 'Mr Dabbings said it's a she.'

'Well, Mr Dabbings is wrong.' Wendy's voice was quiet but firm. 'Our boy is going to be a fireman. Ooh,' she sighed, 'all those buttons – think of the polishing.'

Rukia arranged the Kit Kats in hexagons on the table. Greg took one. She smacked his hand. 'You ruined my honeycomb.'

'Never mind, dear.' Wendy patted her arm. 'Why don't you go and stack some sugar cubes?'

Abbie grinned. Wendy and Rukia had taken to each

other like Flash to floor tiles. The others, too, were chatting away eagerly. The Platts had nothing to worry about. She turned to assure Perdita that the zoo would be fine without them. But she was busy playing chocolate button tiddlywinks with Claire. Abbie grabbed a Kit Kat. *One more week, then Claire'll be history.*

It was a week that flew. On Monday Perdita brought three carrier bags to school with her.

'Super satsumas!' said Mr Dabbings. He emptied them out, spilling rust-coloured rope onto the floor. 'Winnie's weekend hair. I asked Coriander to save the cuttings for my knitting.' The children spent the day untangling Winnie's tresses.

On Tuesday they made lists.

'Don't worry about food,' said Mr Dabbings. 'Mr Hartley has kindly offered to supply all the meals.'

'What?' squeaked Abbie. 'He never told me.' Banana risotto and chicken nugget crumble steamed across her mind. She made a mental list of things to smuggle: *Frosties. Bourbons. Crisps. Bourbons. Lemonade – oh, and Bourbons.*

Marcus offered to bring games.

'Fab apples,' said Mr Dabbings. 'Tiddlywinks, playing cards, maybe a cheeky chess set. But remember, no Nintendos, no Kindles. No iPhones, iPads or iPods. And the only BlackBerries will be those with thorns.'

Terrifica made a list of rain gear. 'Gore-Tex is a must,'

she said, when Ursula murmured that her cagoule leaked. 'Get your parents to buy you one.' Ursula sighed so heavily that a dust particle lost its way.

Henry listed luggage. 'Massive suitcase,' he wrote.

'What for?' said Perdita.

'The treasure.'

Mr Dabbings's knitting needles froze. 'Henry. Let me remind you that the only treasure will be golden sunsets and sapphire seas, which do not fit into suitcases. Is that clear?' Henry was too busy wiping his nose on Ursula's sleeve to answer.

On Wednesday and Thursday they learned about the plants and animals they might find on the island. 'Might' was an important word. Ken turned out to be so remote there was no information on the Internet.

'Emus?' suggested Craig Nibbles when Mr Dabbings asked what seabirds might nest on the cliffs.

'Unlikely, Craig. Emus can't fly.'

'So? They could use ladders.'

Henry had a guess at plant life. 'Honking Muckstems. Puking Jabbers. Venus Girl Traps.' He snickered at Ursula, who fainted with terror, though no one noticed.

On Friday they broke up. Mr Dabbings saw them off at the school gate. To those not going on the trip he gave chocolate eggs clad in woolly green hats. 'These are to remind you of Easter and new life, of chicks and lambkins

– wonders of Nature that you'll sadly be missing.'

Rukia grabbed her egg anything but sadly and skipped off anything but missingly.

The teacher opened his shoulder bag. 'To all my fellow travellers, a gift from me and Mrs D.' He handed out auburn scarves. Each had a name sewn on in sequins.

'So that's what you did with Winnie's hair,' said Abbie. She buried her nose in its itchy-scratchy warmth.

'Fantastic.' Perdita wrapped hers round her neck.

'Aweflicks,' said Henry, whipping Ursula's arm.

Nothing, said Marcus, throwing his into a nearby dustbin.

'Hey!' cried Perdita. 'That's Winnie you're binning.' She fished out the scarf.

'If he doesn't want it, can I have it?' asked Claire. 'I'd be honoured to wear Winnie.'

Perdita pressed it into her hand. 'And she'd be honoured to be worn by you.'

Marcus made a puking noise. Abbie caught his eye. A week ago she'd have told him off, defended Perdita to kingdom come. Now she felt herself swallowing a smile.

He came over. Cupping a hand over his mouth, he whispered, 'Thank goodness you're on this trip. At least there'll be someone decent to talk to.'

He'd just dumped part of her favourite ape. He'd just insulted her favourite friend. But as Abbie headed to the bus stop, her heart couldn't help a little leap. Because, if she'd heard correctly, he'd also just said something slightly nice.

✳✳✳

The two old men waited by the luggage carousel.

'Ooh, I like that one,' said the Emperor in ancient Quechua. He reached forward and grabbed a flowery suitcase.

'Oy!' shouted a woman in modern English. 'Thass mine.' She whacked Chunca with her handbag.

'Yeeaaw!' he yelled in universal language as the woman snatched her case and wheeled it off.

'I think,' said Bacpac, rubbing his master's chest, 'we're supposed to collect our *own* bags, your Stonkingness. That lady thought you were a thief.'

'Me?' roared the ruler so fearsomely that an aeroplane weed on the runway. 'I can hardly be a thief when everything belongs to me anyway. Am I Master of the Universe or what?'

People were staring. Bacpac had to get the Emp out of here. This wasn't the time to remind him that the Universe had moved on.

At last their rucksacks appeared on the carousel. 'We need to get to Bradleigh and find that stoutest crook,' said Bacpac, pulling off the luggage.

The Emperor brightened at the thought of death. 'What are we waiting for?' He stacked his backpack on Bacpac's backpack on Bacpac's back. Then he slapped Bacpac on the backpack. 'Lead on, me old baggage.'

***

'Good news,' said Grandma. She sat down at the prison table.

Klench clutched the sides of his chair. 'Oh, Grandma!' He pulled it towards the table, forgetting that it was screwed to the floor. 'Schnik! But no vorries. Soon I vill be free, thanks to you.'

She lowered her glasses and frowned over the top. 'What?'

Klench clapped his hands. 'Now I have proved I am honest bloke, I vill soon be released, yes?'

Grandma chuckled. 'No, you great chump. You're miles off freedom. But because you passed the 'airclip test, I've got permission to bring a couple more visitors next time, to speed up your recovery.'

Klench's face sagged like a Yorkshire pudding. 'I don't vont to see nobodies. Nobodies at all.'

'Good.' Grandma grinned. ''Coz that's exactly 'oo's comin'.'

5
~

Potted Poop

Breakfast next morning was a noisy business. Bacon was sizzling, Grandma was guzzling and Ollie was grizzling.

'Don't want you to go!' he wailed. Jumping off his chair, he threw his arms round Abbie.

She wriggled free. 'You mean you don't want me to go and find treasure and get incredibly rich while you stay here and do potato prints?'

He nodded.

'Don't worry.' Abbie speared a slice of bacon. 'We're not allowed to look for treasure.'

'Oh.' Ollie stopped crying. 'Bye then.' He skipped off happily.

'Lord, give me strength.' Grandma shovelled fried egg into her mouth. 'When will you get it? There isn't any treasure to look for.'

She yawned. Her false teeth dropped from her gums. Watching her press them back up with her tongue, Abbie lost her appetite. She grabbed the rucksack leaning against her chair and took it into the hall.

Dad was staggering to the front door with a crate in his arms. 'Whoa.' He dumped it on top of another crate. 'That's that lot.'

There were ten in all. Each crate was sealed and labelled.

POTTED HISTORY
Long-life Repasts from the Past

Abbie put down her rucksack. 'I hope those aren't what I think they are.'

Dad patted a box. 'Well. If you think they're bathroom towels from the Iron Age, you're wrong. If you reckon they're ancient Babylonian cheese graters, you're way off track. If, however, you suspect that they're a selection of meals from the tenth century, well ...' His eyebrows did a jig.

Abbie clapped a hand to her mouth. 'Tell me you're joking.'

'I'm joking.'

'Phew.' Her hand dropped.

'Ha! I'm joking that I'm joking. That is indeed our food for the week. One crate a day – breakfast, lunch and dinner – in packets and tins. Cool, eh? I ordered it from an online company that does ready-meals from history.'

'But the monks dug potatoes!' Abbie wailed, imagining the mushy vegetables that were probably sloshing about in those cans. She put her head in her hands. Then she bent down, unzipped a side pocket in her rucksack and took out a pen and notebook.

With all technology banned on this trip, she'd realised she couldn't email articles back to the local paper as she'd done last term from Ecuador. So she'd decided to jot down her thoughts and impressions the old-fashioned way.

Sitting on the bottom stair, she opened the notebook and wrote her first impression.

Wading through mud, singing to brambles – and now tinned sick. Can it get worse?

She sighed. It was more of a *grim*pression. Putting the notebook in her pocket, she went to help Dad load the car.

What with all the boxes and two large rucksacks, it took two trips to get everything, and everyone, to the school. Mum and Ollie insisted on coming. But Abbie drew the line at Grandma, who refused to change out of her dressing gown.

Mr Dabbings was waiting on the pavement by the hired minibus. He wore a woolly green jacket. It had three square buttons down the front that doubled as picture frames. In the top frame was a photo of Wendy's face. The middle one showed her stomach, bulging slightly under a pink overall. The bottom one framed her legs and feet.

Dad pointed to the buttons. 'Hasn't she come to wave you off?'

'Not on your noodles. Buddleia doesn't wake till eight.'

Abbie pulled her Winnie-scarf tighter. Despite blue cracks in the cloud, the air had a mean little nip, as if winter was pinching spring on the bottom before sulking off to bed for the rest of the year.

The Platts pulled up in their battered green van. Perdita jumped out.

Abbie went to help her unload. They'd thought of everything of course: three jerrycans for water, each tied to a rucksack, and two canvas bags. 'Tents? I thought we were staying in cottages.'

'We are. That's the food tent and this one's for the loo.'

Thank goodness they're different colours, thought Abbie. *Wouldn't want to get **those** mixed up.*

Matt and Coriander were lifting out two trolleys from the boot. In her fringed orange cape Coriander looked like a lampshade. Skinny Matt, in his grey boiler suit, reminded Abbie of chewing gum. They wheeled the trolleys over to the minibus.

'Those are for carrying the food boxes,' explained Perdita.

A Landrover drew up with the number plate 'BATTY 1.' Out jumped Terrifica then Ursula.

Terrifica wore a bright red anorak. 'In case I get lost in island fog.'

'In case I don't,' whispered Ursula whose anorak was raincloud-grey.

Perdita put a hand on her arm. 'Haven't your parents come to see you off?'

Ursula blinked. 'They're too busy packing for their Easter trip.' Abbie looked at Mum and Ollie, chatting away to Coriander. They'd never be too busy.

Henry Holler appeared with his parents. Breaking free from his mother's hand, he ran to the minibus.

'Hennie!' cried Mrs Holler, a short lady whose neck was made of chins. 'Huggie for Mummy.'

Henry was already in the driver's seat turning the steering wheel and making car crash noises. 'Lo*serrrr*,' he yelled at her.

'Henry,' called Mr Holler, a breadstick of a man. 'That's no way to speak to your–'

'Eaarrrhhccccchhhh!' screeched Henry.

'My *bay*-bie,' Mrs Holler sobbed as her husband led her back to their car.

A blue Jaguar pulled up. Marcus jumped out and grabbed his rucksack from the boot. Mrs Strodboil came over to Mum.

Abbie glanced through the car window. Marcus's dad was in the driver's seat. Dr Terry Strodboil MSD (Massively Successful Dentist) frowned as his wife hugged Mum. Their friendship made him uncomfortable. Like all bullies, he'd been scared of Abbie ever since she'd given him an earful last term. She waved to him. He gripped the steering wheel and stared ahead. Giggling, she went over to the mums.

Mrs Strodboil was hugging Marcus. 'Enjoy yourself, darling. And forget what your dad said. This trip's about teamwork, not competition.'

'Yeah.' Marcus kissed her cheek. 'Bye Mum.' He flicked his fair hair from his forehead and headed for the minibus. Was that a sniff Abbie heard? Hugging Mum and Ollie, she couldn't help feeling a teeny bit smug. Ten days away from home was a big deal for some of them. But after two weeks in Ecuador last term, she was a hardened traveller. She waved cheerfully as Mum and Ollie returned to the car. Nothing could faze her, nothing could shock.

'Abigail!' Mum rolled down the car window. 'Remind Dad to wash his feet. We don't want his fungus to flare up.'

Abbie ran for the minibus.

She found two seats in the middle.

'Nah,' said Perdita, climbing on behind her with Ursula and Terrifica. 'Let's all sit at the back. We can wave at the cars behind.'

Abbie's stomach shrank. *Aren't best friends supposed to sit together and laugh at private jokes?* She got up grumpily.

Marcus and Henry sat three rows in front of them.

'Good,' said Ursula. 'Now Henry can't stick gum in my hair.' A grey blob sailed backwards and landed on her ponytail. Perdita whipped out some scissors from her snack bag. 'Thanks,' squeaked Ursula, as she snipped out the gum.

Two hours, one loo stop and a bag of Perdita's lice crispies later, they crossed the border into Wales. After another hour, two of Ursula's unsalted rice cakes and three of Terrifica's rock buns, they were pulling into the ferry port. The minibus rumbled over the ramp into the hold of the huge boat.

Climbing off the bus, Abbie's stomach swirled. The air was thick and oily. The boat engine throbbed through the floor and up her legs. She stumbled through a door and up twisty metal stairs, following the others onto deck four.

'Stay together,' said Mr Dabbings as they trooped into the lounge area. 'We don't want anyone getting lost.' But Henry had already run off to the slot machines.

Abbie swallowed as the boat juddered into motion.

'You OK, love?' Dad put his arm round her. 'You look a bit green. Can I get you something?'

Sick or not, this wasn't a chance to waste. 'Maybe,' she said faintly, 'a hot chocolate.' His thumb went up. 'With marshmallows,' she added weakly. 'And chocolate sprinkles.'

He patted his stomach. 'Might make that two.' He turned towards the café.

Coriander tapped his shoulder. 'Forgotten something, Graham?'

He frowned.

'Everyone else. I'm sure we'd all love a hot chocolate. There's plenty of money in the kitty. We all chipped in, remember?' She winked. 'And we wouldn't have any *favourites*, now, would we?'

He blushed.

'No worries.' She winked. 'I'm sure you just forgot that your family's grown, didn't you Father Holybald? Come on, I'll help you.'

Abbie joined the other children at a table where Perdita was shuffling a pack of cards.

'We're playing Cheat,' she said. 'You can join us if you're up to it.'

'Course I am!' Abbie glared at her.

'Sorr*ee.*' Perdita's eyes went wide. 'It's just you weren't feeling well.'

'Oh. Right. Thanks.' Abbie sat down, her cheeks burning. Why had she snapped? Perdita was only being kind. It was just all that stuff with Claire: it had made her nervous, wobbled the rock of their friendship. She picked up her cards.

'I'll start.' Perdita put two cards face down. 'Two tens.'

'Cheat,' said Marcus.

As if, thought Abbie. Marcus would cheat, even when he didn't have to, but Perdita wouldn't, even when she did. You couldn't find a more honest friend. Abbie smiled as Marcus picked up the tens. *What was I worried about?* All that talk about wanting Claire to come – that was just Perdita being her normal, friendly self.

Abbie felt a stab of shame. She'd been so rude to Claire, when her only crime was being nice. *I'll be extra kind next term*, she resolved, leaning back in her seat. In the meantime, why not have the best time ever with the best friend ever?

Dad and Coriander came back with trays of hot

chocolate. As they all reached for their drinks, he winked at Abbie. Sitting down beside her, he slid something into her lap. She glanced down. *A Kit Kat*! He put a finger to his lips.

She winked back. The best friend ... and, occasionally, the best dad too.

***

The ancient Incas climbed off the bus. Considering they were in a foreign country – not to mention a foreign century – they looked remarkably unremarkable in their jeans, brown anoraks and ... OK, maybe the fluffy white ear muffs were pushing it. But what can you do when your boss has a whopping great hole in each ear? Bacpac had bought the clothes the day before, after noting carefully what the average gent was wearing on the streets of England. To pay for the outfits, and the night they'd spent in a Travelodge, he'd traded the Emp's last pair of earrings at a cash-for-gold shop. Ear muffs seemed the simplest way to hide the holes in his lobes.

'There it is, your Superduperness.' Bacpac pointed across the road to a high fence. 'Bradleigh Prison.' Behind the fence huddled a complex of buildings with low roofs and high walls.

Bacpac shuddered, not just from the cold that was nibbling his bones after four and a half centuries in the jungle. It was the colour – or lack of it. In front of him were as many greys as the jungle had greens. The dull concrete of the buildings. The dark bricks of the wall. The greasy pavement, the gritty road.

The Emp whooped. 'Wicked!'

'You can say that again, Master.'

'OK, wicked. Now all we have to do is find that stoutest crook, grab his hand and hold on for dear death. Come on.' Chunca crossed the road.

Bacpac followed, blinking back tears. How could his Luminosity be so eager to die, after four hundred and fifty crazy, exciting, boring, delightful, stressful and on the whole wonderful years together?

He bunched his fists. *Get a grip. If that's what the boss wants, that's what he'll get.* He followed Chunca across the road to a gate in the prison fence.

A man in uniform approached from the other side. 'Yes?' he said, frowning through the fence. He fiddled with his hat.

'We want for meet stoutest crook,' said Bacpac in the English he'd been practising for two months now.

The guard snorted. 'You won't be meeting anyone till I see your visiting order, mate.' Bacpac blinked.

'The letter the prison sent you, allowing you to visit.'

Bacpac had been working hard at jail vocabulary. He got the gist. 'We have no letter. We are fond uncle of Prisoner Klench, come to surprise little nephew.'

'No surprises here, I'm afraid. Can't let you in without a visiting order.'

Bacpac's voice rose in alarm. 'But we travel great far. You cannot turn away.'

The guard adjusted his hat. 'Sorry Grandpa. I don't care if you've walked from Italy. I don't care if you've hiked from India or – I dunno – flown from the bloomin' Amazon. Orders is orders.' He turned to go.

'But we are *favourite* uncle!' cried Bacpac. 'We *must* visit nephew Klench!'

An elderly lady shuffling towards the prison exit looked up. ''Oo?' Her curly grey hair seemed to wriggle. 'Did you say Klench? And nephew?' She hurried towards them as fast as her slippers would carry her. 'Leave 'em to me, Mr Guard. I want a word.' Tilting his hat at the old dear, the guard wandered off.

A few minutes later Grandma was standing on the pavement, pooh-poohing Bacpac's story. 'Uncles? You two, related to Klench? Pull the other one! You look as related as Mars bars to a dumplin'. And you've come from South America? Very suspicious – Klench's only contacts there are dodgier than dodgem cars. The last thing 'e needs is a couple of criminal visitors, now 'e's on the road to redemption.'

'Criminal?' Fire raged in Bacpac's eyes. 'You call my master *criminal*?' He cursed her in ancient Quechua.

There was a squeak from her handbag. 'How dare you eswear at the Grandma!'

'Eshame on you,' squealed another voice.

Bacpac blinked. Chunca gulped. And Grandma smacked the handbag. 'Belt up. What did I say about makin' a scene in public?'

Looking round to check no one had heard, she grabbed the Incas by the hand. 'You're comin' with me, lads. You've got some explainin' to do.'

She marched them to the bus stop. Climbing on the Garton bus, she waved her pensioner pass and explained to the driver that her twin cousins had forgotten theirs … memories not what they used to be … old age no picnic … thanks for the ride.

***

'You gooseberry fool. You plum duff. You apple pushover.'

'Turnover, Mums,' whimpered Klench. 'Apple turnover.' Sitting on the bed in his prison cell, he chewed the edge of a pillow. 'I thought ven I gave back hairclip it vould show I am honest. Zen perhaps I vould be freed. But instead she brought zose stinky heads.' He winced at the memory of the counselling session he'd just endured. Grandma had come into the prison visiting room. Sitting down at the table, she'd explained that the Governor had let her bring some experts along, to encourage Klench on his journey of transformation. Then she'd plonked Fernando and Carmen on the table. They'd lectured him for half an hour on the dangers of greed and gold. He'd hung his head meekly, pretending to listen and admitting that he'd been a vay bad mans.

He'd never been so humiliated in all his life. And nor had Mummy, in all her death.

Now she was silent. You'd almost think she was plotting. Finally, in a silky voice, she said, 'Hubie dubes, I know you vish to turn from crimes.'

He nodded.

'Zat is grand, vizzout a doubt. But have you really vorked it out?'

He frowned. 'Vot you mean?'

'Ven you're free to roam ze street, how on earth you make ends meet? You have had career in crime. Retrainink vill take cash and time.'

He knew he shouldn't ask. 'Vot you gettink at?'

'Treasure.' Mummy rubbed her inner hands. 'If you escaped and found zat isle, you could zen reform in style.'

Klench licked his lips. One final act, to set him up for life. He could sell the treasure and flee to some distant country where no one knew him. There'd be plenty of time for reform after that.

No. Grandma would be livid.

So? He would be loaded.

The choice was clear: reform poor or reform rich.

He nibbled more pillow. 'But Mums,' he said at last. 'Just supposink I agree … how on earth vould I escapes?'

Inner Mummy beamed. 'How indeed, my sveet soufflé? Listen up – I know a vay.'

6

Beard Ahoy

The boat docked at Dublin Port. The children filed down to the hold and onto the bus, tired after the four-hour crossing but quietly excited to be in a foreign country.

Or are we? thought Abbie as they drove off the boat. The afternoon light was fading behind the same grey office blocks and skeletal cranes as you'd find in any English city. It wasn't until they were heading along the river into the centre that she began to spot little differences: elegant bridges, colourful doorways, and statues all over the place. Luckily Dad was too busy messing up Coriander's directions to give a history lecture.

'I said left at the lights, Graham.'

'Oh, right.'

'No, left. *Now* right.'

'Right now?'

'Right *then* – you missed it. OK, turn right here.'

'Right *here*?'

'Oh dear.'

The setting sun proved more helpful, leading them west out of Dublin. The first stars were tickling the sky when they pulled up in front of a yellow house in a little town.

They fell off the bus, silent with exhaustion. Abbie just about made it through her cottage pie and apple tart with extra cream before stumbling up to the girls' bedroom. She got ready for bed and took out her notebook to jot down her first impressions of Ireland. But after one sentence – the cream is epic – the pen drooped in her hand. She fell into bed, where not even Terrifica's volcanic snores could keep her awake.

Breakfast next morning was a farmyard on a plate: bacon, egg, sausage, liver, black pudding ('Dried blood,' said Henry, flicking his onto Ursula's lap) and white pudding ('Don't ask,' said Coriander, pushing hers to the side).

By nine o'clock they were once again heading west. A fine mist blurred the fields and narrow villages of central Ireland. Abbie gazed through the window at fuzzy trees and the smudges of sheep. Leaning her head against the window, she slipped into a doze of land and sky and rushing road. She awoke to gentle hills threaded with low stone walls. The sun flung beams between clouds. A grey line on the horizon thickened into sea as they approached the ferry port of Ballinabeeny.

The name was bigger than the place. There were three whitewashed cottages with tiled roofs, a shop with a bicycle outside and a stone jetty. A single boat bobbed in the water. On the rust-red bow, beside a flaking mermaid, was the name *Fidgety Bridget*.

Coriander went into the shop to buy boat tickets and lunch. The others sat by a stream and decided not to dabble their toes because, never mind April, spring was still in its pyjamas round here. Abbie wrapped her Winnie-scarf closer and thought of sleeping bags and mud and possibly having a good cry. Then Perdita tapped her on the shoulder and shouted, 'You're it,' and the children played tag to warm up while they waited for Coriander to return with sandwiches, crisps and chocolate Hobnobs.

After lunch Mr Dabbings stood on the harbour wall. 'Get your bags, folks. Time to go.' He blew a kiss at the minibus. 'See you here next week.'

A sour fishy smell smacked up Abbie's nose as she hauled her rucksack onto her back. A seagull squawked off the jetty. Fog hung low over the grey-green sea that twitched like living tartan. The door of the nearest whitewashed cottage opened.

She gripped Perdita's arm. 'What's *that*?'

'A beard. On legs.'

It was walking towards them. Perched on top of the enormous beard was a yellow rain hat. Sticking down below it was a pair of yellow trousers tucked into black wellies.

A slit opened near the top of the beard. 'Ahar!' it roared.

'Avast!' And, stopping to face them, 'Ahoy!' An arm shot out from the side. A hand tilted the hat. Beneath the brim two green eyes glittered like flies. 'Well judder me hawsers! What a runtle o' land lubbers. What a muckle o' soil huggers.'

Mr Dabbings stepped forward. 'Well I do like to cuddle a clod, now you mention it.'

'Ha!' Another arm shot out. 'I knew it. Ground clingers, the lot o' ye.' From the shaking fist, Abbie guessed that wasn't a compliment. 'You earthy wormers, you terra firmas

– what brings you to the skirts of Old Granny Ocean?'

Dad reached out a hand. 'Pleased to meet you, um–'

'Cap'n Winkymalarkey O'Rourkemelads!' Dad's hand was ignored. 'Retired pirate, shark-wrestler and squid-squasher. Current Master o' the *Fidgety Bridget* and ferryman to local islands. Where're ye bound?'

'Remote Ken,' said Dad.

'Avoy!' The beard shivered like an electrocuted hedge. 'You're pulling me portholes! It's years since I've hoisted me pintles to that bewarted isle. You urban sprawlers, you shopping-mallers – you won't last ten minutes there.'

Mr Dabbings sniffed. 'We're actually going for ten *days,* thank you, to enjoy the natural world.'

Cap'n Winkymalarkey cackled. 'Oh, it ain't the *natural* world you'll be enjoying, me dewy groggers.'

Mr Dabbings blinked. 'What do you mean?'

The Cap'n threw out his arms. 'Plank up, young drabbers. Load the dunnage, clew the jimmybird and I'll tell 'ee the tale.'

Abbie guessed that meant they were going. Everyone grabbed their rucksacks and followed the Cap'n along the jetty. Stone steps led down to the water. The children climbed the gangplank onto the boat. The grown-ups made several trips to load the trolleys and food boxes onto the deck.

Leaning against the side rail, Abbie saw Henry sidle up

to Ursula. 'Oh no you don't!' She grabbed his arm before he could fake-push the poor girl overboard.

The Cap'n went into the cabin. With a shudder of engine and poop of horn, the boat set off. The wind whipped up, snatching at coats and spraying the deck with foam. Everyone hurried into the cabin, put on life jackets and crowded round the steering wheel.

'So,' said Dad.

'You were saying,' Mr Dabbings coughed.

'About the island,' Matt rubbed his teeth nervously.

The Cap'n steered and stared ahead. 'There be tales,' he said at last, 'of hidden treasure.'

'Yes, yes.' Dad waved his hand. 'We've read about–'

'Mebbe so.' The Cap'n wheeled round. 'But I'll wager me tubscrews ye didn't read there were –' his eyes glinted from face to face, 'GHOSTIES!'

Everyone fell onto everyone else. Dad tumbled into Mr Dabbings. Coriander stumbled into Matt. Perdita tripped over Abbie. Marcus toppled on Terrifica. And Henry seized the opportunity to stamp on Ursula's foot.

When everyone was vaguely upright again, Marcus said, a little too confidently, 'There's no such thing as ghosts.'

'Ha!' The Cap'n's eyes settled on Marcus. 'Is that so, young bobberjack? So tell me why the folks round these parts refuse to visit Remote Ken?' He turned back to the steering wheel.

Dad leaned towards him over Abbie's shoulder. 'Because they've grown up with the stories.' His breath tickled her ear. 'It's always the way. Look at any legend in history and there'll be magic tucked in somewhere. There's even a technical term for it. Hystoria – going hysterical over history.'

'Ahee!' boomed the Cap'n. 'So why the tales o' strange goings-on? Whispers in the woods, ripples in the lake?'

Mr Dabbings waved his hand. 'Oh, just Nature at play.' He smiled round the group. 'I've been reading up. The local climate is thought to result from hot and cold waters meeting to the west of Remote Ken. That creates a warm current called the Atlantic Waft, which can cause unusual weather conditions on the island.' He patted the whimpering Ursula on the shoulder. 'Now good Cap'n, I'll thank you to stop scaring the children and take us to our holiday spot.'

'Calm yer clotterhooks,' muttered Cap'n Winky. 'Just trying to warn 'ee.' His mouth vanished into his beard. For a while he steered in silence. Then: 'Land ahoy!' he boomed.

Peering through the window, Abbie could make out nothing but grey.

'Come. I'll show 'ee where ye'll be resting yer beamscuttles for a ten-day.' Matt took over the steering while the Cap'n led them out of the cabin.

The wind jostled Abbie across the deck. She gripped

the handrail on the side of the boat and stared at the dark shape looming from the sea.

'Look!' cried Henry. But it wasn't the island he was pointing at. Cap'n Winky's hat had blown off. Underneath bits of tape were stuck to his temples. The wind snatched at the tape. The beard shot off and flew away like a great hairy bird.

'Oh,' said the mouth it had left behind. 'Cwumbs. That's not in the scwipt.' The Cap'n clapped a hand to his face.

Coriander laid a hand on his arm. 'I think you'd better explain,' she said firmly.

The Cap'n leaned against the side of the boat. Stripped of his beard, his face was small and pinched. Below wide eyes and sharp cheekbones his cheeks tapered to a tiny chin. 'I told them it wouldn't work.' His voice had gone high and squeaky.

'What wouldn't?' said Coriander.

'The plan.' The Cap'n rubbed his eyes. 'Oh the game's up,' he said wearily. 'Might as well come clean.' He sighed. 'Along this coast, you see, the villages are wather wun down. So the locals hatched a plan to attwact touwists. They put an advert in the paper fow a boatman. Someone who could spin a cweepy tale. The idea was that the stowy would spwead and bwing more visitors.'

'Ha!' Dad crowed. 'What did I tell you? Classic Hystoria.'

Mr Dabbings tutted. 'Exploiting Nature? Shame on you.'

Cap'n Winkymalarkey sniffed. 'Wasn't my idea. I just happened to be here, taking a bweak fwom London. I was twying to find myself.'

'And your chin,' said Marcus.

The Cap'n blushed. 'Please don't. It's no joke having a poor bottom jaw. I'm an actor, you see. But who wants a chinless James Bond? Who'd play Juliet to a jawless Womeo? Audiences were so wude. They laughed me off stage, wuined my confidence. I got tewwible stage fwight.'

Coriander tutted sympathetically. 'Has this job cured you?'

'Dunno. You're my first touwists. The beard helped – until it blew off. Haven't had much pwactice sticking it on. Sowwy.'

'It's OK.' Coriander patted his hand. 'But you shouldn't have scared the children like that, Cap'n Winkymalarkey.'

He hung his small head. 'And by the way, that's not my weal name. It's …' he twisted the toe of his welly boot, 'Bundy Pilks.'

The children hooted.

'Stop that,' ordered Coriander. 'You should never laugh at someone's name. Should you, Mr Dabbings?'

'No.' He shook his head gravely. 'Not even if it's really stupid.'

As Bundy Pilks returned to the cabin, Abbie turned to inspect the island. The edges were flat as a mat. But through the mist she made out two mountains in the middle. Rising in sharp triangles, they peaked at the same height and were separated by a wide V-shaped valley.

The sun broke through the clouds, dropping diamonds onto the sea and scattering the fog in ghostly puffs. Despite the warmth on her face, Abbie shivered. *Not ghostly,* she corrected herself. *Ocean currenty.* The Atlantic Waft was fact. Everything else was fiction.

So why was dread uncurling in her stomach like a slow, black snake?

***

'You chaps are welcome to stay till you're sorted.' Grandma spoke loudly and clearly. 'Aren't they, folks?'

Ollie nodded across the kitchen table. 'Defnutly. Can I take them in for Show and Tell?'

Mum cleared her throat. 'I think it might be hard to explain what two ancient Incas are doing in Garton, poppet.' She glared at Grandma. 'And no, they're not welcome,' she muttered. 'How can we possibly help them?'

Grandma had brought the old men home the previous afternoon. It hadn't started well. When she'd explained that the visitors were Incas who'd survived the Spanish invasion of Ecuador, and that Fernando and Carmen were two of those invaders, the atmosphere had turned a little frosty. But Fernando had apologised in a lovely way – 'I sorry for conquer with all my heart' – and Carmen had refrained from pointing out that he had no heart to be sorry with. After that things improved, not least because the heads knew a little Quechua from their years in Ecuador and could help translate Bacpac's story when his English failed. Chester, too, helped break the ice. Watching him wriggle on Grandma's head, or fly down to help Mum serve dinner, the old men were reminded of monkeys in their jungle home.

But now, at Sunday dinnertime, the tension returned.

''Ow indeed can we 'elp?' Grandma waved her knife at Mum. 'I've been worryin' about it all day. And I've decided we can. I've decided we *should*.'

Mum's fork froze in mid-air. 'Ollie,' she said, 'why don't you go and see how many chocolate wrappers you can find in Dad's study? I'll give you a Wagon Wheel for every ten you bring.'

When he'd gone Mum stared at Grandma. 'If you're suggesting,' she murmured, 'that you introduce the Incas to Klench so that he can hold their hands ...' she let out a long breath. 'Well, isn't that murder? At the very least you'd be a – whatsit? – an accessory.'

'I knew you wouldn't approve,' Grandma laid down her cutlery. 'And nor did I at first. But the thing is,' she sighed, 'growin' old's no lark in the park. Me bones are startin' to creak, me brain's beginnin' to leak – and *I'm* only seventy-three. They're more than six times me age. Imagine 'ow it must feel to be the only survivors of a culture that's long kaput, stuck in a world that's passed 'em by. The kindest thing we can do is 'elp 'em to join their friends and family in the afterlife.'

Bacpac was nodding: he clearly got the gist. Chunca was flicking peas at the wall.

'Besides.' Grandma pushed her plate away. ''Oo's to know? The Incas'll die when they shake Klench's 'and. It'll look like a couple of 'eart attacks. It's the simplest thing – and the best for them. They'll be eternally grateful.'

Mum chewed her bottom lip. 'They'll be eternally dead.'

***

Klench stood over the sink in the prison bathroom. He tipped out the food he'd collected during the day: the prunes and bran flakes saved from breakfast, and the liquorice he'd pinched from another prisoner. He added some tap water and mixed them together. Then he crumbled in a bar of soap, squeezed in some toothpaste, squirted in some hairgel, spooned in some shoe polish ... and opened his mouth.

7

Hurling Henry

The *Fidgety Bridget* sat on the beach, half in and half out of the water. Little waves patted her side. Grabbing their rucksacks, the children climbed down a ladder fixed to the side of the boat. The adults unloaded the rest of the luggage, dropping the food crates onto the beach and stacking them on the two trolleys.

Bundy saluted from the deck. 'See you in ten days – Wednesday at thwee o'clock … ish … pwobably … weather permitting.'

Abbie didn't like the sound of that. 'What do you mean?'

'If the weather's bad, you'll have to wait.' Bundy laughed nervously. 'No one messes with the sea wound here.'

'You mean we could be stranded?' Abbie swallowed.

'What if there's an emergency?' said Marcus.

Bundy shrugged. 'Call me. I'll come as soon as I can.'

'How?' Marcus looked coldly at Mr Dabbings. '*You* didn't let us bring cell phones, *Sir.*'

'I bet there's no signal here anyway,' said Terrifica, her nostrils flaring anxiously.

'Right and right again.' Mr Dabbings smiled. 'Which is why the school bought me this.' He fished out a chunky black phone from his anorak pocket.

Marcus snorted. 'Fat use that'll be. A stone-age phone.'

'No, Marcus, it's a *modern*-age, state-of-the-art satellite phone. As expedition leader I have to be able to contact the outside world. Only in a crisis, of course. I'm sure I won't be needing it, will I, Bundy?'

'No,' squeaked the mini-chinned actor, looking far less than sure and far more than keen to get away. He gave his number to Mr Dabbings, then waved. 'Cheewio, chaps. See you soon … ish.' He went into the cabin to start the engine while everyone pushed the *Fidgety Bridget* back into the water.

They stared in silence as the boat bobbed and shrank towards the horizon. Panic fluttered in Abbie's stomach. *There goes our lifeline, our link to the world.* Never mind the ground beneath them – she suddenly felt adrift, cut loose in space and time. She pictured Brother Donal landing here a thousand years ago. Perhaps the pebbles were smoother now, perhaps the mountains sharper, but little else could have changed. She imagined a thin, ragged man dropping to his knees on the beach to thank God for another safe trip. She pictured three kindly old monks waddling down to meet him, their faces alight, their arms outstretched, all hugs and hot chocolate.

OK, maybe not hot chocolate. But boy could she use one now. A nice little seafront café with armchairs and home-made flapjacks: that would do perfectly. She looked around. *Dream on.* The shingle beach rose gently inland to a band of rocks, dark and chunky as Mum's chocolate brownies. They ended at a line of scrubby grass. Beyond that stretched moorland, a vast bruise of purple-green heather. She shivered. You could see how the stories had arisen. Treasure, Vikings, curses … this place looked made for mystery.

They waited at the edge of the moor while Dad and Matt wheeled the trolleys over the beach. Mr Dabbings was frowning over a map. 'It's the only one I could find,' he said to Coriander. 'Very unclear.'

'This might help.' She turned it the other way round. When he looked just as baffled, she took it gently from him. 'That stream on the left leads over the moor to a lake between the mountains. The cottages should be there.'

Cottages. A fine word – almost as good as café. A smile rose inside Abbie as she pictured herself sitting by a roaring fire with Perdita in the cosy house they'd agreed to share, toasting the marshmallows she'd sneaked into her rucksack.

'We must stick together,' said Coriander. 'There'll be bogs.' She scanned the moor. 'Like over there.' She pointed towards a bright green patch of grass on the right. 'You really don't want to fall into one of those.'

'Mum should know,' said Perdita proudly. 'Tell them about the time you fell into the Okavango swamp.'

Coriander shuddered. 'I wouldn't be here now if it wasn't for that passing crocodile.'

Not entirely comforted, Abbie focused on the ground as they set out over the moor. The heather flattened beneath her trainers, then bounced back, boosting her stride. A watery sun warmed the back of her head. She fell into an easy rhythm, punctuated by the peep of invisible birds. If you didn't think too hard or look too closely, this was almost, at a pinch, what you might call, very nearly, not too bad.

The land rose gently, its smooth surface broken only by fiery bursts of gorse and huge boulders scattered over the moor as if by giants in a tantrum.

'Erics,' said Dad happily. 'Those rocks were carried down from the mountains in the Ice Age.' He winked at Abbie. 'Bit of a *pre*historian too, your old dad.'

'Actually,' said Matt, 'they're called erratics.'

'Oh.' Dad sniffed. 'Well, as you know, my expertise lies in people, not stones.'

After nearly an hour they reached a ridge on the moor.

'Wow,' said Abbie. In front of them a rocky slope dropped to a grassy area. Beyond it lay a pebble beach, then a lake.

The mountains rose either side, their reflections trembling in the blue-green water. She shielded her eyes. 'What are those?' On the grass below them five grey domes stood together, surrounded by a low circular wall.

Dad whistled. 'Beauties.' He left his trolley at the top of the slope and climbed down the rocks. The others followed.

Up close the beauties turned out to be buildings. The walls were made of thin flat stones, layered horizontally. Four of the domes were about twice Abbie's height. The fifth was taller and wider. All five had rectangular doorways.

'Beehive huts.' Dad stroked the biggest dome. 'Built by the monks a thousand years ago.' He shook his head in wonder. 'Some job, quarrying that lot.' He nodded towards the rocks sloping down from the ridge.

'How come there are five?' said Marcus. 'I thought only three monks lived here.'

'These were probably built before they came, by a whole team from the monastery. Maybe as a bolt-hole in case of invasion.' Dad patted the wall. 'Not a lick of cement between the stones. Look at that craftsmanship.'

But Abbie was looking at something else – or rather she wasn't. 'Where are the cottages? I thought *they* were by the lake.'

Dad winked. Mr Dabbings smiled. Abbie went cold.

Last Christmas she'd been sure she was getting an iPhone. She'd even spotted the rectangular parcel under the tree. But it had turned out to be a six-pack of tights from deaf Aunt Brassica who lived in Swansea and bred prawns. Oh, the disappointment.

But that was nothing compared to this. 'I'm not sleeping in a pizza oven!' she wailed.

'As promised,' said Mr Dabbings, ignoring her, 'simple self-catering. They're roomy and dry with a south-facing aspect.' He sounded like a medieval estate agent.

Dad patted the hut. 'If they're good enough for men of God, they're good enough for you, young lady. The monks lived in them for years. We can jolly well do it for ten days.'

'So you knew about this. Why didn't you *tell* me?'

Dad shrugged. 'You never asked.'

She couldn't deny that. So she settled for some high-voltage glaring and waited for the others to complain. But no one did. They were too busy running in and out of the huts, testing for echoes and ancient graffiti.

'How about this one, Abbie?' Perdita stuck her head out of a hut. 'We can spread some heather on the ground for mattresses.'

Abbie stooped through the entrance. Hardly the cottage she'd imagined, but she had to admit it was snug. The air was warm, the earthen floor firm. The walls curved over protectively like a giant cupped hand. *Could be worse*, she thought grudgingly. *And it'll be fun sharing with Perdita.* Besides, what was the choice?

The huts were identical except for the largest one, in which a stone bench jutted from the wall.

'Would this have been Father Kenneth's hut?' asked Marcus. 'Bigger and more luxurious?'

Abbie winced at the medieval idea of luxury.

Dad shook his head. 'As senior monk, he'd have set an example of humility. He'd never take the best accommodation. This was probably used communally – for prayer or storing food.'

'Good job we've got a tent for that,' said Coriander. 'We'll need all the hut space for sleeping. Hey girls, why don't we put it up? The boys can help Matt with the loo tent.'

That sounded only fair. The girls rushed out before the boys could protest.

'I'll be construction director,' said Terrifica, as Coriander unfolded the canvas.

Perdita laughed. 'I don't think so. Mum's put up tents all over the world. Siberia, the Sahara – you name it.'

Terrifica sniffed. 'Well I've done it in Guides.'

Abbie snorted. 'Who cares about *Guides*?'

'I do.' Everyone turned. Ursula was sitting down hugging her knees. 'I'd love to be a Guide.'

Perdita crouched next to her. 'Why aren't you?'

'My parents.' Ursula put her chin on her knees. 'They can't take me.'

'Why not?' said Terrifica. 'It's only once a week.'

'They're out every night train–' Ursula clamped her lips shut.

'What for?'

'Nothing.'

Coriander was kneeling down, laying out tent poles. 'That's a shame, dear.' She sat back on her heels. 'If transport's the problem, I'd be happy to take you. Maybe I could chat to your parents when we get back.'

'No.' Ursula paled to paper.

Abbie smiled sympathetically. She was an expert on uncool parents. Ursula's must be off the scale. What on earth could they be training for? Shouting nicknames in public places? The nose-picking Olympics?

Following Coriander's directions, and ignoring Terrifica's, the food tent was soon standing in the centre of the hut circle. The boys returned from helping Matt set up his latest invention over the ridge on the moor. Inside a little brown tent was the Soilet, a little wooden seat with a hole in the middle that formed the top of a vertical pipe. With lively sound effects from Henry, Matt explained how waste travelled down the organic pipe deep into the earth. After a few weeks the pipe would dissolve, leaving no litter and fertilising the soil.

'Wait till you hear about the loo roll!' Mr Dabbings's sideburns danced. 'Matt's brought a stack of leaves soaked in a special liquid that makes them soft, strong and biodegradable. Kind to the behind and sound under-ground.'

Marcus rolled his eyes at Abbie.

'Aoww!' came a loud whimper – or was it a quiet scream? Henry was jabbing Ursula's arm with a tent peg.

Perdita rushed over. 'Stop it, you big–'

She froze. Henry was in the sky. Ursula had grasped his waist and lifted him above her head. For a moment he hung frozen in the air. Then he flew three metres over the grass and landed on his bottom.

Ursula covered her face with her hands. 'Oh no.'

Henry blinked at her in terror.

'How did you do that?' gasped Abbie as Coriander ran over to comfort him.

'My parents. They're ...' Ursula chewed the inside of her cheek.

'Well, spit it out,' barked Terrifica.

'Wrestlers.' Ursula burst into tears.

'Mumm*eeee*!' wailed Henry, burying his face in Coriander's shoulder.

'Sssh.' She wiped his tears with a plait. 'It's OK.'

'Serves you right,' said Perdita briskly. She turned to Ursula. 'Why didn't you do that months ago?'

'I ...' Ursula was shaking. 'I hate violence. And showing off. You should see my parents. Wherever we go, they roar and shout and make a scene – in supermarkets, cafés, libraries. It's all publicity for their stage show.'

It was the longest, loudest speech she'd ever made. And it explained so much: why she hid behind others, why her clothes were the colour of porridge. *Poor thing*, thought Abbie. *With parents like that, who wouldn't want to disappear?*

'Priceless!' Terrifica honked like a goose. 'Ooh, bagsy not share a hut with you. I might wake up on the ceiling.'

Perdita glared at her. 'Don't worry, you won't. Because *I'll* share with Ursula.' She took the tiny girl's hand. 'You can teach me some wrestling moves.'

'Hey!' Pity went sour in Abbie's mouth. 'I thought *we* were together.'

Perdita's eyes went wide. 'We can't let Ursula go with ...' she pointed at Terrifica who was still hooting away. 'She'll just tease her all night. Come on, it's only for sleeping.'

Being offered the biggest hut was no compensation for sharing with Terrifica. That evening, after a meagre meal of potted turnip soup and crackers, Abbie abandoned the singsong round the fire Matt had lit on the beach. Despite Mr Dabbings's best efforts on his guitar, she *wasn't* happy and she *didn't* know it, so why on earth should she clap her hands?

Lighting a candle from the cinders at the edge of the fire, she headed off to bed. She slipped into her sleeping bag, took out her notebook and wrote:

Lumbered with Battgirl, thanks to Perdita,
my BFF–WISH (Best Friend Forever – When It
Suits Her).

Then she slammed the book shut and blew out the candle.

***

Klench sat at the back of the bus, grinning and groaning.
The grin was at the ease of his escape. The groan was at
the ache in his guts. The prune-bran-liquorice-soap-
toothpaste-hairgel-polish mixture had done its job. The
warder had taken one look at Klench rolling around the
floor of his cell and called an ambulance. The hospital was
twenty minutes away and, in the rush, no one had thought
to put a potty in the vehicle.

As the traffic lights turned red, Klench had whimpered,
'I must go.'

'We-e-ell …' The prison officer looked at the awesome
tum rumbling before him. An accident wouldn't be pretty.
'I really shouldn't do this but …' Handcuffing Klench's
wrist to his own, he told the driver to stop at a public toilet.

At the cubicle door, Klench gasped, 'You comink in or
vot?'

'We-e-ell.' The prison officer looked at the green face
trembling before him. It was a poo he'd rather not view. 'I
really shouldn't do this but …' Unlocking the handcuffs, he

pushed Klench into the cubicle.

Ten minutes, three wind concertos and four barrels of eau-de-cowpat later, Klench emerged. 'Zat,' he sighed, 'iss better.' He went to the sink, washed his hands and held them out for the handcuffs.

Seventeen seconds, two Chinese burns and a kick up the backside later, the prison officer was in the cubicle, stripped of his jacket and handcuffed to the toilet roll holder.

'And zat,' sang Klench, 'iss *much* better.' Stuffing the officer's mouth with toilet roll, he squeezed into the jacket and fished out a pair of dark glasses from a pocket. He gave a little wave. 'Cheerie pip – or perhaps I should say toodle *loo!*'

Now Klench gazed out of the bus window, rubbing his stomach.

'No pain no gain, my superbrain,' Inner Mummy reminded him.

He winced. It was all very well for her. Swanning about in his head, she could enjoy the plus of freedom without the minus of gut rot. Still, the foul mixture was almost out of his system. 'And it iss good to be on ze runs again,' he murmured, clutching his belly. 'Literally.'

∗∗∗

Grandma and the Incas were watching TV. Or rather, the two old men were gawping from the sofa while she explained for the umpteenth time that there wasn't *actually* a tiny man inside the box. 'It's called technology,' she said vaguely. 'Cameras and satellites and cables and– *WHAT*?!' She leapt out of her armchair. 'I don't believe it!' A mugshot of Klench filled the screen.

'The escape happened this afternoon,' said the newsreader, 'on the way to the hospital.' His grey hair stuck out in alarmed tufts. 'Police are warning that he's dangerous and shouldn't be approached by members of the public.'

'You try and stop me.' Grandma shook her fist at the

telly. 'Of all the …' She grabbed the Sunday crossword, scrunched it into a ball and hurled it at the screen. 'To think I believed 'e was reformin', when all the while 'e was plannin' to escape!' A furious tear rolled down her cheek. Chester slipped down her forehead to mop it up.

When Bacpac had translated the news, Chunca put his head in his hands. 'Now my death is over.'

8

Nature's Pick 'n' Mix

'Knockety knock!' A voice crashed into Abbie's dream. She was a raisin cooking in a cake, hot and squashed and smothered in flour.

'I said knock knock.'

She opened her eyes. The flour turned into her sleeping bag. The squash turned into Terrifica, who'd rolled across the floor of the hut and flung an arm across her chest.

Pushing her away, Abbie blinked in the sunlight pouring through the entrance. 'Who's there?'

Dad's outrageously cheerful face appeared. 'Friar.'

'Friar who?'

'Friar-*ing* pan! Geddit?'

Abbie goddit. She goddit that she was lying in a stone pimple, on the nose of sweet nowhere, with an un-best friend, a doofus dad and a bruised bottom.

'Sleep well, girls?'

Terrifica sat up, her yawn drowning out Abbie's groan. 'Superdedoops.'

'Great stuff. Brekkie's ready.' That got Abbie out of her sleeping bag faster than you could say 'toast triangles'. Throwing on jeans and a jersey, she stumbled outside.

It was surprisingly warm. She breathed in the sweetness of grass still wet with dew. Birdsong glittered on the air. A pale mist draped the lake. Stretching out her arms, she had to admit there were worse ways to start the day.

Perdita and Ursula were already at the lake, paddling and shrieking at the cold. Swallowing her annoyance, Abbie too headed down to the beach, where the bonfire had been relit from last night.

Dad, Matt and Mr Dabbings were sitting around eating from wooden bowls.

Coriander was stirring a pot in the embers. 'Morning, dear.' She ladled some grey goo into a bowl.

Abbie wrinkled her nose. 'I'll just have toast, thanks.'

'Toast – what's that?' Dad winked at Coriander. 'Remember the menu's tenth century this week. None of your Hovis back then, my girl.' He licked his wooden spoon. 'Barley grain and milk. Yum. And way healthier than sliced white.'

Scowling, Abbie took the bowl.

He leaned over. 'Apart from the Tesco sugar,' he whispered. 'Not exactly Dark Ages but I sneaked it in to liven things up.' Swallowing the sweet, creamy and not entirely un-delicious porridge, Abbie allowed a little grin.

Perdita strode over. 'Sleep well?' She whacked Abbie on the back.

'Nhhllk.' Porridge flew everywhere.

'Excellent,' said Ursula, coming up behind. 'That was a Whopperslap,' she told Abbie.

'Urse has been teaching me some wrestling moves,' said Perdita.

Urse? Abbie spluttered again.

'Perdita's a natural,' said Urse.

'What a surprise,' Abbie muttered. But they were too busy doing something with elbows and shoulder blades to hear. She screwed up her eyes until the two of them shrank to vague, unimportant blurs.

'Hey, lemon face.' She hadn't noticed Marcus coming down from his hut. 'You OK?'

She nodded quickly.

'This'll cheer you up.' He pulled a blue rag from under his jumper. 'Can you believe it? Henry was cuddling this all night!' He dangled it between finger and thumb.

Abbie's hand flew to her mouth. Henry Holler – loud-mouth, bully and (until yesterday) class toughster – had a blankie?

Perdita turned to them. 'Where *is* Henry?'

They found him further down the beach, sitting with his arms round his knees. 'I wanna go ho-wum,' he sniffed.

Perdita snatched the blanket from Marcus and dropped

it onto his lap. 'I think you lost this.'

'Mr Binkles.' Henry snuggled it to his face. Marcus snorted.

Perdita glared at him. 'That was mean of you.' She turned and marched back to the huts. Ursula scuttled behind.

'Miss Goodie three-plaits,' muttered Marcus.

Abbie felt a blush creep up her neck. *Perdita's right. It was mean.* She blinked at the lake. *So why didn't I say so?* Little waves ruffled the water.

A low note cut the air. They looked back. Mr Dabbings was standing in the middle of the hut circle, blowing a curly horn.

Marcus grinned. 'Marching orders.' They ran back along the beach.

'Welcome,' said Mr Dabbings as everyone gathered round, 'to a truly delicious day.' He smacked his lips as if the air was made of chocolate. 'This morning we're going to pick 'n' mix from Nature's snackbar.'

'Awebics!' shouted Henry, who'd cheered up now that Mr Binkles was tucked safely under his T-shirt. 'Mine's a Lion Bar.'

'No, Henry. Coriander and I will introduce you to some of the edible plants on the island. We'll gather them for lunch, just like the monks did.' Everyone groaned.

'Either that,' said Dad, 'or you can stay behind and help me and Matt wash up medieval style – twigs and water plus natural disinfectant.'

'Which is?' said Abbie suspiciously.

'Saliva.'

Everyone shrieked with disgust except Henry, who said, 'Awelicks, I'll stay.' In the end Terrifica agreed to stay too and make sure that no one spat on anything so she could earn her No To Nasty Habits badge.

The others packed water bottles and cagoules in their rucksacks and followed Mr Dabbings up the slope. Abbie ignored Perdita's request to wait while she emptied a stone from her shoe. *That'll serve her right for ignoring me*. But it didn't, because Ursula waited instead and showed Perdita a special foot flick to get rid of stones without removing your shoe.

When everyone had climbed over the ridge, Coriander scanned the moor. 'Let's head for those woods.' She pointed to the nearest mountain. A cluster of trees hugged the base. Above them the slope rose steeply, speckled with boulders and scrub. Towards the top the vegetation gave way to bare rock that tapered to the peak.

Abbie strode across the moor, taking deep gulps of air until it felt as if she was breathing from her toes. Her irritation with Perdita faded. Thin clouds whispered across the sky. The air was warm, the heather still. And suddenly she was full. All her worries and wants, yesterdays and tomorrows, dissolved into the shimmering, brimming here-and-now.

'So.' Marcus fell into step beside her. 'The treasure.'

Abbie blinked.

'Imagine if it was still here.'

Tomorrow came flooding back. Wants did a U-turn.

'We'd be loaded for life.'

Abbie pictured his huge house. 'You already are.'

Marcus had the sense not to reply.

'It *would* be amazing to find it, though,' she murmured, as reporters and cameras jostled across her mind.

They continued in silence, jumping over the stream they'd followed yesterday and heading for the mountain. Abbie fell into a dream, imagining what she could buy with money from the treasure. *Plasma TVs for every wall. Holidays wherever and whenever I like. Bourbons galore … Bourbon factories galore!* And think of the articles she could write that would fly round the world … *The New York Times, The Sydney Herald, The Mongolian Mail on Sunday.* She'd be the richest, most famous young journalist in history.

'Bog!'

She looked up. In her reverie, she'd fallen behind. Coriander had already reached the woods and was pointing to the left, where a bright green patch lay in front of the trees.

Abbie shivered. It wasn't that close, but she'd been in her own little world. What if she'd wandered towards it and … *Don't!* She ran to catch up with the others.

When everyone had gathered by the trees, Mr Dabbings looked round gravely. 'Now remember kids, these woods aren't used to humans. I want everyone to tread softly. If we're kind to Nature, she'll be kind to us.' Abbie imagined blackberries queuing patiently to jump into a jam jar.

She followed the others into the woods. Stooping between the wriggly branches of oaks, she felt like an intruder. Every snap of twig shattered an ancient stillness. Every footstep crushed a world of roots, insects and living earth. She held herself in tight and small and crept through the gloom.

They came to a clearing where spears of sunlight stabbed through the trees.

'Ha!' cried Mr Dabbings. 'Dotty Normans.' He pointed to a cluster of spotty brown umbrellas on the trunk of a tree. 'We can make soup.'

'No!' Coriander grabbed his arm. 'Those are Grim Zitters. They cause dreadful diarrhoea.'

Mr Dabbings frowned. 'I'm sure they're Dotties. Look at the tilt of their hats.'

Coriander shook her head. 'Definitely Zitters.'

'Normans.' Mr Dabbings's voice was cold. 'I know my fungi thank you.'

'OK,' said Coriander gently, 'we'll agree to differ. But better safe than sorry, eh Bran?'

Mr Dabbings's face went tight. His eyebrows bunched.

His lips pursed. He crossed the glade to a fallen log. Sitting down, he folded his arms. His breathing came in sharp little bursts.

Coriander went over and put a hand on his shoulder. 'Sorry, Bran, but we can't risk it. Why don't you go back to the moor and make up poems about moss while I find some herbs for lunch?'

The teacher stood up. Without a word he marched out of the woods. The children followed in silence. They'd never seen him lose his cool. And it wasn't cool.

***

Ollie threw a Caramel Swirl at the board. The white king fell over. 'Ha, you die!' He was teaching the Incas a version of chess in which, to win, you had to hit the opponent's king with a chocolate.

Chunca picked up the king. Shaking his head, he gabbled to Bacpac.

'Master say, what is point of dying in game? When can he die for real?'

Grandma looked up from the crossword. 'When I've worked out where Klench 'as escaped to. In the meantime, we're stuck 'ere.'

'Why?' said Ollie. 'I want to go out.'

'I've told you,' said Mum, 'we're not going anywhere till Klench is caught.'

'But I'm *borrrrred.*' He threw a Vanilla Fudge at her.

'Ow!' She rubbed her nose. 'Don't be a baby, Oliver. You're six years old.'

'So? *He's* four hundred and fifty.' Ollie pointed to the antiquated Emp who was lobbing Quality Streets through the window and knocking out caterpillars on the lawn.

***

The lady in the camping shop coughed. 'I'm not sure that one will quite, er, accommodate you, Sir. Better go for the two-man.'

'But I am vun mans.' Klench pulled down his dark glasses and scowled at her. 'I think perhaps you are tryink to rip me offs. And zat makes me sad.'

The lady gulped. Sad wasn't the word she'd use to describe the expression in those piggy eyes, beneath the black Afro that must surely be a wig. It so didn't match his pasta-pale skin. Not that she was about to ask. He clearly wasn't a man for small talk – or indeed small anything. 'It's just with your, um, build, you'd have more, er, breathing space. I assure you, Sir,' she lied, 'most single campers go for the double tent.'

Mollified, Klench opened the wallet he'd found in the prison officer's jacket.

Inner Mummy, who had a degree in counting money, did a quick sum. 'Sixty-five you can afford,' she declared.

'But time you cannot. Grab ze tent and hit ze trail. Cops vill soon be on our tail.'

9

Troubles and Bubbles

Lunch was a bad mood bring-and-share. The first offering was from Mr Dabbings. Returning from the moor he stormed off to his hut, still furious at being out-fungied.

The second was from Dad. He stood outside the food tent waving a bowl in one hand and a stick in the other. 'I've been scraping this for half an hour and it's still caked in porridge!' he shouted at nobody in particular. A skylark called Nobodyinparticular Jones burst into tears and changed her name to Sue.

Matt came out of the tent. 'I offered your dad some Scour Flour,' he explained to Abbie, holding out a handful of brown powder. 'You mix it with water and it cleans the dishes perfectly.'

Dad wagged his stick. 'That's cheating. The monks didn't use chemicals.'

'I told you,' said Matt, 'Scour Flour's only bramble thorns mashed in vinegar. Both were around in medieval times. The monks could easily have made up this mixture.'

'Ha!' Dad jabbed his stick in the air. 'But we don't actually know if they did.'

'Suit yourself.' Matt shrugged. 'I'm off to light the fire.' He turned towards the beach then grinned over his shoulder. 'Don't worry, I promise I'll do it medieval-style, with flint and steel.'

Dad looked as if he'd like to mash Matt in bramble thorns and vinegar.

The third grumpster was Terrifica. She'd found a patch of nettles near the camp and wanted to boil them to make tea. But she'd forgotten to bring her garden gloves and had to abandon her Picking Cruel Plants Sensibly badge.

Henry too was miserable. After the blankie incident, he'd tried to restore his tough image by picking the nettles with his bare hands. Now he was sitting against the wall of his hut whimpering. Coriander had collected some dock leaves to rub on his stings but he wouldn't let go of Mr Binkles.

'Why do I have to share a hut with him?' Marcus grumbled. 'I'll never sleep with him snivelling into his blankie.'

Only the Platts and Ursula seemed happy, which made Abbie the mother of all bad mooders. 'Thanks for including me,' she snapped, as Ursula explained a move to Perdita that involved knees and ankles.

'I will if you like.' Ursula crouched down and tickled the

back of Abbie's knees. Her legs buckled. Ursula kicked the back of her heels.

Abbie's legs shot forward. 'Yoww!' She plonked onto her bottom.

'The Bumparump.'

Perdita clapped. 'Classic. Winnie would love it.' She helped Abbie up. 'Hey, there's a thought. Urse could teach the orangs to wrestle. Great idea, don't you think Abbie?'

Yeah. Abbie rubbed her bottom. *And while you're at it, why not invite her to come and live at the zoo?* 'I'll help Dad with lunch,' she muttered, hobbling off to the food tent.

Inside Dad was sitting on a crate, trying to unscrew a Potted History. 'Phew.' He wiggled his fingers. 'You need a bionic wrist for this. Hey Abbs, go and get Ursula, would you?'

Her face crumpled. 'Not you too.'

'What?' Dad put the pot down. 'I just thought, because she's–'

'Strong and amazing and everyone's new best friend.'

'What are you on about?'

A tear squeezed out. 'Well, Perdita's anyway.' Abbie brushed it away angrily. 'Sharing a hut with her, learning those stupid wrestling moves.'

'Oh, come on.' Dad patted the crate. She sat down next to him. 'You know what Perdita's like. Friends with every-one.'

'Except me,' Abbie sniffed.

'Nonsense.' He put his arm round her. 'But if that's how you're feeling, you should talk to her. I'm sure she'll put your mind at rest. And in the meantime ...' he glanced at the tent door. 'Tenth-century tonic.' He fished a Yorkie bar out of his pocket.

Abbie's eyes widened. 'That's not medieval. It's Nestlé.'

'Says who?' Dad winked. 'I'm the history expert; *I'll* tell you what it is.' He broke the bar in two. 'A Celtic medicine, found in a peat bog, preserved for a thousand years.'

Abbie took her half, grinning. 'You're not so bad for a dad.'

'But remember,' Dad brandished the other half in the air, 'it comes with an ancient curse. If you tell anyone about it, your head falls off. You have been warned.'

Dad might be a choco-sneaking superstar, but he'd been useless on the Perdita front. Talk to her? When? Ursula was stuck to her like a hairclip. Even at lunch they were sitting on the wall finding new ways to push each other off.

Anyway, why should I go crawling? thought Abbie. *Perdita's upset me: it's her job to apologise.* Abandoning her bowl of pease pudding not-very-hot, she went down to the beach where Terrifica and Marcus were skimming stones.

'Four ... five ... six.' Terrifica sighed. 'I need eight bounces for my Stone Skimmer's badge.'

'Who's to know?' said Marcus.

Terrifica's jaw dropped. 'But that's cheating. I'll lose my Honest and True badge.'

'Not if you don't tell anyone.'

'That's double cheating. I'll lose my Usually Honest and True badge.'

'Not if you don't tell anyone.'

'I'll lose my *Nearly* Usually Hon–'

Abbie left them to it. The sun was high as she wandered along the beach. Tiny waves crinkled the lake.

Hearing laughter, she turned round. Perdita and Ursula had come down to the beach and were playing Piggy in the Middle with Henry. Her chest went tight. *Even he's better than me now.* First Claire, then Ursula, now Henry – what had she done wrong? Flicking through the last few weeks in her mind, she came up with the worst possible answer. *Nothing.*

She sat down by the water and ate the last chunk of Yorkie. Sweet misery sank into her tongue. *Should I talk to Coriander?* And say what? 'Hey, why has your daughter stopped liking me?' What was the point? Coriander couldn't force their friendship. And nor could Perdita. An ache filled her throat as she realised that Perdita wasn't to blame. She couldn't help her feelings. And if she'd suddenly gone off Abbie – well, it wasn't her fault.

Abbie reached into the lake and snatched a handful of pebbles. 'It's never her fault!'

The stones glittered in her palm. Closing her eyes, she fanned the flame that Marcus had lit that morning. Imagine, by the teeny-weeniest chance, that the treasure was still here. And imagine, by the jammy-wammiest fluke, that she found it. *Ha!* The class would be at her feet. The world would be at her toenails. And Perdita would be on her knees, begging to re-best their friendship.

'Well, you can beg your bottom off, Miss Two-face, because I've gone off you too. In fact I'm completely sick of you!' Abbie flung the pebbles at the lake. Tiny explosions shattered the water. Jumping up, she turned to go.

What was that? She spun back round. A movement in the middle of the lake. A bubble breaking the surface. Another, and another. *A fish?* The bubbles were spreading. *A school of fish?* More like a university, the way they were popping and dancing outwards. Waves were growing too, carrying the bubbles to the edge of the lake.

Abbie backed away. The bubbles had reached the shore and were snapping onto the pebbles, sending up spurts of foam. She scuttled up to the undergrowth at the top of the beach, then turned and ran. As she approached the huts, the waves began to calm. The bubbles shrank to the middle of the lake, petered out and vanished. The water returned to its gentle movement: a restless denim of crisscrossing lines.

The grown-ups were sitting on the beach. Thank

goodness – they must have seen it too. They'd have the explanation.

In fact they had several. Mr Dabbings said it was Nature letting off steam, whatever that meant. Dad said it was the Loch Ness Monster on holiday eating beans. Coriander suggested underwater plants giving off gases. 'Like the Whiffaweed of Wataronga. I once dived into a bloom off New Zealand. I was looking for the Bearded Trout. But I gave up because of the smell.'

'This didn't smell,' said Abbie. 'And why did the bubbles come and go so fast?'

Matt had the best answer. 'Hot springs. Those two mountains are classic volcanic cones. There must be magma near the surface. And when the water comes in contact it heats up and bubbles.'

Mr Dabbings scratched a sideburn. 'You mean we could, um … erupt?'

'No.' Matt smiled. 'I'm sure the volcanoes are long

extinct. Nothing to worry about, Bran.'

Sitting round the fire that evening, you could almost believe it. The children's skinny shadows licked the beach. The fire cackled and spat, barbecuing their potted boar sausages into bliss. The dusky air was warm. Marcus was thanking goodness that Henry was moving to Coriander's hut so that she could tell him bedtime stories. Mr Dabbings was strumming his guitar and singing a long-distance lullaby to his unborn babe.

And Abbie? Oh she was just watching the flames fidget into the sky and wondering where to start her own private treasure hunt.

***

Klench's face stared blankly from the telly.

'Police are following several leads,' said the newsreader whose hair flew in all directions, as if following those leads.

Grandma threw her slipper at the screen. 'In other words, they 'aven't a clue. Where's 'e got to, the Jammy great Dodger? There aren't many places a whopper like that can 'ide.'

***

'What the hell ...? Ah thought you were in jail, Tubman.' Brag Swaggenham, oil tycoon and billionaire baddie, sat up straight in his chair. If he'd known the call was from his old partner in crime, he wouldn't have answered. He hadn't forgiven Klench for their capture in the Amazon jungle just four months ago. He was still sore about his near-imprisonment. He was still sore about the huge sum he'd paid Klench for an operation to change his fingerprints and stretch his fingers. And he was still sore. While the operation had worked technically – he could now fit twenty more rings on each hand – his fingers still throbbed, despite Klench's promise that the pain would wear off.

'I escaped,' Klench squeaked down the satellite phone he'd nicked from the camping shop. 'And I have learned about an island zat hides priceless treasure.'

Brag wasn't surprised at either piece of news. Klench was the cleverest crook he knew. He glanced at the jeweller working in front of him and pressed the phone to his ear. 'So what's your plan?'

'Take me to island and I vill give you cut of loots.'

Brag pulled his cowboy hat down over his forehead. 'Now why would ah do that – after all that pain you caused me?'

'Becoss zat pain also saved your bacons. Vizzout your new finkerprints, you vould be locked up for life. Like I voss.'

Brag frowned. Fair point. He'd got off free when they couldn't match his prints to his crimes, while Klench had landed up in jail.

Pulling a gun from his belt, he pointed it lazily at the jeweller. The poor man got the message. He huddled over the new ring he was engraving for Brag, humming loudly to make sure he didn't hear a word of the conversation.

'So where's this island?' Brag whispered down the phone.

Klench snorted. 'As if I tell before you give me lift. Vhere are you now?'

'Monaco. Bumping up mah finger wardrobe.'

'Perfect. You can pick me up on Vednesday. Fly me to island in your private helicopter and I vill locate treasure. Believe me, it vill fetch more money zan I can spend in vun lifetimes. You are velcome to leftovers.'

Brag's blue eyes narrowed. Either Klench was telling the truth, in which case they'd both make a killing. Or he was lying, in which case … there was nothing to lose but a tank of helicopter fuel. A smile cracked his tanned face. 'See ya Wednesday, Gutbutt.'

10

The Hunt is On

Mr Dabbings couldn't have been more helpful. His timetable next morning suited Abbie perfectly. After a breakfast of corn meal and milk – or in Abbie and Dad's case, secret rice crispies in the tent – Mr Dabbings announced that everyone would go off alone to catch Nature's Newshour.

He waved his arms as if conducting an orchestra. 'Hear the headlines in the wind. Watch the live un-coverage of mist. Interview the rabbits, badger the badgers.'

Henry scrunched Mr Binkles. 'Do we have to go alone?'

'Of course. Nature speaks differently to each of us, Henry. When it comes to noticing, two is a crowd.'

Abbie couldn't agree more. Tucking her notebook into the pocket of her shorts – it would come in useful for jotting down clues – she looked around. *Where do I start?*

The trick was to think like a monk. What had Dad said? They'd brought out the goblet every day from a secret place. So it had to be hidden from general view but easy for them to get to.

The coast? She hadn't seen any caves or cliffs, and surely it was too far for the monks to traipse over the moor every day.

The lake? Three old men in dresses would hardly be up to diving.

The moorland? Her heart sank. It could be buried anywhere under all that heather.

Except … the monks would need to locate it easily. So they'd have had some sign, some landmark. And while there was plenty of land, there weren't many marks: just gorse, a few trees and those huge scattered rocks.

Abbie screwed up her eyes. *Come on monks, give me a clue.*

For a moment she went blank. Then a brown-robed grandpa shuffled into her mind. 'Ooh, me poor old bones,' he murmured, rubbing his back. 'Ooh, me poor old eyes.' He hobbled away into darkness.

Thank you! Abbie opened her eyes. The goblet must have been within easy walking distance of the huts. And it must have been clearly marked for their dimming eyes, with some sort of sign that would weather the rain and wind – and, with any luck, the centuries too.

By the time she set off across the moor, Abbie was planning her outfit for the *Hiyaa* TV show.

At the first boulder she found lichen in the shape of Africa.

At the second boulder she found bird poo in the shape of a Walnut Whip.

At the third she found Marcus. He was kneeling down, examining the side of the rock. 'Whoa!' He jumped up, brushing off his trousers. 'You gave me a shock.'

If I was an inventor of paint colours, thought Abbie, *I'd make a new red called Embarrassed Marcus.*

He cleared his throat. 'I was just, um, listening to this boulder.'

Abbie snorted. Since when was Marcus into Dabbings-style Nature? 'Rubbish. You were looking for treasure.'

Marcus stumbled backwards. 'No ... I mean, what? ... I mean ... how did you know?'

Abbie felt herself blushing a new sort of pink called Because I Was Too.

'Great minds, eh?' Marcus whistled. 'Well I won't tell if you don't. And seeing as we've caught each other, why don't we look together?'

They ran to the next boulder. And the next. And the one after that. They found puddles. They found moss. They found a rock shaped like a croissant. They found tussocks that looked like Jedward.

And they found Terrifica. She was staring through a magnifying glass at a vein of quartz on a boulder. 'Yes,' she admitted. 'But if I *did* find the treasure, I'd use it to earn my Rich and Generous badge.' She turned a shade called Terrific Liar.

'You mean you'd give it to charity?' said Marcus.

'Of course.' She turned a deeper shade of Terrific Liar.

Three boulders later they found Dad. 'Oh dear,' he mumbled, turning a colour called Whopping Great Cheat. 'I'm supposed to be a responsible adult. Please don't tell Mr D.'

They didn't have to. Because at the next boulder they found him copying shiny squiggles on its surface into a notebook. He went the brightest red of all: Caught-In-The-Dabbings.

Dad traced the squiggles across the rock. They ended at a snail. Everyone folded their arms and smirked at the teacher.

'OK, OK!' He threw down his pencil. 'But my motives are pure, I promise. If I found the treasure I'd spend the money preserving this island's natural splendour.'

'But it's already being preserved,' said Abbie.

Mr Dabbings scuffed the ground with his sandal. 'Er yes. Until now. But how long before progress sticks its ugly nose in? Before pylons spring up and crisp packets choke the seagulls?'

No one looked convinced.

Heading back to the huts, Abbie swung between relief and disappointment. *Thank goodness I'm not the only sneak on the block. But poop the competition.* Because one thing was clear: the hunt was on. Whatever the others might pretend, she could bet her sweet Bounty bar that they wouldn't give up now.

And so could Mr Dabbings. Back at the huts he blew his horn.

Coriander appeared over the ridge of the moor. In her shiny yellow poncho she looked like a happy pepper. 'I've been listening to mud by the stream.'

Matt returned from the nearest mountain where he'd been watching granite erode. Henry came out of the Platts' hut where he'd been weightlifting Mr Binkles. Perdita had been at the beach chatting to pebbles. So, of course, had Ursula.

'That's cheating,' said Abbie. 'You were supposed to go alone.'

'Talking of cheating.' Mr Dabbings coughed. 'Time for a meeting.' He blew the horn in an impressive but pointless way, as everyone was already there.

He explained that half the party had been caught looking for treasure. Henry looked glad. The Platts looked sad. And Ursula looked at a beetle who was wing-wrestling his cousin.

'So.' Mr Dabbings rubbed a sideburn. 'Seeing that some are already at it, I've decided on a change of plan. From now on the treasure hunt's official.'

The cheer was so loud that a startled cloud ran away to Scotland.

'How about two groups?' said Coriander. 'Better to work

in teams than sneak off alone. Two adults, three children in each.'

Abbie could have hugged her. A chance to make peace with Perdita. No doubt Urse would make up the threesome – but it could be worse.

Which is exactly what it turned out to be. When Henry bagsied to go with Perdita, and Abbie told him to shove it, he burst into tears and ran up to the moor. Perdita lured him back with the promise that he could be on her team.

So that was it. Abbie didn't bother asking if she could be the third. She couldn't bear to hear again how Ursula needed protecting from Terrifica.

Who right now was telling Marcus that if they were going to be team-mates he'd jolly well better keep the Girl Guide law and be friendly and helpful, which meant sharing any clues he found because, if he didn't, she'd write to the Countess of Wessex who was the President of Girl-Guiding and practically the Queen.

'Thank goodness you're with us,' he said as Abbie joined them, which cheered her up in a sour sort of way. 'Let's grab your dad too. He's the history boffin – he'll know where to look.'

Abbie and Marcus found him in the food tent making parsnip paté crackers for lunch. 'I'd be delighted to join you,' he said, throwing them each a bag of smokey bacon crisps.

Marcus gasped. 'This isn't monk food!'

Dad grinned. 'They kept pigs and grew potatoes, didn't they? But if it makes you uncomfortable, Abbie and I are happy to help.' He held out his hand.

Deciding he was very comfortable, Marcus opened his packet.

After lunch everyone went up to the moor. They sat in a circle to finalise teams. Matt and Coriander insisted on being together as man and wife, two-in-one, plaited for life, blah-di-blah.

Mr Dabbings went quiet. He got up and wandered back to his hut while the others thought up team names. They came up with:

The Slightly Platt-Hollers: Perdita, Ursula, Henry, Matt and Coriander.
The Hartley-Battboilings: Abbie, Marcus, Terrifica, Mr Dabbings and Dad.

Mr Dabbings returned with his guitar. He'd put on his Wendigan, a woolly jacket with five buttons down the front shaped in the letters W, E, N, D and Y. While he gazed out to sea and sang 'My Poppets Lie over the Ocean', the others played, 'What I'd do with the Treasure'.

'I'd buy this island and turn it into a Guide camp,' said Terrifica, 'where people could learn to *Be Prepared*.'

Dad said he'd write a book called *Indiana Hartley: How I Dug Up the Truth.*

'I'd rule the world,' said Henry, a little off topic.

Coriander said she'd turn Remote Ken into a holiday park so that the zoo creatures could roam as free as birds, even though they were all animals except for the birds.

Matt agreed, adding that he'd build an open-air heating system so that the zoo creatures could be as snug as bugs, even though they were all animals and birds except for the bugs.

'Me too,' said Perdita. 'And with the money left over I'd buy a Guide uniform for Urse.'

Ursula was so moved she had to miss her turn.

Everyone looked at Abbie. 'I … I dunno.' She hugged her knees and stared at the ground. Perdita hadn't even thought of her. *That's it. Our friendship's officially dead.*

'Hey.' Marcus leaned over. 'If I won, you could have half the money.'

She didn't believe him for a second. But just at that moment it was the kindest thing anyone could have said.

On the way back to the huts, Coriander suggested they make reed whistles before starting the treasure hunt tomorrow. 'We'll be wandering all over the island. We need to be able to contact each other. If a fog came down we'd be in trouble.'

No one could argue with that, though Mr Dabbings looked annoyed that he hadn't thought of it first. They walked round the lake until they found a cluster of reeds and spent the rest of the afternoon learning from Matt how to cut notches for the mouthpiece using a stone.

That evening, after a meal of potted mole stew, they sat round the fire and practised peeping on their pipes. There was such a racket that a family of midges who'd booked a lakeside table had to cancel their dinner for eight hundred and ninety-four.

***

'... And three fifty change,' said the shopkeeper. 'Thank you, Madam.'

Grandma scooped the money across the counter towards her purse. Three coins dropped onto the floor. 'Blast!'

The young man behind her picked them up. 'Your treasure, Ma'am,' he said, handing them back.

'Much obliged.' She frowned. "Ere, what did you say?'

The man repeated it.

'Of course!' She punched him in the shoulder. 'That's it.' She pressed the coins into his hand. 'There you go, chuck. Treat yourself.'

The young man stared as the old lady danced out of the shop, shouting, 'I'm on your trail, you crafty crumpet!'

Shaking his head, he turned back and bought a Toblerone.

***

Klench sat in the darkest corner of the Welsh motorway service station, munching his fifth chocolate-chip muffin.

'Zat's enough, you pastry puff,' barked Inner Mummy.

He looked at the clock on the wall. 'But it's only seven forty-four and nineteen seconds, Mums. I must get through whole night before Brag collects me in mornink. Besides, I need to stock up for trip.' He shivered at the thought of all the long-life food he'd packed in his rucksack.

'Any more snacks vill raise suspicion – zen goodbye to expedition.'

She was right. He'd got this far without being recognised. Just a few more hours to keep a low profile. Grabbing the four Danish pastries, six burgers and five turkey subs he'd bought for dinner, Klench crouched down and squeezed himself and his rucksack under the bulging leather seat, with which he merged so well that the short-sighted cleaning lady, who came every hour on the hour, thought he was part of the furniture.

11

Choco-sneaks

Next morning everyone was up bright and early – or at least early. Abbie felt as bright as the inside of a Hoover bag, thanks to Terrifica's night-travel. The large girl, wrapped in her sleeping bag and snoring like a rhino, had kept rolling across the floor and slamming into Abbie. After the fourth slam, Abbie had escaped to the stone bench where she'd lain safely, if lumpily, for the rest of the night.

Yawning, she dressed and shuffled out of the hut. The air was sharp and still. Only the lake danced to its silent music, wriggling and swirling in tricky little currents.

Over a breakfast of hard-boiled eggs and corn cakes they discussed the rules for treasure hunting. Excitement grew until Dad reminded them that there was practically zero chance of finding the goblet because there was practically zero chance it was there.

Marcus said that practically zero wasn't *actually* zero, so there was a very small chance, say 0.0000001 per cent.

Mr Dabbings said, 'Please Marcus, it's too early for maths.'

Matt said they should spend the mornings treasure hunting and the afternoons doing joint activities, to keep good relations between the teams.

Coriander said that was a great idea: the most important thing was that everyone stayed friends.

Abbie said nothing on the outside but plenty on the inside as Ursula showed Perdita a Sneaky Belter.

Collecting a jerrycan from the food tent after breakfast, she strolled past them to the lake. The jerrycan was for water. The stroll was for spying.

'Where shall we look first?' It was amazing how much louder Ursula's voice had become. Three days ago it would have sounded like, 'Where shall we look first?'

'Mum suggested the mountain, just above the woods,' said Perdita, who couldn't whisper if she tried. 'There must be plenty of nooks and crannies – perfect for hiding treasure. Oh, hi.' She waved at Abbie. 'Are you spying on us?'

Dung buttons. Abbie frowned in a 'How dare you suggest such a thing?' sort of way.

'Why don't you join us?' said Perdita. 'Your team could go one way round the mountainside and we could go the other. We'd cover the area in half the time.'

'Nah.' Abbie smiled coolly. 'We've got a *totally* different idea.' She sauntered back to the food tent, swinging the jerrycan in a calm but firm, carefree yet determined way. 'Quick!' she hissed, ducking into the tent. 'We need a plan.'

Mr Dabbings was sitting on the floor, stroking a round stone. 'If I screw up my eyes,' he murmured, 'that could be Wendy's tum.'

Terrifica snapped her fingers. 'No moping, Sir. We need to organise. I'll be chairperson.' She blew three times on her reed whistle. 'Dyb dyb dyb, chin up chaps. Let's put on our thinking caps. Hands up with suggestions.'

Marcus's hand went up. 'Who said you could be chairperson?'

Terrifica twiddled her pencil. 'That's a question, not a suggestion. Mr Hartley, as monk expert, where do you think they might have kept the goblet?'

'We-e-ell.' Dad scratched his beard. 'Somewhere hidden yet obvious.'

Terrifica nodded. 'Easy but difficult.'

Marcus gave a slow handclap. 'Genius.'

Terrifica glared at him. 'I meant easy for the *monks* to find but difficult for anyone else. Somewhere near the huts. What about the lake?'

'If you're suggesting scuba diving,' said Abbie, 'you've won your Stick It In Your Pipe badge.'

Dad smiled. 'I'm sure Terrifica doesn't mean *in* the water, love, but round it. How about we split up? Half our team goes one way round the lake and half the other.'

'I'll come with you,' said Abbie quickly.

'How nice. Fond of your old dad, eh?'

'Mm-hmm,' she replied, eyeing the rectangular bulge up his sleeve.

Mr Dabbings took a pair of knitting needles from his rucksack. 'If you don't mind, I'll stay and man the fort. This baby jacket won't knit itself, you know.' He held up a patch the shape of Australia.

'Fine by me, Bran.' Dad patted Abbie on the back. 'Let's head to the right of the lake.'

'Hang on.' Marcus raised his hand. 'You can't expect me to go with–'

But Dad and Abbie were off.

A few clouds lay across the sky like ripped sheets. On the left the lake stirred gently, nudging the beach with little waves. The pebbles merged on the right with thick undergrowth.

'This is like looking for a needle in a haystack,' said Abbie, 'except there's no needle.'

'Nice to be together, though. Just us two.'

'Yeah. You're great, Dad.' She squeezed his arm affectionately.

'You too … hey!' But she'd already pulled the Crunchie bar out of his sleeve.

They munched round the lake. Flies buzzed. A crow creaked from a distant tree. Pebbles crunched under their trainers.

'Dad.'

'Yes, love?'

'Don't you feel bad about this secret food? You're the one who wanted to eat medievally. The others'll go mad if they find out we're cheating. You wouldn't even use Matt's Scour Flour.'

'Matt!' He stopped.

Abbie stared at him. Matt was his closest friend, the man who'd drop anything to mend his computer or fix his car. But the way he'd said it, you'd think Matt was a fly that needed swatting. 'What would we do without Matt, eh?' He kicked a pebble. 'Always has a plan. Handy as a hanky, smart as a phone, kind as a clementine.'

Abbie had never thought of small oranges as particularly caring. But she let it pass. Dad clearly needed to get this off his chest.

'I mean,' he folded his arms, '*I'm* supposed to be the medieval expert round here. But he keeps scoring points with his Scour Flour and Soilets and silly old Erics.'

Abbie overlooked that one too.

'Oh he *seems* all quiet and helpful. But underneath he's just showing off. And if that's his game, he jolly well can stick it up his–'

'Dad!' Abbie clutched his arm. 'Look.' Bubbles were popping in the middle of the lake. 'The hot springs.'

'Ha!' Dad stabbed the air with his finger. 'There we go again. We all had our theories but who was right? The

142

Marvellous Mr Matt, of course.'

Abbie pulled him back as the bubbles spread to the shore, bursting onto the beach. It was the strangest sight: not a breath of wind and the lake boiling like water in a pan. Panic rose in her chest. What if Matt had been right *and* wrong? Right about the volcano, wrong about extinct? What if it had been building up for years, waiting for this moment to erupt?

She grabbed Dad's hand. 'Let's go back.' Not that it would help. If the volcano blew its top, huddling in a hut wouldn't save them. But at least they could eat Dad's chocolate supplies before melting into lava.

By the time they reached the camp, though, the bubbles had subsided and the lake was back to its gentle dip and swell.

There was no sign of the others. 'Any more chocolate?' asked Abbie.

Dad winked. But on the way to the food tent, he froze. 'Listen.' With a finger on his lips, he turned towards the wall that surrounded the huts. They crouched down.

'Zitters indeed!' A voice was coming from the other side. 'They were definitely Normans. She humiliated me in front of the children, Wendikin.'

Abbie peered over. Mr Dabbings was sitting with his back to the wall.

Dad sprang up. 'Gotcha!'

'Aaagh!' The teacher dropped his phone. Snatching it up, he gasped, 'Gotta go, Wendo. Kiss Buddleia for me – no, it'll strain your stomach.' He made a kissy noise and ended the call.

Abbie smiled sweetly. 'I thought the phone was for emergencies, Sir.'

Mr Dabbings ran his fingers through his hair. 'Yes, of course. I was just, er, checking there wasn't one at home. You never know with babies.'

Dad raised his eyebrows. 'What d'you think, Abbs; should we tell the others?'

Mr Dabbings stood up. 'Had a good walk?' He tapped his foot. 'It certainly looked like it, with that snack to spur you on. You should have seen the wrapper sparkle when I happened to glance across the lake. Quite lovely. What do you think; should I tell the others?'

Dad held up his hands. 'OK, point made. How about we call it quits? You keep our secret, we'll keep yours.' Mr Dabbings nodded. They all shook hands.

A shrill sound pierced the air. Terrifica was running up from the beach blowing her reed whistle. 'Yoo hoo lot!' Her cheeks were flushed, her nostrils flared. 'Have you seen Marcus?'

'I thought he went with you,' said Abbie.

'We had an argument by the lake.'

Not you too, thought Abbie. Everyone seemed to be at

it – falling out in lumps like manure from a tractor.

'I said he should wade in and look for glinting,' Terrifica explained. 'He told me to wade in myself. I said, "I can't, I'm busy directing." He said, "You mean dictating." I said, "What's your problem?" He said, "You are." And then the lake started to bubble and he said "Stuff you!" and ran off along the beach. So I just carried on. I thought he'd come round the lake and join you.' Shielding her eyes with her hand, she surveyed the landscape like a bossy pirate. 'Oh my woggle, where can he be?'

In his hut, it turned out. Abbie and Terrifica found him sitting on the ground playing chess with himself.

'Checkmate.' He shook hands with himself. 'I won,' he said, looking up triumphantly at Abbie. 'And I only cheated twice.'

'I was worried about you,' said Terrifica. 'You shouldn't rush off like that.'

Marcus frowned. 'Did you say something, Abbie? I thought I heard a voice.'

'It was me,' said Terrifica.

Marcus arched his eyebrows. 'Wow, Abbie, how do you do that without moving your lips? That's pretty cool. But then *you* are pretty cool.' He glared at Terrifica. 'Unlike *some* people round here.'

She glared back. 'Well, I agree with that!'

As Terrifica huffed out of the hut Abbie couldn't help

a little grin. *How about that, Perdita Platt? Look who's popular now.*

***

'Are you sure?' said Mum. She was tucking clean sheets into Chunca's bed while he tucked into lasagne downstairs. Being royalty, the Emp had made it clear to Bacpac (who'd made it clear to Fernando, who'd made it clear to Mum) that he expected to be treated like – well – royalty.

'I'm sure.' Grandma stuffed a pillow into a case. 'I thought you'd be glad if I took them off your 'ands for a few days.'

'Well, I suppose I am.' Mum rubbed her forehead with a weary hand. 'But how will you cope? The language, the constant demands.' She pointed to the tin of Cadbury Heroes that Chunca had ordered for his bedside table.

'Easily.' Grandma punched the pillow. 'I booked an 'otel in Margate for a week. The staff can run round after 'im while I go paddlin' in the sea.'

Mum smoothed the sheets with her palms. 'Then what? You can't bring them back. Now Klench has vanished, there's nothing for them here.'

'I'll chat to Bacpac. Tell 'im the best thing they can do is fly back to the jungle. If they're goin' to live forever, they might as well do it there.'

When Mum had gone to fetch clean towels, Grandma

146

opened her handbag and checked the three plane tickets to Ireland that she'd bought.

***

The helicopter propellers whirred to a stop. Klench paused in his seat, savouring his last moment in the cockpit before braving the ghastly outdoors.

'Get outs,' barked Inner Mummy.

Sticking out his inner tongue, Klench grasped his rucksack and clambered off the helicopter. It was all right for her, sitting in her inner armchair while he did the dirty work of treasure hunting on this freezing scab of an island.

Well, maybe not so freezing. The sun warmed his face as he scanned the beach. Definitely scabby, though.

Klench turned back to the cockpit. 'I phone you ven I find ze goblet,' he shouted up at Brag.

The cowboy clicked his tongue. 'You better, Bulgy Boy. Ah'll be lying low in Wales, waiting for your call. And before you try any ol' tricks – like phoning someone *else* – remember, ah have ma contacts. Ah'll know where to find you. And ah sure don't appreciate a broken promise.' Doffing his cowboy hat, he started up the propellers, grinning as the wind messed up Klench's perfectly parted lemon hair.

12

Awetricks

It was a cold, quiet and infuriating lunch.

Cold because there was no fire. By the time the Slightly Platt-Hollers returned from their morning hunt above the woods, everyone was starving and couldn't be bothered to wait for Coriander and Matt to get the fire going.

Quiet because Marcus was still ignoring Terrifica; Mr Dabbings was knitting in silent shame after the phone fiasco; and the seagull salami was simply beyond words.

Infuriating because the Slightly Platt-Hollers kept grinning at each other and tapping their noses.

Abbie couldn't stand it. 'We get the message,' she cried as Perdita winked at Henry. 'You'd better tell us what you found, otherwise we'll just head up the mountain too.'

'Go on then,' said Henry. 'Why waste time asking us?'

Abbie had to admit that was a surprisingly smart question from a boy with a blankie up his T-shirt.

'It was probably nothing.' Perdita nudged Ursula.

'At least, nothing worth mentioning.' Coriander sucked

her cheeks.

'So you might as well mention it.' Dad dropped a piece of seagull salami casually on the ground. 'Then we can join up again, work together. You know the saying. More minds make … er, faster finds.'

'Actually, we don't,' said Matt.

'Pleeese.' Dad gave up on casual and clasped his hands together. 'I'll give you some of my cho–'

'Dad!' Abbie kicked his ankle.

'We don't need their help,' said Terrifica. 'We'll find it ourselves, won't we, team?'

'But not till tomorrow,' Perdita reminded them. 'Remember the rules. Afternoons are all together. No sneaking off in teams.'

Of course, it all depended what you meant by teams. Which is why, when Coriander suggested that they collect enough firewood to last a few days – 'You never know how long this lovely weather will last' – Abbie found herself climbing over the ridge with Marcus.

'I mean we're not actually a team,' she murmured.

'No. We're two-fifths. Forty per cent.'

'Or two people who happen to be walking in the same direction.'

When they were on the moor, Marcus grabbed her arm. 'Right. Did you see where they went this morning?'

Abbie pointed to the mountain above the woods, where

she'd spotted the Slightly Platt-Hollers on her walk round the lake. 'You realise this is cheating,' she said nervously.

'Oh yeah? What about all their nudging and winking and not telling us what they found? That's not exactly honest.'

They walked in silence over the moor. Flies glinted like metallic dust round Abbie's head. A rabbit froze then fled, shivering a trail through the heather.

'Anyway,' said Marcus as they reached the stream. 'What if we both just *happened* to be looking for firewood up the mountain and we both just *happened* to find something? That wouldn't be cheating, would it?'

Abbie frowned. It sort of would. But if she scrunched up her eyes and squashed up her brain, it sort of wouldn't either.

Half an hour later they reached the woods.

'Let's collect firewood here,' said Marcus, 'on our way back.'

They slipped between the trees. Like the last time she'd come here, Abbie felt as if she was invading a private world. Secret scents laced the air: soft sad moss and sweet decay. She crept round bluebells that glowed as if lit from within, and roots like the knuckles of clenched fists. There was something so alive about the stillness: the brambles locked in silent battle, the strange little crackles and whispers. It was as if the trees were watching, holding their breath.

Marcus seemed to feel it too. Tense and low, he tiptoed ahead.

And froze. Voices.

Now it was Abbie who held her breath. *Ghosts.*

Of course. It all made sense. These woods were haunted.

Abbie's heart punched into her throat. Marcus crept

behind a tree and beckoned. Somehow her legs took her to him. Crouching down, they peered into the gloom.

Giggles. Not very ghostly ones.

'We fooled them,' said a voice.

'Awetricks!' said another.

'Not really *tricks*,' said a third. 'Just a bit of fun.'

Abbie's hand flew to her mouth. In a clearing ahead of them, Perdita, Henry and Ursula were collecting wood.

Abbie gawped. Marcus put a finger to his lips.

'We didn't *actually* lie,' said Perdita, throwing a branch onto a pile. 'We said we hadn't found anything, which we hadn't.'

'Not our fault if they thought we had.' Ursula yanked up a root with one hand.

Abbie bunched her fists. All that nudging and winking – it was pure bluff. Outrageous! She stepped forward. Marcus gripped her arm. Shaking his head, he pulled her away towards the entrance of the wood.

Back out on the moor, she snarled, 'How dare they? The unbe*liev*able cheats.' Tears of fury pricked her eyes.

Marcus stopped. 'No they're not.' He flopped down on the heather. He was actually smiling! 'Perdita's right. They didn't lie. We're the ones who assumed they'd found something.'

'But that's what they *wanted* us to think.'

Marcus lay on his back. 'Course it is,' he said, putting

his hands behind his head. 'And good luck to them. They're just misleading the enemy.' He laughed. 'It's even got a name in war. Propaganda.'

Enemy, war – is this what it's come to? A stone settled in Abbie's stomach. How could she explain to Marcus that, while it might not be *officially* cheating, it still wasn't right? He'd never understand. Cunning was in his bones. But Perdita? She didn't have a sneaky cell in her body: at least, that's what Abbie had thought until now. She sat down next to Marcus and hugged her knees miserably. In almost a year of friendship Perdita had been a tower of honesty and openness. And now that tower was crumbling.

Was I wrong about her? About all of them? Because it struck Abbie that all the Platts were in on this. Matt and Coriander, whom she'd grown to love and trust like family, had winked and nudged along with the rest of them.

The stone turned in her stomach. 'Well, I'm going to tell them what I think of their little game.'

'No.' Marcus propped his head on an elbow. 'Think about it. If they've tricked us, it's only fair we trick them back. And if they catch us, we just turn round and say they started it.' He grinned. 'Relax, Abbie. The fun's just beginning.'

Oh, but it wasn't. Not even the wolf burger and chips could cheer her up that evening. Nor the packet of Fruit Gums that Dad slipped her way when no one was looking.

Nor the sunset that set the sky on fire. Perdita's betrayal twisted in her chest, dark and sharp as the mountains that stabbed the burning clouds.

Lying on her stone bed that night, she reached for her notebook and scribbled by candlelight:

Perdita Platt, you lousy traitor,
I'll get you back, sooner or later.

***

Chunca took the leprechaun-shaped peppermill from the table and tried to stick it through the hole in his right earlobe.

'No. It's to spice up your food.' Grandma showed him how to twist the bottom so that pepper came out.

Chunca got twisting. Black flakes freckled his Irish stew.

'That's enough,' warned Grandma.

But Chunca was enjoying himself. Pepper blanketed the stew. He took a mouthful. 'Pwwffhhh!' he gasped in ancient Quechua, leaping from his chair.

The barman of the pub hurried over. 'Everything all right, fellas?'

'Not used to Irish food,' said Grandma, passing Chunca a glass of water. 'Foreigners.'

The barman nodded. 'Plenty of those round here. Americans mostly, in search of their origins.'

Grandma was too tired to explain that it wasn't their origins these Americans were after, but their endings. It had been an exhausting day. First the early morning lift to the train station, pretending that they were catching the eight-fifty to Margate. Then the nine-ten to Stanstead Airport, the flight to Shannon and the hour's bus ride to the town of Killyboon on the north-west coast of Ireland.

When the barman had gone Chester dived from her head and mopped up the worst of the pepper from Chunca's plate. 'Eat up,' yawned Grandma, while Chester sneezed back up to wig duties. 'Busy day tomorrow.'

***

Klench lay in his tent. He shone his torch beam on the wall. A daddy-long-legs, who'd always dreamed of going on stage, leapt into the spotlight and tap-danced across the canvas.

'Bravo,' said Klench. The daddy-long-legs bowed. Klench squashed him with the torch. 'Schnik,' he murmured, regretting it immediately. 'Now I have no companies.' He turned over uneasily.

'Nonsense.' Mummy opened an inner eye. 'I am here, but give me break. I cannot alvays stay avake.'

'I know zat, Mums,' he muttered. 'In fact I vish you'd sleep all ze times. I mean I have no *livink* companies.' He let out a whimper.

'Oh, stop!' Mummy sat up in his brain. 'I told you, zere are no ghosts here. Go to sleep, my dumpy dear.'

But he couldn't. He'd been on edge ever since arriving on this island. First that nerve-wracking creep across the moor, praying he wouldn't bump into the school party. He mustn't be spotted. Unarmed and alone, he'd be easily overpowered. No doubt they had some way of contacting the mainland and could call the police. Luckily he'd made it across to the woods without seeing a soul. But he'd been so busy scanning the horizon he'd almost walked into that bog at the edge of the trees. Only Mummy's inner shriek had alerted him.

Then there was the misery of stumbling through the dense undergrowth till he'd found this clearing.

And beyond the sweat and strain of putting up his tent, there was something else. He'd felt it the minute he'd entered these woods: an alertness in the air, as if the whole place was alive.

'Only birds and forest creatures. Settle down now, flabby features.'

How could he, after that terrible afternoon trying to hide and hunt at the same time? His metal detector hadn't so much as burped as he'd circled the lower slopes of the mountain. And as for the heat – he'd sweated almost as much as his ex-prison colleague Dampy Staines, who'd ended up in solitary confinement after his cell-mates rioted. Who'd have thought April would be so warm at this latitude? He was stinky, clammy and restless.

Sighing, he closed his eyes. Crime was so complicated. When he'd found the treasure he'd settle on some tropical island and set up a little business. Yes, a bakery-cum-launderette where customers could eat pastries while their clothes were cleaned. 'Nosh 'n' Vosh,' he murmured. Comforted, he fell asleep and *dreamed* of Grandma's grateful smile as he presented her with a complementary profiterole atop a freshly washed dressing gown.

13

Look Who's Cheating

Abbie swung her legs down from the stone bench. Yawning, she climbed out of her sleeping bag. Not such a bad night; she must be getting used to her bumpy bed. She pushed back the curls that smeared her forehead and slipped on shorts and a T-shirt.

It wasn't much cooler outside. The sun glittered like a feverish eye through lashes of faint cloud. Abbie pressed two fingers into the nape of her neck where an ache was flowering. Yesterday came rushing back: the shock and sorrow of Perdita's not-quite-cheating.

Dad was clattering about in the food tent. Abbie slunk past to avoid breakfast duties and headed for the lake. She stopped at the wall where a Fruit Gum lay abandoned from last night. Bringing it to her mouth, she had second thoughts and stuck it in a crack in the wall, where a family of spiders cheered at the surprise delivery of a new red sofa.

At the edge of the lake she bent down and splashed her

face and hair with water. She stood up and threw her head back. *Aah, shampoo advert.*

'Hey, loo brush!' She wheeled round. Dad was waving a spoon from the tent. 'Come and help me scramble eggs.'

'In a sec.' Abbie ran her fingers through her hair. *Of course,* she thought, her mind clearing, *the thing to do is confront her, get things out in the open.* Marcus was wrong. They had to stop all this sneakery: nip it in the bud before it got out of hand.

She came back up the beach and across to Perdita's hut. 'Hello. Anyone awake?' She stooped through the entrance. Perdita was standing in the middle.

Ursula was wrapping her three plaits round her neck. 'The Stranglehold,' she told Abbie. 'For stopping burglars.'

'What if they haven't got plaits?'

Perdita shook her hair free. 'Then they shouldn't be burgling. That's unfair.'

'*Talking* of unfair.' Abbie put her hands on her hips. 'We know what you were up to yesterday, with your nudges and nose-taps and "nothing-worth-mentionings". You were trying to put us off. I can't believe you'd do that.'

'I'm sorry.' For the first time ever, Abbie saw Perdita blush. 'It was meant to be a joke. But you're right, it was a bit sneaky. Wasn't it, Urse?'

'Yes.' Ursula slid her hands sheepishly into her pockets.

Then she whipped out a blue wrapper. 'Just like this!' She pulled out a gold wrapper. 'And this. *And*,' she held up a yellow wrapper, 'this!'

Perdita stared at the Yorkie, Crunchie and Fruit Gum papers.

'Secret supplies.' It was Ursula's turn to put her hands on her hips. 'I found these lying around. So I spied on you and your dad. And I saw you scoffing chocolate in the food tent. Not very observant, are you?'

'Well, you're not very ... observable!' was all Abbie could think to reply.

'Incredible.' Perdita shook her head at Abbie. 'Why didn't you tell me before, Urse?'

'I didn't want to get Abbie into trouble,' the tiny girl said nobly. 'Plus,' she added with a grin, 'I thought it would be great for blackmail.'

Perdita grabbed Abbie's arm. 'You're coming with me.' She marched Abbie outside and across to her parents' hut.

'Mum, Dad, you won't believe–' Perdita froze in the doorway.

Coriander was standing with a small box in her hand. Matt sat with a bigger box in his lap.

'Matches!' Abbie ran in and snatched the box from Coriander. 'And firelighters.' She scooped the box from Matt's lap. 'Flint and steel, eh? What a total lie!'

Matt rubbed a finger over his teeth. 'Not total,' he said

in a small voice. 'We did it medievally at first, but it took so long.'

Coriander chewed a plait. 'We thought you wouldn't mind. We brought these as back-up, in case it rained and the firewood got wet.'

'But it hasn't rained.' Abbie folded her arms. 'And the firewood's dry.' *This is fantastic,* she thought. *Spin it out.* 'It's very dry. Very dry indeed.'

'We just thought–' whispered Coriander.

'What? What was it you just thought?' Abbie tapped her foot. 'What thought was it that just thought itself into your thoughts?' Her eyebrows arched. *I'm brilliant at this. I should be a teacher.*

Matt blinked at the ground. 'We just thought it would be good to speed up the cooking. Everyone's so hungry all the time.'

'But you didn't tell Dad. You tried to impress him, made him feel useless.' Abbie wagged her finger in a teacherly way. 'That was mean. And naughty.' She almost added, 'Stay behind and tidy the cloakroom.'

Coriander snapped out of her shame. 'It's thanks to your dad and his medieval mush that we're all starving.'

'Oh no we're not – at least, not all of us.' Perdita held up the chocolate wrappers. 'Look what Urse found.'

Coriander's eyes widened. 'You cheats,' she murmured, sounding more envious than angry.

Abbie snatched the box of firelighters from the ground. '*You* cheats!' she shouted. The noise brought the others into the hut.

'What's going on?' said Dad. 'We're all waiting for breakfast. You need to light the fire, Coriander.'

'Allow me!' Abbie brandished the firelighters.

'Why don't we just have *chocolate* instead?!' Perdita waved the wrappers.

Everyone stood in silence while guilt and outrage played ping-pong across their faces.

At last Mr Dabbings clapped his hands. 'All righty. It seems both teams have been up to their tricks. We'll have to revise the rules. From now on, *everyone* can use matches instead of having to light their candles in the fire – and *everyone* can share the remaining chocolate.' Before anyone could argue, he turned to Matt. 'How about you get the fire going now, twenty-first-century style? I'm sure a good breakfast will calm things down.'

But even Dad's Dairy Milk and porridge couldn't clear the air. The teams sat apart on the beach, whispering together and glaring at the enemy, until Coriander stood up.

'This is awful!' She threw out her arms to the Hartley-Battboilings. 'We can't spend the rest of this trip at war. Let's forget treasure hunting today and have some fun together.'

Dad jumped up. 'Good idea. We need to build trust

again. And I've got just the thing. I was saving it for a rainy day but it'll be even better in sunshine. It's what the monks did to get closer to God and each other.'

'Boresticks!' shouted Henry. 'I'm *SO* not praying.'

'That's not what I meant.' Dad grinned. 'Though now you mention it, the *Annals of Donal* do say that angels joined in, to reward the monks for their holiness.'

An hour later Abbie *was* praying for angels. But she must have failed the holiness test because there wasn't a heavenly helper in sight and it felt like a metal bar was turning in her shoulders. 'How could the monks enjoy this?'

Dad, who'd decided he'd be most useful supervising, stopped on his rounds. 'They had no choice. No Potted Histories for them, my girl.'

His 'just-the-thing' was making flour from some barley seeds he'd brought along. Everyone was sitting in a circle, crushing the grain between two pebbles they'd collected from the lakeside.

'The monks used stones as well,' Dad told the sweating grinders. 'They shaped them into simple hand mills called querns.' He looked over Abbie's shoulder. 'Come on Abbs, give it more welly.' He slapped her on the back.

'Ow!' She rubbed her shoulder. 'What's the point? I'm using more calories making the flour than I'd get from eating it.'

Dad chuckled. 'Think of the poor monks. They had to grow the barley, pick it and pull off the husks before they even *thought* about grinding.'

Abbie scowled. Dad's trust-building exercise was doing just the opposite. Querning, or whatever you called it, had *not* brought her closer to God or anyone else. Her fingers closed round the pebble in her right hand. It *had*, however, brought her closer to grinding Dad to a pulp.

But he'd moved on. 'Now,' he said, 'how about a prize for the quickest querner?' He strolled round the circle. 'Not bad, Terrifica … Nice technique, Coriander … Hey!' He stopped behind Ursula. 'Mega.' He held up her bowl, full of pale brown powder.

She blushed. 'It's the arm wrestling. I practise every morning against myself.'

Dad took a Mars Bar from his pocket. 'Congratulations, Quern Queen.'

'Wow, thanks.' Ursula held it reverently by her fingertips. Then she tore off the wrapper, broke the bar in two and gave half to Perdita.

Creep. Abbie scowled. And that went for Dad too. How could he reward the enemy? Building trust was one thing, sharing supplies quite another.

Marcus caught her eye. 'Stuff this,' he muttered, scooping up his barley pile and flinging it at the lake. 'I'm going for a swim.'

Five minutes later, while the adults gathered the grain piles to make porridge for lunch, the children were splashing around in their shorts and T-shirts.

All except Abbie. She sat at the edge of the lake doodling in her notebook while tiny waves tickled her outstretched legs.

'Come in,' called Marcus. 'It's brilliant.'

She shook her head. All that querning had worn her out. Yawning, she stood up. A stroll along the lake, a bit of peace and quiet – that would do nicely. She'd had quite enough of team-building for one lifetime.

***

'Ask your master what 'e wants on 'is T-shirt.' Grandma and the Incas were in a souvenir shop in Killyboon. They'd spent the morning buying supplies for the trip to Remote Ken. After trading in one of Chunca's golden bracelets, they'd bought rucksacks, hiking gear and a few tins of food. Now Grandma had spotted a Design-your-own-T-shirt shop and decided that the Incas might as well die in style. 'You can 'ave somethin' written on specially – a sort of epitaph.'

Bacpac didn't understand the word. So, loudly and slowly, she'd given some examples: 'I ♥ Ibiza' or 'Rock 'n' Roll Gran'.

***

Above the huts, on top of the moor, a boulder wriggled into position. An unusual boulder, covered in mint-green moss and holding a pair of binoculars.

'Ze children are splashink in lake,' the boulder murmured, adding almost wistfully, 'havink funs.'

'Funs?' barked Inner Mummy. 'Vot is point of zat? Vy zey vaste zeir time on pleasure, ven zey could be seekink treasure?'

'Don't ask me. I never vaste time.' From the way he sighed, you'd almost think Klench regretted it. 'But look.' The binoculars shifted to the left. 'Not everyvun is svimminks. Zere is Miss Meddle.' That was his pet name for the girl who, twice now, had foiled his wicked schemes: the first time last summer in the Platts' Museum of Hair, and the second before Christmas in the Amazon jungle. 'She is strollink off round lake.'

Klench lowered the binoculars. 'Not much excitements. I guess zat means zey have found nothink.' That was good news. The bad news was that neither had he. But at least, wandering over the moor, he'd come to the ridge and spotted the camp by the lake.

Mummy had been delighted with the discovery. 'Spyink, Hube, now zat's ze ticket. If zey find a clue, just nick it.'

But no joy yet. Packing away the binoculars, he lumbered back over the moor to his tent in the woods and a measly lunch of four long-life doughnuts.

14

The Hiding Place

Abbie strolled along the beach to the right of the lake. The shrieks and splashes of the swimmers faded beneath the buzz of flies and hush of tiny waves against the shore. Sunlight danced tiptoe on the trembling water.

She walked faster. Her back straightened; her lungs filled with soft, warm air. 'It's OK,' she told a bramble bush, 'it really is.' So what if she'd lost her best friend? The sun would still rise. Leaves would still fall. And a Pringle would still nearly fit on her tongue. It wasn't the end of the world, just the tiny part she'd shared with Perdita. 'And good riddance to that,' she said, swinging her arms. 'I'd had enough anyway.'

For a moment the bramble believed her.

Beyond the spot she'd reached with Dad yesterday, the lake curved round to the right. A new sound joined the murmuring afternoon: a low roar like distant traffic. Shielding her eyes with her hand, Abbie gazed up at the mountain on the right. About halfway up a waterfall burst from the rock, spilling down in thick white lines like paint.

Sweat tickled her forehead. The back of her neck burned. Her head was beginning to throb. *I should go back.* But she'd come this far. Might as well get a proper view.

A little further on she reached the bottom. The waterfall bounced into a pool to the right of the beach. In front of the fizzing wall the water lay dark and deep. It flowed out into lacy streams, strewn with large stones, that rattled across the beach and fed the lake.

Abbie knelt by the pool. Bending over, she scooped water into her mouth. Then she lay on her back beside the water, perched her notebook on her stomach and tucked her hands behind her head. *Bliss.*

The roar of the waterfall was strangely soothing: a duvet of sound round her ears. Spray pecked her face. She looked up. High clouds drifted like cigarette smoke. A seagull wheeled in the echoing blue.

And suddenly she was wheeling too, looking down on the island – on herself and the others, plotting and scheming over treasure that didn't exist. 'How sad are we?' she asked a fly as it landed on her stomach.

The fly rubbed its front legs as if to say, 'Where shall I start?'

She sat up and opened her notebook.

I hereby vow, she wrote, to stop this wild goblet

chase and spend the rest of the trip treating every living thing with love and respect.

The fly flew onto the page. She squashed it.

She gazed into the pool, gleaming and calm before the waterfall's fury. Her shoulders sank with sudden exhaustion. All the bickering and trickery of the last few days; all the nights interrupted by lumpy beds and Terrifo-snores; all the fresh air and mushy food … a huge yawn tumbled out. *But I can't sleep here. What if it's dark when I wake up?*

There was one way to stay awake. Laying her notebook on the beach, she slipped off her sandals and stood up. 'One, two, three –'

She crashed into freezing darkness. Her arms thrashed up through the shocking blur till she surfaced, spluttering and laughing. 'Wahoo!' She pushed her hair out of her eyes. 'Wahaa!' Holding her breath, she went under again, trying to touch the bottom. But her feet pedalled endless silky water. Her chest nearly bursting, she came up again.

Perdita will love this, she thought, flipping onto her back.

Perdita. Her ex-best friend. In the thrill of discovery she'd forgotten. She pictured Perdita coming here with Ursula to learn some stupid wrestling move like the Spraylock or the Gushcrush.

'Never!' she yelled into the din. 'This is *my* secret.' She swam towards the waterfall. Taking a huge breath, she dived. Water slammed down on her, solid as concrete. And then she was through, gasping and snatching great gulps of air.

She'd come up into a kind of chamber hidden behind the waterfall. Two metres in front of her the pool met a wall of jutting, blocky rocks. They must form the bottom of the mountain. On the right the chamber was bordered by thick undergrowth. To the left the water lapped against boulders and mossy rock.

Abbie swam over and hauled herself up onto a boulder. Dangling her feet in the water, she gazed at the waterfall from behind. It drilled down in a shouting, shimmering curtain.

'Wow!' She was surprised to hear herself. But tucked inside the clamour was a kind of silence: the sort you get in a classroom that's so noisy you can say 'Bottom burp,' in a perfectly normal voice, knowing that your neighbour will hear but the teacher won't.

She shivered in the gloom. Standing up, she wrung out her T-shirt and squeezed her dripping hair. She ought to get back. But the thought of diving into those wriggling depths again made her teeth chatter. She looked to her right. She could get out by walking over the boulders to the edge of the chamber. There was a small gap there, between the waterfall and the mountainside.

Abbie stepped carefully over the slippery boulders

towards the edge of the waterfall. Sunlight streamed through the gap onto the rocks projecting from the back wall of the chamber.

Between two of the rocks lay a vertical crack. A shaft of sunlight filtered through, lighting up some sort of cave behind.

Her stomach flipped over. *You couldn't design a better hiding place.*

Crazy. No one organised scenery except God and Steven Spielberg.

She gasped. Of course! It was the other way round. *Because* it was so secret, this was the perfect place *for* hiding something.

Her heart hammering, Abbie crept towards the back wall and squeezed through the crack. For a maddening moment it was pitch dark. She breathed out slowly, letting her eyes adjust to the weak light that trickled through.

She was in a dome-shaped cave. The walls of reddish mud and rock had crumbled in places, leaving an earthy rubble round the edge. The floor, too, was smooth, packed mud. Water plopped on her head. The air smelt like wet socks. By the Hartley system of measurement, the space was about four Abbies long and two wide. The highest point must be a Dad and a half.

That was all. No goblet dripping with rubies and diamonds.

'Poop!' she yelled.

'Oop … oop … oo,' echoed the walls.

'It must be here!'

'Ere … ere … ere,' the cave agreed.

She looked round again and tried to think monk. *The ground.* Perhaps they'd buried it. But where? Kneeling down she began to dig, clawing and scraping with her fingers. Mud squeezed under her nails. Her fingers ached.

She sank back on her heels. She'd made a hole the size of a tennis ball. The treasure could be anywhere. She needed help: tools to dig, lights to see. *And company.* Because a cold dread was leaking into her stomach – a feeling that she wasn't alone. She wheeled round.

Nothing but rock, dripping and mud.

She dug her fingernails into her palms. *Get a grip.* It was just the gloom and cold: the shock of the water and thrill of this find. But no matter what she told herself, the shivering wouldn't stop. She longed to be back at the huts.

Jumping up, she squeezed out of the cave. She turned and paused to memorise the position of the crack between the rocks. Then she picked her way across the boulders to the edge of the waterfall. Icy spray nipped her skin as she slipped through the gap and back out into the dazzling afternoon.

She ran back along the beach, jumping from stone to stone across the network of streams. At the spot where she'd lain by the pool she picked up her notebook. Crack between 3rd and 4th rocks, she scribbled, cave in mountainside. She drew a quick sketch of the back wall of the chamber. Then she slipped on her sandals and legged it back to the huts.

***

Bundy Pilks shook his head. 'No way, maties. Look at that water. Way too choppy. Can't take Bwidget out in that.' He was standing on the jetty at Ballinabeeny pointing at the sea.

'But we've got to get there asap,' said Grandma, who'd been driven to the port with the Incas by the landlord from Killyboon.

'It is matter of life and death,' added Bacpac, proud of the phrase he remembered from his BBC lessons. 'Or death and life,' he said, looking suddenly confused.

'Sowwy chaps. No can do. Give me a wing at dawn tomorrow. If it's calm, I'll take you first thing.'

Grandma punched his number irritably into her phone. Then she ushered the old gents back to the car and told the landlord they'd have to come back tomorrow.

Bacpac translated. The Emp scowled at Grandma.

'Don't blame me,' she snapped. 'And anyway, you've waited four centuries – what's another day?'

***

Sitting on his reinforced air-bed, Klench pulled off his hiking boots and socks.

'Schnooff!' Mummy wrinkled her inner nose. 'Don't you dare make such a stench! You dishonour name of Klench.'

'I cannot help it. Zere is novhere to vosh in zese voods.' He unzipped the tent door, rolled up the flap and stuck his feet outside.

'Zat von't do, you great gnu. If you vont zem clean and bright, you should vosh in lake tonight.'

He nodded slowly, loath to admit that, as usual, her idea was excellent. Besides bathing, he'd be able to search the beach for treasure while the school party was asleep.

In the meantime, to relieve the stink, he took a bottle out of his rucksack and poured Dettol over his feet.

15

Sit Down and Shut Up!

Abbie tore along the beach. Blood roared in her ears, as if an aeroplane was taking off inside her head. Her right hand sweated round the precious notebook.

As the huts came into view she stopped to catch her breath. A giggle burst out of her. *Wait till everyone hears what I've found.*

Because everyone *would* hear. Her chest swelled with noble pride as she vowed to bring unity once and for all. *Goodbye sneaking, so long competing.* It was time to lay down all rivalry, forget silly squabbles and band together to find the treasure.

Wiping sweat from her forehead, she approached the huts. Perdita, Ursula and Henry were crouching by the lake, too busy making mud sculptures to notice her.

'How's my Edie?' Henry was shaping a low ridge of mud into a crocodile.

'Great,' said Perdita. 'But her tail's a bit thin. Hey, Urse, your Winnie's brilliant. How did you make the mud look so hairy?'

Anger burned up Abbie's throat. How dare they? Edie, Winnie – all the zoo animals – they were *her* special friends. 'That's nothing like Winnie,' she snapped. 'The arms are way too short.'

Perdita looked up from her python. 'Oh, hi. Where were you?'

'Nowhere.' Abbie whipped her notebook behind her back.

'What's in there?' Ursula frowned.

'Nothing.' Abbie brought the notebook back and dangled it casually by her side. 'I'm starving. Hope Dad saved me some lunch. Bye.'

And before they could ask why her face was so red or her hair so damp, Abbie was strolling towards the huts with a hand in her pocket, a whistle on her lips and the notebook up her T-shirt. *Welcome back, sneaking,* she thought furiously. *Hi again, competing.*

She went into Dad's hut, her heart hopping like a frog in a frying pan. The air was hot and stale. Mr Dabbings sat cross-legged on the ground. He was knitting what Abbie guessed was supposed to be a scarf but looked more like a Curly Wurly.

'*There* you are, Abbs.' Dad was lying on his sleeping bag. 'I was just beginning to–'

'Quick. Get the others. You won't believe ... wait till I ... *get* them!'

Dad looked as if he was about to say, 'Now hang on young lady, that's no way to talk to your father, if you want other people you can jolly well fetch them yourself, I'm not your servant you know, a little respect wouldn't go amiss and by the way please stop standing on my sleeping bag.' But the urgency in her voice, and the madness in her eye, made him jump up instead. Thirty seconds later all the Hartley-Battboilings were gathered in the hut.

'Emergency meeting,' Abbie said in a trembly voice. 'You'll never guess what I–'

'Hang on,' Terrifica tutted. 'Procedure.' She brought out her whistle and blew. 'Dyb dyb dyb, listen well. Abigail has news to–'

'For goodness sake!' snapped Marcus. 'Why do we have to go through this rubbish every time?'

'He interrupted!' cried Terrifica. 'He's always interru–'

'No I'm not! And what about you, barging in all the time like a bull in a handkerchief?'

'*Neck*erchief!' wailed Terrifica. 'Guides wear *neck*erchiefs!'

'Well you need a *mouth*erchief. Maybe that would stop you braying like a donkey.'

'He called me a donkey! *Do* something teacher.'

'Well I – now then.' Mr Dabbings waved his arms. 'Please, Terrifica. Kicking isn't kind. And Marcus, punching doesn't help a rose to bloom.'

'Cut it out!' yelled Dad, trying to separate them.

'Pig!' cried Terrifica, whacking Marcus on the arm.

'Buffalo!' he shouted, stamping on her foot.

'Walrus.'

'Squawking halfbeak.'

'Gassy aardvark.'

'STOP!' roared Abbie.

Terrifica stopped whacking. Marcus unstamped his foot. They slunk apart.

'SIT DOWN AND SHUT UP.'

They did. And no one said a word until she'd told the whole story and shown them the sketch in her notebook. 'The cave's behind these two rocks.'

'Oh wow,' breathed Marcus.

'Oh double dyb,' murmured Terrifica.

'Oh sparkly raindrops on new-cut grass,' gasped Mr Dabbings.

'Oh cut the gush,' cried Dad. 'Grab any diggers you can find – sticks, toothbrushes, knitting needles. Let's go!'

'Wait,' said Abbie. 'It'll be dark soon.'

'So?' Marcus arched his eyebrows. 'Are you *scared*?'

You bet, thought Abbie, recalling the cave. It had been spooky enough at midday. Her skin prickled as she remembered the drip of water, the dim chill, the feeling of being watched. Imagine all that in the shadow of night. But she couldn't let Marcus see her fear. 'Course not. It's just that we can't dig in the dark.'

Marcus's hands flew to his head. 'Aaagh!' He turned on Mr Dabbings. 'Well done, *Sir*, for not letting us bring torches.'

Everyone scowled except Abbie, who thanked the teacher silently for the perfect excuse.

'Candles?' he suggested in a small voice.

Everyone smiled except Abbie, who cursed the teacher silently for perfectly ruining the perfect excuse, and Terrifica who clasped her hands in horror. 'No way! A Guide never roves by candlelight. What if we set fire to the undergrowth? I'd be thrown out, de-woggled for life.'

Abbie thanked Terrifica silently for perfectly unruining the perfectly ruined excuse. 'She's right. And there's nothing to lose by waiting till morning. The other team doesn't know about the cave. It's been there for a thousand years: it'll be there another night.'

Not even Marcus could argue with that.

It was so warm that evening they didn't bother with a fire. Everyone climbed to the top of the moor to eat cabbage cake and watch the sunset fan across the sky like the wings of a fiery eagle.

'It's crazy really,' said Coriander. 'All of us still hoping there's treasure when we haven't found a single clue in five days.'

Marcus nudged Abbie so hard that her cake flew from her hand. It landed in a bog where it lay for three thousand two hundred and fifteen years until it was found by a cockroach called Brian Prosser who used it to prove his theory that the human race was wiped out by bad picnics.

'Look at that sky,' said Matt, taking Coriander's hand.

'Stunning.' She leaned against his shoulder.

'Like a whopping great goblet of gold,' murmured Mr Dabbings. Nine faces turned on him. Five were curious, four furious. 'I mean ...' he chewed his lip, '*heavenly* gold.' He blinked round. 'I mean ... maybe *that's* what the monks meant by the treasure – the setting sun. Yes!' He clapped his hands, warming to the theme. 'Maybe they sat here like us, wowing at the sky, and wrote a prayer about God's sunset being like a golden cup, dripping with jewels. Maybe

Brother Donal found that prayer and … and got carried away, and imagined there really *was* a cup, and described it in the *Annals* as if it was real and … and that's how the legend began. Phew.' He mopped his brow with a knitted hanky.

Abbie stared at him. She'd always thought his brain was made of tofu. But this was impressive. This was chocolate-up-the-sleeve crafty.

A bit too crafty. 'Whatever,' said Matt, yawning. 'At any rate, we're clearly wasting our time. We might as well give up looking and spend the last few days having fun together.'

'Definitely,' said Coriander.

Now what? Abbie looked anxiously at Marcus.

'How about a game,' he said quickly, 'to round off the hunt? First thing tomorrow, each team collects as many gold things as they can from Nature – to celebrate the island's, um, environmental riches.'

'Great idea!' cried Dad. 'And the winners get the box of Ferrero Rocher chocolates I just happened to bring along for a rainy day.'

***

Grandma was sitting with the Incas in the garden of the bed and breakfast at Killyboon watching the sunset. Cupping his hands round his mouth, Chunca shouted at the sky.

'What's 'e on about?' said Grandma.

Bacpac sighed. 'My Master tell Granddad to get our rooms ready. We coming up soon.'

'Grandson of the sun, eh?' Grandma gazed at the huge orange ball sinking slowly in the sky. 'Does 'e really believe 'e'll end up there? What does 'e reckon it's like?'

Bacpac sighed. 'A golden palace with three hundred flush toilets and melted chocolate in taps.'

'And you?' Grandma studied Bacpac's kind face. 'What do you think?'

The old servant bit his lip.

'Look,' said Grandma softly, 'are you sure you want to go through with this? You could always – you know – *forget* to 'old 'ands when the time comes.'

Smiling sadly, Bacpac shook his head. 'What Master want, I want. If he want to die, I want to die too, whether I want to die or not.'

Grandma squeezed his arm. 'For a load of nonsense, that sort of makes sense. What a pal you are. You remind me of Chess.' She patted her head. 'You'd do the same for me, wouldn't you chuck?'

Chester wriggled madly. It was hard to tell if he was agreeing with Grandma or trembling with horror at the thought.

***

Darkness was falling in the woods as Klench packed for his night-time wash. He eyed the soaps on his inflatable dressing table. Which one to take? Oven Cleaner, Creosote or Marmite? He settled for Oven Cleaner – it might be the cruellest to cuts and scrapes, but it definitely gave the best scour.

His alarm clock was set for 3 a.m. What to do until then? He'd slept all afternoon and finished his supper (three long-life strudels, four lardy cakes and, to shut Mummy up, half a carrot). Taking a magazine, a blindfold and a box of pins from the dressing table, he settled down to fill the remaining hours with his favourite game of Pin the Tail on the Policeman.

16

Not Exactly Stealing

'Yeeaggh!' Abbie spluttered awake. Cold was crashing onto her head, soaking her curls and freezing her brain. 'Get off!' She sat bolt upright.

'Ha!' Terrifica was standing over the stone bench with an upturned bucket. 'You jolly well deserved it. How could you oversleep on a day like this?'

Abbie was just about to tell Terrifica what *she* jolly well deserved, when she remembered what day 'this' was. Pushing off the soggy sleeping bag, she stood up and stretched. At least the water had jolted her from a restless sleep full of strange rustlings at the edge of her dreams. 'What's the time?' She squeezed out her curls.

'Time to get rich! Come on. Everyone's waiting.' Terrifica clapped her hands. 'Thrillingtons or what?'

Abbie grinned. *Just wait till we come back with the goblet*, she thought, imagining the look on Perdita's face. But until then, they had to play it cool. The Slightly Platt-Hollers mustn't suspect a thing.

Throwing on shorts and T-shirts, they stooped out of the hut. The newly risen sun spilled orange across the sky. The rest of the team was round the smouldering fire, eating barley flake cereal and trying to hide their excitement from Coriander and Matt.

'*There* you are.' Dad shoved bowls at Abbie and Terrifica. 'Get this down you and we'll be off.'

'Hang on,' said Coriander. 'You can't start before us. Our team's not ready.'

'Oh dear, what a shame.' Dad tutted sympathetically. 'Never mind, I'll save you a Ferrero Rocher.'

'What have you got in there?' Coriander frowned at the bulging rucksack he'd slung over his shoulder.

'Oh, just a few spoons and forks for digging up,' he coughed, 'er, shiny shells and things.' He clapped his hands. 'Ready for the off, team?' He winked as subtly as a lighthouse.

'Suppose so.' Mr Dabbings yawned as quietly as a foghorn.

'See you later.' Marcus waved as sincerely as a snake.

'Wait.' Abbie chewed as daintily as a piranha. 'I've forgotten something.' Her notebook – for finding the cave again and jotting down any more clues.

She ran back to her hut and unzipped the top pocket of her rucksack. It was empty. Frowning, she opened the other pockets. Nothing. She rummaged in the main bag. Not there. She shook out her sleeping bag. Nope. Scrunching her hair, she thought back to yesterday. She'd shown it to the team in Dad's hut. *Then I brought it back here, I swear. I was putting it back in my rucksack when Ursula came in and …*

Ursula! She bit her finger, remembering how the tiny girl had asked on the beach what was in her notebook. *No!* She rushed out of the hut.

Henry and Ursula were heading for breakfast.

Abbie grabbed her shoulders. 'Where is it?'

Ursula wriggled free. 'What?'

'My notebook. You've got it, haven't you?'

'No,' said Ursula, turning faintly pink.

'Well one of you has.'

Henry shook his head.

'OK,' snarled Abbie, 'where's Perdita?'

'Having breakfast?' Henry blinked innocently.

'You know she's not – and so do I. I know exactly where she is!'

Henry sniggered. 'So why bother asking?'

'My notebook!' Abbie yelled. Everyone at the food tent looked up. 'My private, personal stuff – Perdita *stole* it.'

Matt and Coriander rushed over.

'What did you say? Perdita would never steal.' Coriander blinked at Henry and Ursula. 'Would she?'

Henry scrunched Mr Binkles. 'Well …'

'Not exactly,' mumbled Ursula.

'How can you *not exactly* steal?' Abbie stamped her

foot. 'Either she did or she didn't.' The other Hartley-Battboilings came up, filling the air with outrage.

'I mean … it was all three of us.' Henry dug the ground with the toe of his sandal.

'Well why not?' said Ursula indignantly. 'It was obvious you found a clue yesterday. Why didn't you tell everyone, when we'd agreed to work together again?'

'What clue?' Coriander exchanged a baffled look with Matt.

'When Abbie came along the beach,' said Henry, 'she had "clue" written all over her face – or at least in her notebook. You should've seen the way she shoved it behind her back.' He sniffed. 'But Perdita said no, if she *had* found something, she'd have told us.'

It was Abbie's turn for some squirmy footwork.

'So Henry and I followed you,' said Ursula. We listened outside your dad's hut while you debriefed your team. We heard all about the waterfall and what you'd found there. Then I followed you back to your hut and–'

'Saw where I put it,' snarled Abbie, 'so you could steal it later!'

'*Borrow*,' corrected Henry smugly. 'So we could prove to Perdita you'd been hiding a clue.'

Abbie recalled her rustling dreams. 'You mean you nicked it from my bag?'

Ursula couldn't help a tiny smile. 'In the middle of the

night. Easy peasy with Terrifica snoring like that.' Her smile collapsed. 'But when I woke Perdita and showed her, she was furious. Said we should put it straight back.'

'I knew it.' Coriander breathed out with relief.

'Until she read through the notebook – all those things you'd written about her – *and* the sketch. Then she was even more furious. With *you*.' Ursula allowed another teeny smile at Abbie. '*So* furious that she copied it. Then she put your notebook back so you wouldn't know we'd taken it. And at sunrise she went to find the cave. We were supposed to stay here and, oops –' she blinked at Henry, 'pretend we didn't know.'

'But she *didn't* put it back,' cried Abbie. 'I've looked in my rucksack.'

Henry shrugged. 'Not hard enough. Better look again.'

'No way!' Marcus wagged his finger furiously at Abbie. 'Don't you see? He just wants us to waste more time so that Perdita can find the treasure. She's probably in the cave right now, digging away.'

'Quick!' cried Dad. 'We need to get there before she … Oh Sweet Mother!'

Which wasn't dismay at the thought of Perdita finding the goblet but amazement at the sight of something else. Striding over the brow of the moor, arm in arm with two old gents, was his – oh, sweet – mother.

***

190

Klench stared at the sketch in the notebook he'd stolen so neatly. 'Cave in mountainside,' he murmured. 'Oh no. Zere are two mountains and each has many sides. Cave could be anyvhere. Vhere to start lookink?'

Mummy rolled her inner eyes. 'Vhere d'you think, my dimvit dearest? If in doubt, zen try ze nearest.'

Klench scowled. It was all right for Mummy, sipping her early morning inner tea. She wasn't the one who had to slog up a slope to find this cave. He shut the notebook savagely. She hadn't even congratulated him on his brilliant burglary.

'Vy should I?' she snapped. 'It voss luck zat made you look, and see ze girl return ze book.'

Yes, but it was *his* keen ears that had alerted him during his three o'clock bathe. Wallowing in the lake like a pale whale, he'd heard angry voices coming from one of the huts. He'd slipped out of the water, donned his mint-green dressing gown, scuttled over in the soft starlight and crouched by the entrance to listen.

As an expert in eavesdropping, he'd quickly worked out that the speakers had stolen a notebook. As a master of meddling, he'd soon realised that the figure who scurried out of the hut holding a candle in one hand and something else in the other, was returning that notebook. As a specialist in spying, he'd easily followed the someone to another hut and watched from the entrance while they fumbled for a rucksack and unzipped a pocket. And as a black belt in burglary, he'd crept in smoothly afterwards, felt for the rucksack and pinched the book.

But as a hater of Nature, he was dreading following the clue. All that dirt and digging – it was enough to make an apple crumble.

Talking of which … he opened his cool box. 'For energy, Mums,' he said miserably. 'Zere is much excavatinks to do.'

17

Bad News Bearers

Abbie blinked. What she saw made no sense. It was a picture of mismatches, like a cabbage on the moon or a cat swimming through Debenhams. *Grandma can't be here. She's at home.*

Abbie screwed up her eyes. Was her brain playing tricks, inserting a memory of Grandma in front of island scenery? But she had no memory of Grandma wearing calf-length hiking breeches, with binoculars round her neck and a T-shirt that said SURF BABE.

Neither did she recognise the two old men. The one on Grandma's left wore white earmuffs and a T-shirt that said I RULE, OK? The man on his left wore a T-shirt with an arrow pointing to the right and the words HE RULES, OK? This poor chap was stooping under the weight of two rucksacks. Both men had skin the colour of caramel and black hair flecked with grey. They stopped in front of the speechless campers.

'Hi-de-Hi,' said the man in earmuffs, in a way that

suggested he'd been watching old BBC comedies.

'Hail fellows and well met,' said the man under the rucksacks, in a way that suggested he'd been reading Shakespeare plays.

'Any chance of a sarnie?' said Grandma, in a way that suggested there'd better be. Her grumpy voice banished Abbie's last doubt. This was no hologram. This was flesh-and-blood Grandma: now mopping her brow with Chester, now clacking her teeth with impatience.

'Cat got yer tongue?' She tutted at Dad. 'And you can stop starin',' she said to Abbie. 'That's no way to greet the Son of the Son of the Sun.'

Abbie tried to, she really did, but when Grandma slapped Mr Earmuffs on the back and said, 'This is Chunca, King of the Incas,' her jaw couldn't help but drop. And when Grandma whacked Mr Rucksacks on the arm and said, 'This is Bacpac, servant of the King,' her eyes couldn't help but pop.

Dad stepped forward. 'Mother,' he said gently, 'it's great to see you, it really is. But I think you've had too much sun.'

'Sun.' Chunca waved at the sky. 'Hi Granddad.'

'What 'e means,' said Grandma, 'is that 'e's descended from the sun god Inti.'

'Sun-*shine*.' Chunca pointed at Grandma. 'My besto.'

She grinned. ''E thinks I'm the bee's knees.'

Dad took her arm. 'You need to lie down, Mother.'

Grandma shook him off. 'I'm tryin' to 'elp 'im die, you see. And it's provin' quite a mission, I can tell you.'

Chester bounced on her head in agreement.

'Aagh!' 'Urk!' 'Eek!' and 'Yeurch!' shouted Terrifica, Ursula, Henry and Marcus. Or was it Ursula, Marcus, Henry and Terrifica? Or maybe Marcus, Henry, Ursula and … *Oh, who cares?* thought Abbie. The point was that they'd never actually met Chester. OK they'd *seen* him – but a battery-powered tonsure was a far cry from a living patch of chest hair. And right now Grandma was causing enough embarrassment without Abbie having to introduce him.

There was no choice, though. So she did it quickly,

keeping explanations to a minimum. As for their reactions
… well, it was hard to tell because, as soon as she'd finished,
she closed her eyes and prayed she was in a Doctor Who
Easter special. But when she opened them again there
was no Tardis waiting to whisk her to Planet Sensible, just
Grandma, now spouting some hootiefruit about ancient
prophecies, stoutest crooks and holding hands.

Abbie had to admit it was a good story – until the last
two words.

'*WHO*?!' she said as calmly as she could.

'I knew 'e'd come 'ere,' said Grandma, 'in search of
treasure, even though I told 'im it was nothin' but a
fairytale. 'Ere Corrie, you OK?'

Coriander's hands were pressed against her cheeks.
'Perdita!'

'Out there with Klench!' gasped Matt. 'No!'

'Now calm down.' Dad put a hand on Matt's shoulder.
'We've been searching this island for nearly a week. And
there's been no sign of company.'

Oh hasn't there? While the others murmured their
agreement, Abbie's throat filled with dust. The growing
unease she'd felt on this island, the sense that they weren't
alone … had someone been watching them all along?

And not just any old someone. She clasped her head
as memories crashed in. Klench holding them hostage in
the Hair Museum. Klench trying to trim their brains in

the Amazon jungle. Klench with a gun. Klench with a bun. And now a new nightmare, Klench on the run. He was out there somewhere – and so was Perdita.

'This is all my fault,' she mumbled. 'If I'd shared the clue, she wouldn't have gone off alone.'

Coriander moaned. Matt groaned. And Grandma bunched her fists. 'Ooh, just wait till I get me 'ands on 'im. I'll smack 'is bum to kingdom come. I'll clip 'is ears for twenty years. I'll squeeze 'is knees to … to …' She looked round for help.

'Mushy peas!' cried Mr Dabbings with surprising enthusiasm for a peace-loving man.

Coriander sniffed to her senses. 'We have to find Perdita before Klench does.' She stepped forward and grabbed Abbie's arm. 'We're going to that cave right now. And the minute we find her –' she turned to Mr Dabbings, 'phone Bundy. We're leaving this island immediately.'

Grandma folded her arms. 'I'm not leavin' anywhere without a sarnie. Me and the lads missed breakfast.'

'For goodness sake! Our daughter's … and you're … oh, there's no time for this.' Coriander grabbed Abbie's right hand.

Matt grasped her left. 'Take us to Perdita.'

Abbie nodded, blinking back tears. Everyone followed them down to the lake except Grandma and the Incas.

'Help yourselves,' Dad called over his shoulder, pointing

to the food tent. 'But don't go anywhere till we get back. I can't have you wandering off as well, Mother.'

'Alright, keep yer 'air on,' shouted Grandma, which was a bit rich as Chester had already shot off her head towards the food tent.

Abbie ran along the beach. The others crunched behind her like frantic cornflakes. Tears blurred the shingle into a wobbly grey curtain. She blinked furiously. She had to stay focused. Klench could be anywhere: round the next bend, behind a bush, perched up a very strong tree.

Marcus caught up with her. 'What's all the fuss?' he panted. 'Is this guy really so bad?'

'Worse,' she mumbled, realising that the other children and Mr Dabbings had never met Hubris Klench. How could she describe the depth of his depravity, the height of his horridity, the width of his wickedosity? 'Smuggler. Kidnapper. Bank robber. Brain shrinker.' The list was endless. But her breath wasn't. She waved her arms to indicate more crimes and ran on.

Her chest was exploding. She pushed herself harder, hoping the pain would suppress her panic. What if Klench had caught Perdita? What if he'd forced her at gunpoint into the cave to dig up the treasure? A sob escaped her. Never mind their recent quarrels: Perdita had been the best friend of her life.

Another sob slipped out. The life that Klench had done

his best to ruin. Every time she thought they were safe he popped up again – indestructible, unstoppable, everlasting as a giant gobstopper. A sudden anger flared in her chest, fuelling her stride, scooping energy out of nowhere.

The beach curved to the right. And there was the waterfall, crashing and sparkling down the mountainside.

A shriek cut the air. Abbie spun round. Coriander was sitting on the beach. Her hand was cupped over her left ankle. She was wincing with pain. Abbie ran back.

'I tripped,' said Coriander. 'I'm OK.' But her face was ashen. Taking Matt's hand, she tried to stand up. 'Ow!' She collapsed. 'My ankle.'

Matt rubbed her shoulders. 'Try again,' he urged. But when he hoisted her up her leg crumpled.

'You go on,' she gasped, flopping down on the beach. 'You've got to find Perdita.'

'I can't,' said Matt. 'What if Klench finds you?'

'You must. What if he finds Perdita?' They stared at each other.

'We'll have to split up,' said Abbie. 'Half come on with me, half take Coriander back. We mustn't leave anyone alone.' Their only advantage was numbers. If Klench had picked up a gun somewhere – which knowing him was likely – their one hope was to overwhelm him. 'Who's coming with me?' she said as calmly as she could over the fireworks of fear inside.

Matt looked frantically from her to Coriander. *What a choice*, thought Abbie: *protecting your wife or rescuing your daughter*. In the end she decided for him, saying he'd be most help making a stretcher.

Mr Dabbings eagerly offered to carry one end. 'Much as I'd love to meet this appalling villain, you understand, and teach him the Love Rainbow. Which is, Henry?'

'Kindness, happiness, helpfulness, cheerfulness, friendliness, gentleness and lentilness.' Henry finished wrapping his blankie round Coriander's ankle and said he'd go back too, so that Mr Binkles wouldn't get lonely.

Terrifica said she'd hold Coriander's hand and 'earn my Florence Nightingale badge'.

Dad put his arm round Abbie. 'I'm with you, darling. Not letting you out of my sight.'

Marcus joined them. 'Me too. I'm not giving up now.'

On Perdita thought Abbie, *or the treasure?* But she was too grateful for his company to ask.

'Nor me,' said Ursula, 'not if Perdita's in trouble.'

Coriander smiled through her pain. 'What a friend you are.'

The words stabbed Abbie, hot and true. She'd got Perdita into danger and Ursula was volunteering to get her out.

No. If anyone's going to rescue Perdita, it's me. She turned and strode on towards the waterfall.

***

'Disgustin'.' Grandma dropped her potted pigeon cookie on the groundsheet. Chester took it outside, dug a hole and buried it, accidentally destroying a woodlouse shopping centre. 'There must be somethin' tastier. If I know Graham, 'e's bound to 'ave a bit of choc stashed somewhere.' She rummaged round the tent, peering behind crates and lifting the edge of the groundsheet. 'Ha!' Tucked in a corner was a plastic box. ''Oo fancies a Ferrero Rocher?'

Sitting on Bacpac's lap (emperors are allergic to the floor) Chunca beamed. Of the few English words he'd learned, 'Ferrero' and 'Rocher' were by far the most interesting. No one had bothered to tell him they were actually Italian. He opened his mouth. Bacpac unwrapped the choc and popped it in.

Grandma sat on a crate, munching thoughtfully. 'Wonder where that scoundrel could be?'

***

On the mountain, as it happened, just above the woods. 'Give me break,' Klench panted. 'I am out of puffs.'

Mummy jabbed his bottom with an inner poker. 'Get a move on lazy breeches, if you vont to find ze riches.'

Oh boy did he vont. Taking a deep breath, Klench lumbered on, fuelled by the thought of unearthing his passport to freedom and respectability, when his life – and her death – could start all over again.

18

Where's Perdita?

Abbie marched ahead, a poisonous soup of guilt and fear bubbling in her chest. She pressed her knuckles into her eyes. She had to hold it together, get them to the cave. The waterfall roared like growing dread. At last she reached the pool at the bottom and waited for the others.

Ursula arrived first. 'This is all my fault,' she gasped. Her face was streaked with tears.

'What?' said Abbie sharply.

'I should never have taken your notebook. I'm sorry.'

Relief flooded Abbie. Ursula knew how she felt – was even taking the blame! Time to swallow her pride, forgive and forget, hug and make up. 'It's too late now!' she snapped.

Ursula bit her lip and nodded miserably.

Why did I say that? If Abbie had burrowed underground and swallowed earth, she couldn't have felt more like a worm.

She hid her shame with efficiency. 'We have to assume

the worst,' she said when Dad and Marcus arrived. 'That Klench *has* found Perdita in the cave and that he's got a gun. Our only hope is to surprise him. We go through the waterfall. Three of us wait by the crack in the rocks while one goes into the cave and distracts him. Then the others creep in and grab him.'

'Who'll go in?' said Marcus. Everyone looked down and found a particularly amazing pebble to stare at.

'Me.' Everyone looked up and found a particularly amazing Ursula to stare at.

'Wow,' said Marcus.

'No.' Abbie was shocked to discover that she'd spoken. '*I* will.' She licked her lips. 'I've handled Klench before.'

Dad gripped her arm. 'No way! I wouldn't dream of letting you do that.'

'But you'd dream of letting Ursula?' Abbie pulled away.

'Um, of course not. I mean … *I'll* do it.'

'No,' said Abbie. 'We need the strongest people to grab him – that's you and Ursula. And Klench knows me – I'll be more of a distraction than Marcus. She turned to Ursula. 'I bet you know some good rear attacks.'

'There's the Backstabber. And the Buttboot.'

'Perfect,' said Abbie, though she doubted even Ursula could boot *that* butt.

'Hang on,' said Dad. 'I said no. I won't allow this, Abigail. Your mother would never speak to me again. *I* would never speak to me again.' His voice trembled. 'As your loving father and parent-in-chief, I absolutely forbid–'

But she was already running in front of the pool. She jumped from stone to stone across the streams and reached the gap at the far edge of the waterfall. Taking a deep breath, she slipped through.

Marcus and Terrifica followed, staring round the chamber in wonder while Dad rushed through. Before he could grab her, Abbie dodged towards the back wall.

The morning sun threw a dimmer light than yesterday. Feeling rather than seeing her way to the crack, Abbie froze. *I can't go in.* She spread her hands on the rocks either side to steady herself. *I have to.* Cold stone pressed into her palms. *I could be shot.* She shivered. *So could Perdita.* She looked behind. Marcus and Ursula were blocking a furious-faced Dad.

Clenching her fists, Abbie slipped into the cave. Her breath came in little gasps as she blinked round. Slowly the darkness took shape as …

Nothing. No Perdita. No Klench. Just dripping water and crumbly red walls.

Her fists opened. Her shoulders dropped. She breathed deeply, letting the tension leak out. 'Come in,' she yelled above the hollering water. 'It's safe.'

Dad burst in and grasped her by the shoulders. 'I'll give you safe, my girl! Don't you *ever* do that again.' He hugged her.

Ursula put a hand on her arm. 'Wait till I tell Perdita what you did.'

Abbie smiled in a frowny way. Then she frowned in a smiley way. Ursula was the enemy. Why would she sing Abbie's praises? It didn't make sense. *If she'd gone in first, I'd never have told Perdita.*

Perdita. Where was she? Abbie shouted into the darkness. The waterfall shouted back.

Dad dumped his rucksack and brought out candles. Handing them round, he took a matchbox from his pocket and lit them. Light flickered wickedly round the cave.

'Maybe Perdita came and went,' said Marcus.

Abbie looked at the ground. Apart from the hole she'd made yesterday, the mud was smooth. Strange – if Perdita had come here, why hadn't she started digging? *Did she never make it? Did Klench nab her on the way?*

She swallowed. 'We have to go.' Her voice was flat, a lid on the panic that was boiling inside.

Marcus had already taken a spoon from his rucksack and was kneeling down, scooping out mud. He looked up, dismayed. 'But the treasure!'

Ursula bent down and snatched the spoon from Marcus's hand. 'What's more important – a battered old cup or Perdita?'

Marcus sank back on his heels. 'OK,' he said in a small voice.

Abbie was the last to leave. While the others stooped through the entrance, she lifted her candle and glanced round for a final check. Shadows capered on the walls.

She caught her breath. At the back, amid the earthy rubble, was a crack in the wall. Small enough to overlook, just big enough to squeeze through.

Abbie walked over to the crack and stuck her head through. 'Perdita?' She turned round. 'Guys,' she called, 'come back!' Bending down, she pushed through the gap and stood up. She was in a passage about two metres wide. The ceiling arched just above her head. The wet red walls gleamed in the candlelight. 'Perdita?' She took a few more steps forward. 'Are you there?'

She turned her head. 'Quick,' she yelled back out through the entrance, 'there's a tunnel!'

There was a thud. Then a series of quick dull knocks. Then a tumbling, thumping, scraping. Then a sharp pain as something hit her head. Wheeling round, she screamed. Mud and rocks were falling. The entrance to the tunnel was closing up.

***

'That's enough!' Grandma slapped Chunca's hand away from the Ferrero Rocher box. 'They'll rot your teeth.'

Bacpac translated. The Emp gabbled back in ancient Quechua. 'Master say who care? When he die, whole body rot. And please he die soon. Why wait? Let us find stoutest crook right now.'

Grandma sighed. 'I don't see why not. Graham's takin' ages. Come on.' Picking up her binoculars, she headed out of the food tent. 'Let's go up to the moor and 'ave a scout round. That crafty old crab can't be too far away.'

***

In fact, he was just above the woods, looking up the mountain slope. 'Crack betveen third and fourth rocks,' Klench read from the notebook, 'cave in mountainside.' He shook his head. 'Vich rocks? Vot cave? Ziss must be wronk mountain.'

Inner Mummy snorted. 'Do not try to make excuses, just because you're out of juices. I see boulders just up zere. Move zat butt, you vast éclair.'

19

Caved In

Shielding her face with her arm, Abbie staggered back towards the tunnel entrance. Mud and crumbly rocks rained down, blocking her path. 'HELP!' she screamed. 'DAD!' But the more she yelled, the faster they fell. Could her voice have caused this, destabilised the already soft walls? She stumbled backwards into the passage, screwing up her eyes, coughing and gagging and tasting mud.

At last the avalanche stopped. The candle trembled in her hand. Shadows reared like cobras over the fallen rocks. For a second her mind was blank. Then dazzling waves of panic crashed through. With shaking hands she stood the candle on a rock and scrabbled frantically at the rubble. A few small stones trickled down. Nothing else would budge. The entrance was completely sealed. Not a chink of light broke through.

'Daaaad!' she moaned, shoving herself against the rocks. 'Maarcus!' But it was pointless. Even if they heard, how could they break through from the other side?

Besides, they'd already left the cave. What if they hadn't noticed she'd lagged behind? What if they were through the waterfall and heading back along the beach, unaware that she wasn't?

Her legs gave way. She sank against a rock and clutched her stomach, winded by terror. Her cheeks felt cold. She must be crying. Closing her eyes, she took short sharp breaths while waves of sickness shuddered through her.

When the shivering had calmed a little, she opened her eyes. Behind her lay the barrier: blocky, unbreachable. You'd think it had always been there. Ahead of her lay … what?

She licked the roof of her mouth, sticky with fear. Bending down, she picked up the candle. The flame thinned. She cupped her hand round it. *Don't go out.* Her only light, her only hope in this nightmare.

Working saliva into her mouth, she headed down the passage. She could see about two metres ahead. Beyond lay thick darkness. 'Perdita?' she said, not too loudly, for fear of dislodging more rock. Silence. She filled her lungs with dank, stale air and focused her mind on one goal: moving forward.

The walls either side had a sickly yellow sheen, like frozen milk. Running her fingers along their lumpy skin, she thought back desperately to geography lessons. *Minerals – deposited by flowing water.* Perhaps a river had carved this tunnel. Perhaps it had run right through the mountain and out the other side. *Please!* She walked faster.

Unless … a fist of fear punched her chest. What if the mountain was made of limestone? What if water had trickled down from the surface, carving out holes and passages that led nowhere, like the inside of a giant Crunchie bar? What if others had come along here looking for treasure … and never got out? What if she found skulls and ribcages and earbones – did ears even *have* bones? – and … 'Perditaaa!' she wailed, no longer caring what she dislodged. This was all her fault. If only she'd told everyone about the cave. If only she hadn't drawn that sketch. If only she hadn't wandered off yesterday. 'I'm sorreee!'

The ceiling dripped. The walls gleamed. The mud sucked her sandals.

She blundered on, the candle in her right hand. With her left hand she shielded the precious flame. Every few steps she called Perdita's name. The tunnel curved right, then left, then went straight on. Left again, right again, straight. The air became colder. The candle burned lower. Colder, lower, further.

'Please!' she begged the darkness. 'Let me go!'

'Oh.'

She stopped. Was that an echo?

'Loh … ello … hello?'

'PERDITA!' She rushed on in the gloom. 'Where are you?'

'Here.'

'Where?'

'I don't know!'

Abbie tried to think calmly. *If Perdita came in the same entrance as me, and the tunnel hasn't forked, she must be just ahead.* 'Don't move.' She rounded the next corner.

'My candle went out.' Perdita's voice was getting louder.

'I've got one. I'm coming.'

'I can hear you squelching.'

A bend to the left. A blur in the darkness. Two brown eyes, a pale teary face and – 'Abbie!' Perdita's arms were around her neck. 'Oh, thank goodness.' She stood back, crying and smiling. 'I was too scared to go on in the dark so I turned back.' She squeezed Abbie's hand. Her teeth gleamed in the candlelight. 'The treasure must be in here somewhere. If we go back and get more cand–'

'We can't.'

'Can't what?'

'Go back.' Abbie held her arm. 'There was a rockfall. The entrance is blocked.'

Perdita froze. Her eyes glowed, huge and unblinking. She closed her lids, as if tucking the news underneath. 'Blocked.' Her voice was flat.

'We have to go on.' Abbie swallowed. 'And find a way out.'

Perdita opened her eyes. 'Out,' she echoed dully. A drop of water fell on her head.

'Come on. There isn't much light left.' The candle was down to its last few centimetres. Taking Perdita's hand, Abbie led them through the dripping gloom.

At last Perdita said, 'How did you know I was in here?'

Abbie looked over her shoulder. 'I couldn't find my notebook. I guessed you'd taken it.'

'But I put it back in your rucksack so you wouldn't know. You must've missed it.'

Abbie was sure she hadn't. But what was the point of arguing? They'd done nothing else on this island and look where it had got them.

'I'm sorry we took it,' said Perdita. 'But I was so mad when I read it. Why did you write that stuff about me? And why didn't you tell us about the cave?'

''Coz I was mad too.'

'I know. Like you have been this whole trip. Why?'

Abbie stopped. *Does she really not know*? She turned round. 'Because you went off with Ursula, of course.'

212

'What?' Perdita scrunched her eyebrows. 'I didn't "go off". I was only trying to help – trying to cheer her up.'

'You dumped me to share a hut with her. *And* teamed up with her for the treasure hunt. Was all that just cheering up?'

'No. That was because she's nice, which you'd have found out too if you'd stayed around.'

'You didn't want me to!'

Perdita stared at her. 'Of course I did. *You're* the one who didn't want to. So I gave up. I thought ...' her eyelids fluttered, 'you'd had enough of me.'

Abbie's jaw dropped. 'You're joking.'

'Actually,' said Perdita in a thick voice, 'I'm not in the mood right now.'

'I mean, I thought *you'd* had enough of *me*, the way you hung around Claire, then Ursula – then even Henry.'

'I was making friends with them, not unmaking friends with you.' Perdita shook her head in bemusement. 'Why would I? How could I? You're brilliant.'

'I am?' Abbie stared at her. 'Well ... well so are you.'

Perdita held out her hand. 'Friends again?'

Abbie squeezed it. 'Friends.' They were trapped in a tunnel with no way out. But still a ridiculous relief spread inside her: a bubble of light that seemed to rise and expand, shrinking all her hurt and anger, squeezing it out of her chest and away through the darkness.

The darkness that wasn't so dark.

She turned round and looked down the passage. The blackness really did seem to be lifting to a greyish gloom. It couldn't be from the candle: the flame was guttering and thinning. Could there be another source of light?

They rounded a bend. 'Hey!' She pointed ahead. 'Is that …? *YES!*' About five metres ahead a circle of light pooled on the ground. It came from a hole in the roof of the tunnel.

'Oh,' breathed Perdita. 'Thank you. *Thank* you!' They hurried on as fast as they could without killing the candle flame.

'Hey!' Reaching the light, Abbie felt a tug from behind. A draught of air was pulling at her back. The candle went out. Dropping it, she looked up. The hole was just above her head. 'Quick!' she yelled. 'I'll give you a leg up!'

'No, you go first.' Perdita was struggling too, bending forwards against the backward pull and cupping her hands to make a step for Abbie.

'No!' shouted Abbie. 'You're lighter and thinner. You can get through the crack and pull me up.'

'Not against this wind!' screamed Perdita. 'It's getting stronger.'

Rooted in terror, stupid with horror, Abbie knew one thing. She'd got Perdita in here; she had to get her out. With a strength born of desperation, she crouched down; grabbed Perdita round the knees and shoved her upwards.

Perdita's fingers gripped the edge of the hole. Yes …

'Aaaaagh!' Abbie was yanked backwards in the draught. For a second Perdita hung by her fingers from the lip of the hole. Then she lost her grip and dropped back down into the passage. The air went still. Then the pull became a push, the stillness a rush. With a sound like a gunshot, the girls were hurled forwards and upwards in a blast of hot, wet wind.

***

'Where could she have gone?' Dad shielded his eyes and peered up the beach.

'We last saw her in the cave, right?' said Ursula. 'And she's definitely not there now. We must've just missed her.'

They'd been heading back along the beach before they'd noticed that Abbie wasn't behind them. They'd shouted, searched the undergrowth, blown their reed whistles, run back through the waterfall and peered round the cave – but there was no sign of her.

'Maybe she found a different way back,' said Marcus. 'Maybe she called but we didn't hear her over the waterfall.'

'Perhaps she found Perdita,' said Ursula, 'and they're back at the huts already.'

'Let's hope so,' said Dad, rubbing his beard nervously. 'I guess we'd better go back and check.'

***

Up on the moor, Chunca peered through the binoculars. 'It's a small world,' he said, chuffed at remembering another phrase from his BBC lessons.

'That's 'coz they're back to front.' Grandma took the binoculars, turned them round and peered through. A rabbit jumped across her vision. She trained the glasses over the moor, the woods and then up. 'Ha!' Wobbling up the mountain, high above the woods, was a football-shaped figure. 'There 'e is, the great melon! Knew 'e wouldn't take long to find.' She patted her head. ''Ow about a chocky, Chess?'

Chester dived into her rucksack, brought out the box and popped a Ferrero Rocher into everyone's hand.

'Eat up, boys,' said Grandma. 'We've got quite a trek.' Gazing up at the mountain, she dropped her wrapper absent-mindedly. Then she set off over the moor.

20

Bigmouth

Abbie blinked. The daylight was dazzling after the gloom of the tunnel. Her head throbbed, her face was hot. 'Ow!'

'Sorry,' Perdita was sitting on her foot. She wriggled off.

'Where are we?' said Abbie. 'What happened?' They'd landed in a heap of arms, legs and bruised bottoms on a patch of scrubby grass. In front of them was a tangle of nettles and brambles. She didn't recognise this part of the island.

If it is the island. Despite the heat, a shiver ran through her. *Have we died? Is this Heaven?* What a let-down. Since when did Heaven have nettles and thorns? *Oh no. Does that mean it's–*

'Hell,' boomed a voice. 'Now I'm in doo doos.'

The girls spun round. There was no one there: just a massive grey rock looming from the grass about three metres in front of them. It stuck out from the bottom of a steep mountainside. Halfway up the rock was a hole, rimmed by a band of reddish stone. Was that where they'd been flung out? But how?

Abbie clutched Perdita's arm. 'There must be someone inside,' she whispered, pointing at the hole.

'Let's go,' hissed Perdita. They turned back towards the brambles.

From behind came a snorting, sniffling sound, like a hundred bulls with colds. The girls were sucked backwards in a whoosh of warm air.

A rumble rippled up from the ground. 'Excuse *me*. A little thank you wouldn't go amiss.'

Abbie knew she should run or crawl or fly – whatever it took to get away. But her legs had other ideas.

Perdita too was turning round slowly. 'How …?' She trailed off, her mouth agape. They'd been dragged right back to the rock. The hole was just above their heads.

Closing her mouth to stop her heart jumping out, Abbie stood on tiptoe and peered through the hole into a dark cave. As far as she could see it was empty.

'Oohoo!' rumbled the voice. She leapt back as hot air blasted into her face. 'Ahaha. Tickly.' The rock gurgled, as if water was bubbling deep inside. 'Haven't had a laugh in years. Lost the habit, you might say.' More gurgles. Abbie shrieked. The rim of the hole was wriggling like … like lips round a mouth! She stumbled backwards and fell on her bottom.

The gurgles subsided. 'Not that I'll be laughing much longer. But at least you're safe – for now.'

'We are?' squeaked Perdita, helping Abbie to her feet.

'Thanks to me.' The rock-lips pressed together. 'Wouldn't you say?'

'Er … yes. Thank you.' Abbie nudged Perdita.

'Very much. Indeed. Um, what for?'

'What *for*?' bellowed the rock-mouth. The girls ducked as more hot air shot out of the hole. 'Only saving your lives. I was supposed to swallow you. But you stuck in my throat.'

'We were in your *throat*?' Abbie's hand flew to her own. She remembered the wind that had sucked them back down the tunnel, like – yes, now she thought about it – a huge intake of breath, and then thrust them up and forward. 'You mean,' she gasped, 'you *coughed* us out?'

A windy sigh escaped the cave. 'Couldn't keep you in. You choked me up. Brought back so many memories.'

Abbie blinked. The craziness of this conversation was conquering her fear. 'Of what?'

'Oh nothing much.' The cave gave a rasping laugh, like rocks sliding over each other. 'Only friendship, loyalty, love – all that fluff Father K can't stomach. You'd think he'd have mellowed after all these centuries.'

Centuries? Father K? Jigsaw pieces crashed round Abbie's mind. 'How *many* centuries?' she whispered.

'Hmm, let's see. Not that I can, these days. I'm blind as the bats inside me.' Another laugh burst out. 'What year are we in now?'

Perdita told him.

'You're kidding. Well, doesn't time fly when you're having fun?' Another snort escaped, ruffling Abbie's curls. 'Eighty plus a hundred, plus lichen, plus more hundreds, divide by erosion, minus leap years … oh at least a thousand.'

'You mean–' Abbie gulped, 'you're a – you *were* a – *monk*?'

There was a slow hiss as the cave sucked in air like a weightlifter gathering strength. Then words rattled out. 'In nomine Patris, et Filii, et Spiritus Sancti, yes indeedie. Brother Finbar, servant of the Most High – priest of the people, former holy man, current rock-star, pleased to meet you, top o' the morning, Amen.'

The girls gaped at each other, their mouths frozen Os.

After swallowing three gnats, Abbie mumbled, 'Pardon?'

The cave repeated itself.

'But,' Perdita's lips warmed up, 'if you *were* a monk, then you must be a …'

'Oh *puh-lease*.' The cave groaned. 'Do I *look* like a ghost? Do I waft and woo-hoo? How could I pass through walls? I *am* walls. Try putting your hands through *me*, sunshine, and they'll never pray again.' Laughter echoed out, deep and dark as an underground river. 'Think of me more as a fossil in progress. Nine parts mountain, one part monk. Lucky for you, my heart's still softish.'

Abbie breathed slowly, trying to take it all in. At last she said, 'You don't really, um, look like a monk.'

'And you don't look like dinner. But that's what you were meant to be. As I said, I had orders to swallow you.'

'Orders?' A chill ran across Abbie's shoulders. 'Whose orders?' She glanced wildly round the glade.

'If you want my help,' muttered the mouth, 'you'd better stop interrupting. There isn't much time. I told you, I'm already in the poop. So I suggest you sit down, shut up and hear me out.'

***

'This is a nightmare.' Dad put his head in his hands. 'We leave in search of one missing person and come back to five – six if you count Chester.'

'And seven if you count Klench,' said Mr Dabbings. The way Coriander looked at him, he wished he hadn't.

Dad, Marcus and Ursula had returned to find everyone who wasn't missing sitting in Abbie's hut. Which meant they now needed *two* search parties: one to find Abbie and Perdita and one for Grandma and the Incas who, they agreed, must have gone off to look for Klench.

Dad insisted on looking for the girls. 'Mother'll be OK. Klench wouldn't lay a finger on her.'

Matt was torn between going with him and staying to look after Coriander.

'Stay,' said Ursula. 'I'll go. I promise we'll find Perdita.' Dad's eyebrows rose. 'And Abbie,' she added quickly.

Which left Mr Dabbings as the only remaining adult to lead a search party for Grandma. 'I'd love to,' he said. 'Really. But I'd be much more use manning the fort.'

'I'll do that,' said Matt. 'And Coriander will woman it.'

'And I'll child it.' Henry stroked Coriander's ankle. 'Mr Binkles needs my support.'

'You're not *scared* are you, Sir? Don't worry, I'll protect you,' said Marcus. 'Diddums,' he added under his breath.

Mr Dabbings's sideburns drooped. 'But I'm so behind on my knitting.'

'Nonsense.' Terrifica grabbed his hand. 'I'll come too. A Guide knows no fear.'

'Besides.' Dad punched Mr Dabbings's shoulder. 'If

you did happen to meet Klench, Bran, your phenomenal peace-making skills might well make him surrender and earn you a major international police award.'

Mr Dabbings looked round the nodding faces. 'Really?'

'Ooh yes.'

'Definitely.'

'No question,' said everybody with a sincerity that would fool absolutely nobody except a really clueless teacher.

***

'Last one, lads.' Grandma gave them each a Ferrero Rocher. 'Good job we're headin' into shade. It'll be cooler in the woods.' She popped her chocolate in her mouth and regretted it. 'Ooh, I'm parched. Any water left?'

Chester shook his curls. Bacpac held up his empty bottle. Chunca drank his down to the last quarter then threw the bottle into the air. Water scattered on the ground.

'Thanks a bunch,' muttered Grandma.

'Ancient Inca custom,' Bacpac explained. 'Emperor offer last drops to Granddad so that he send rain to fill bottle.'

'No offence,' snapped Grandma, 'but Granddad doesn't seem to listen much.' She pointed at the cloudless sky. 'Come on. We've got a mountain to climb.' Dropping her chocolate wrapper, she headed into the woods.

21

A Tragic Tale of Tableware

'Oh it was peachy,' sighed Finbar the cave. 'When we first arrived there was never a squabble, never a tiff. All three of us were one.'

'How can three be one?' said Perdita.

The cave mouth tutted, a squelchy sound like a boot rising from mud. 'If you'll just let me finish ... I'm talking peace and love, sister. I'm talking major hoorays at escaping those Vikings. I'm talking one long hooley: thanking God like there was no tomorrow.'

Perdita couldn't help butting in again. 'You don't sound very – well – *monkish*. I thought they said things like 'thee' and 'thy' and 'wouldst thou pass the butter?''

'Ha!' snorted Finbar. 'Fooled you. That's how we *wrote*, so that people in future would read our manuscripts and think we were super-sacred. Holier than Thou, you could say.' Chuckles rippled out, flattening the grass in front of the girls.

Abbie wished he'd cut the corny jokes. But she guessed the suggestion wouldn't go down well.

'And we were for a while. Holy, I mean. Brother Oisín was cool as a cellarful of cheese. And our boss, Father Kenneth – what a leader. When he talked you listened, when he ordered you obeyed. A mighty man of God indeed.' The cave lips trembled. 'Until he forgot the God bit.'

Abbie frowned. 'The *Annals of Donal* said he was gentle.'

'Gentle?' Air gusted out of the cave. 'Oh, he put on a show in front of Bro Do. And in front of us too, at first. But as time went on, power went to his head. Started throwing his weight about, skiving off work. Told us God needed him twenty-four seven. "Brother Fin," he'd say, "The Lord wants a chat. Knock me up some breakfast, would you?" or "Brother Oisín, I can't plant the barley. God wants my hands muck-free for prayer."'

Good one. Abbie imagined trying that after dinner: '*Sorry Mum. God wants my hands Fairy-Liquid free for prayer.*'

'But pushing us around,' said Brother Finbar, 'only pushed us together. The more Kenneth bullied, the closer we got. He became jealous of our friendship. And that made things worse. He ordered us to weed the crops, knead the bread, fish and farm till the cows came home – which they only did when *we* fetched them. The final straw was when he used the goblet as crockery.'

The girls gasped. So the treasure was real – it had really

existed! They hugged their knees and held their questions. Even Perdita knew better than to interrupt now.

'One day we found Father Kenneth in his hut. And can you believe it – he was slurping soup from the Goblet of Dripping!' There was a hissing sound as Finbar drew an outraged breath. 'Sacrilege. But when we protested, Kenneth just laughed. "Zip it, losers," he said, "God told me not to waste good tableware." Well!' The lips pursed. 'That

did it. Oisín and I decided to rescue the Lord's treasure from this nut job and take it to safety. Not back to Ireland – that was fast becoming a Viking resort – but maybe some quiet little island to the west.'

Abbie couldn't help a smile. America was hardly a quiet little island.

'So we plotted our escape in secret. Except it wasn't, thanks to my big mouth.' The rock-lips sagged like a sad banana. 'Father Kenneth met us on the moor one day. "Nice plan, Fin," he said. "And thanks for sharing it. Overheard you talking to Oisín. So I've hidden the goblet from your grubby little paws." Ooh, the sneer on his face. Oisín and I saw red. A scuffle broke out and – I swear this is true –'

'What?' Perdita shuffled forward on her bottom.

'Father Kenneth fell into a bog. No one pushed him, honest to God. There wasn't so much as a nudge. You've got to believe me.'

'Course we do,' said Abbie reassuringly.

'We weren't murderers. But we weren't stupid either. "Tell us where the treasure is," shouted Oisín. "*Then* we'll pull you out," I yelled. "Not on your nellynoo," hollered Kenneth, trying to get out by himself. We hesitated – just for a second. But it was a second too long. When we reached out to grab him, he was up to his chest. And the more he struggled, the faster he sank. "Curse you," he screamed, "I'll get you for this! I'll drag you down. I'll hunt you and hound you from under the ground. This land won't have peace while I'm still around!" And then …' the lips paused, 'he was gone.'

Abbie pictured a thrashing soup of monk and marsh slowly settling into green calm. She shuddered. Horrible. But if Kenneth really was so awful …

A nasty little question slunk into her mind. *What would I have done?* It was like one of those magazine quizzes to test how lovely you are.

> Your worst enemy has fallen into a bog. Do you:
> a) Reach out to rescue him/her
> b) Watch him/her sink, or
> c) Run away.

'Well,' she said, moving on swiftly, 'at least you and Brother Oisín could live in peace.'

The red lips shrank to a jelly bean. 'You'd think so. And at first we did. We agreed to forget about finding the goblet and live out our days on the island. But the weird thing was, as the weeks passed we began to find fault with each other. Oisín's calm turned to laziness.'

'And I bet he got fed up with your big mouth,' said Perdita helpfully.

Abbie thumped her arm. 'Now look what you've done,' she hissed as the mouth clamped shut.

'Sorry,' said Perdita. 'I was just getting into the story. Please go on.'

The rocky lips opened a crack. 'Well now you mention it, that *is* what he said. We began to argue about everything: whose turn it was to cook, whose prayers were better, who God loved more. I knew our quarrels were stupid but I couldn't stop. In fact I almost enjoyed them. You know the feeling?'

Oh boy – like I know my own brother. Abbie glanced at Perdita and felt a blush rising. *Or my best friend.*

Finbar's voice dropped. 'It was as if Kenneth was still around.'

Abbie swallowed, trying to coax water into her throat. 'How? He was dead.'

The cave-mouth sighed. 'Death. We think it's so simple when we're alive. One minute there, one minute gone, to angel choirs and eternal rest. But it wasn't like that with Kenneth. They say there's no peace for the wicked. Well, his body may have gone, rotted into earth. But it was as if his character – his spirit or essence, whatever you call it – lived on. As if his greed and selfishness and jealousy had leaked into the earth, poisoned our food and polluted our air. As if we were eating and drinking and breathing them in.'

The air was hot and still. Bushes sat like sentries. The grass stood in stiff blades.

'One day,' the cave-mouth coughed, 'after a nasty tiff

over whose turn it was to quern, I'd had enough. I decided to give up monking – kick the habit.' Finbar paused while the girls laughed dutifully, though it was the last thing they felt like doing. 'All I had to do was find the goblet and nick the boat while Oisín was asleep. I'd row back to Ireland, buy a nice little pad in the new Viking town of Cork.' He was talking more quickly and quietly. 'I searched the island, found the cave behind the waterfall. And like you, I thought the goblet would be there. But as I stepped inside, a rock fell and hit me on the back. My spine cracked and I collapsed.'

Abbie shivered, remembering the rockfall that had blocked up the passage. She'd thought that her shouting had loosened the stones. But had something else been at work?

'I cried out for Oisín.' A rattle crept into Finbar's voice. 'But he couldn't hear me. So I lay there and waited to die.'

'What a horrible end,' murmured Perdita.

'Horrible, yes. End – no such luck. My body just sank into the earth, as if something was pulling me down. And here I've lain ever since, condemned to this living death.'

'What do you mean?' whispered Abbie. Sweat nibbled the back of her neck.

'Kenneth was a powerful man. And his words were powerful too. He *did* drag me down, just like he said he would. And he's hounded me ever since. I can feel him in my limestone, taste him in my quartz. For a thousand years he's been filling my veins, taking me over. He almost took you over too – till you fought back with friendship.' There was a whistling sound as Finbar struggled for air. 'Told you he'd be livid. He's clogging me up. Can't fight any more. But you can.'

From inside the cave came a dull thudding sound. Abbie ran forward and pressed her palms against the rock. She stood on tiptoe. 'What are we supposed to do?' she yelled into the gloom. Great clods of mud and rock were falling, piling up on the floor.

'Your only hope …' the lips were slowing, as if freezing over, 'is your friendship.'

'What are you on about?' yelled Perdita.

But Finbar spent his last breath doing what he loved best. 'Kenneth always said … I was a bigmouth. Well not any more.' The cave was a slit. 'Ha … good one … me.' The girls stared in horror as the lips fused to a thin red line.

***

'Deep breath, chaps. It's all uphill from 'ere.' Emerging from the woods, Grandma pointed up the mountain. Klench was a green blob clambering towards the rocky heights. 'For a lardy lad, 'e's pretty nimble.' Licking her dry lips and squinting in the sunlight, she set off up the slope. Chester wriggled between sunhat and sweatband duties. Chunca followed, then Bacpac who reached out his arms and pushed his master valiantly from behind.

***

Dad pressed his fingertips into his forehead and scanned the beach for the bazillionth time. 'Why would she just wander off?'

'Maybe she found something,' said Ursula. She clamped her lips over the dreadful alternative. That something – or some*one* – had found her.

***

'There.' Marcus pointed across the stream. A square of golden paper glinted in the heather. 'Another wrapper.'

'Litterbugs,' said Terrifica. 'Look how they've broken the Guide Landscape Law.'

'Good job,' said Marcus. 'Otherwise we'd have no idea where they went.'

Mr Dabbings fiddled with a strap of his rucksack. 'If it *is* them. I mean, we're assuming the old folk left this trail. But what if it was that villain?' He glanced round nervously.

'Doesn't matter. If it was, they probably spotted these wrappers too, and followed him. So either way we're on the right track.' Marcus waded through the stream and picked up the Ferrero Rocher paper.

'No.' Terrifica followed and snatched it from his hand. 'I

232

hate to do this but …' she bent down and tied it to a sprig of heather, 'we should leave it here. Then if anyone needs to find us, they'll know where we've gone.'

Marcus shook his head. '"Anyone" could be Klench. What if *he* sees the wrappers and follows *us*?'

Terrifica shrugged. 'We have to risk that. A Guide always stays in touch.'

'*I* know!' Mr Dabbings put up his hand as if he was the pupil. 'How about I go back to the huts and tell the others where you've gone? Then you can keep the countryside clean *and* follow the trail.'

Marcus and Terrifica strode back through the stream.

'Nice try, Sir.' Terrifica took his left arm.

'But you're the responsible adult.' Marcus took his right. And, for once in complete agreement, they marched him through the water, across the moor and towards the woods.

22

Stick-in-the-Mud

'Finbar?' Perdita tried to prise the red line apart with her fingers. 'Say something!' She pressed her fists into the rock. 'You can't just close up!'

Abbie put a hand on her shoulder. 'What if he didn't? What if he was closed up?'

Perdita sprang back. 'We have to get out of here! Which way back to the huts do you reckon?' She looked round the glade.

Abbie tilted her head to listen. Beneath the buzz of flies came a low, distant roar. If the tunnel had brought them through the mountain and out the other side, that could be the sound of the waterfall.

She followed it to the right, leading them round the base of the mountain through bracken and brambles that scratched like cats. Nettles stung, thistles chafed, the sun burned the back of her neck. Her head throbbed with thirst and confusion. *A rocky monk? A monky rock? Friendship the only hope … of what?* It was all too much to take in.

As they rounded the mountain, the view opened out.

'Yess!' Abbie threw out her arms. Ahead of them, beyond a thicket of trees and bushes, lay the lake. The girls crashed through, oblivious to thorns, and tore across the beach.

Abbie waded up to her waist, bending down to scoop great mouthfuls of water. She ducked under, closing her eyes as the cold wrapped her neck, punched her brain, bounced round her head and filled her bones. She came up for air, threw her head back and whooped. 'Bliss!' She whooshed armfuls of water at Perdita who shrieked and splashed back. They floated on their backs and gazed into glittering blue.

'Hey,' said Abbie. 'You realise that if Finbar couldn't find the treasure, the Vikings probably couldn't either.'

Perdita frothed up water with her feet. 'So?'

Abbie stood up. 'So it could still be here.' Lifting her palms, she watched silver threads stream through her fingers. 'When Finbar said friendship's our only hope, maybe he meant that if we all work together – properly this time, no arguments – we'll find the treasure. It kind of ties in with all that crazy stuff about the monks ruining everything by quarrelling.'

Perdita splashed her. 'You can't be serious. We just nearly died in a tunnel, got coughed out of a cave – and you're still talking treasure hunts!' She turned towards the beach. 'I'm going to find Mr Dabbings. He needs to phone for the boat right now.'

Abbie smacked her hands on the water. 'I'm just saying one last look, while we wait for it to come. No sneaking or cheating.'

Perdita wheeled round, her eyes huge with outrage. 'How stupid can you get?' She bunched a fist against her ear. 'Hello? Earth calling Lettuce Head.'

Abbie clenched her own fist. 'Hear you loud and clear, Weed Brain.'

'Fine!' Perdita stomped onto the beach. 'Do what you want. I'm out of here.'

'Hey, wait for me.' Abbie waded after her.

Or rather tried to. 'What the–?' She felt the ground soften beneath her. 'My foot!' Mud was oozing over her sandals, between her toes. With a huge effort she pulled out a foot and tried to step forward. But now the other one was stuck. A bubble popped in front of her. Another on her left ... and now they were snapping and spreading in all directions. 'Help!'

Perdita spun round and dashed back to the water's edge.

Waves were growing, carving foamy lines across the lake, slapping against Abbie's waist. Mud sucked at her shoes, her heels, her ankles. 'I'm sinking!' she screamed.

For a second Perdita froze. Only her eyes moved from the lake to the beach as the horror of her choice sank in.

Then she crashed into the water. She managed a few steps before the mud took hold. She stretched out her arms to Abbie. But it was no good. Between them lay a metre of churning, sobbing water.

Sobbing? That's what it sounded like: a soft moan that rose and fell with the waves. Except that as it grew louder the waves grew smaller, as if feeding the sound with their energy. Abbie tried to lift her foot again. This time it jerked up from the mud. She sprawled forwards and crashed into Perdita.

Holding hands, they staggered to the edge of the lake. The mud was firming beneath them. The bubbles were shrinking, the waves subsiding. Gently they pushed against Abbie's back, nudging her out like liquid knuckles.

The girls dashed up the beach. From the safety of the undergrowth they turned and stared at the muttering water.

Because muttering it was – apparently to itself. 'Couldn't keep 'em in … choked me up … ah, the memories.'

Abbie's hand flew to her mouth. *Those words – just like Brother Finbar's!* And suddenly she knew. Grabbing Perdita's hand, she held it high, as if they were Olympic rowing champions. 'Yes,' she shouted, 'we're friends!'

Perdita gaped at her as if she'd finally popped her pretzels.

'Friends?' Irritable little waves slapped the shore. 'Waste of time. Nothing but trouble if you ask me.'

Courage rose in Abbie. 'He says he's sorry, Brother Oisín.'

Perdita gasped. Abbie put a finger to her lips.

The waves crisscrossed in confusion. 'What … who … where?'

'Brother Finbar.' Abbie pointed behind her. 'He's round the mountain there.'

The waves froze in stiff little peaks, as if holding their breath.

Abbie frowned. 'Didn't you know? He's in a cave – I mean, he *is* a cave.'

The water resumed its rhythmic surge. 'All I know is he never came back.'

Perdita found her voice. 'He – he couldn't. He was injured in the cave. He lay there calling for you.'

'You're. Kidding. Me.' Each word broke the surface in a bubble. 'When I. Was calling. For *him*.'

'Why?' said Abbie.

The waves broke in white frills. 'Did he tell you about our row?'

'Whose turn to quern,' said Perdita.

A sigh rippled the water. 'I bet he said it was mine. That was Brother Finbar all over. He could talk a fly into a web, a pig into sausages. But not this time. I'd had enough of his lip. When I told him so, he stormed off. To hell with you, I thought. To hell with our holy life. I decided to find the goblet and leave.'

'Just like him,' said Perdita.

'I knew it!' A shadow darkened the gleaming water. 'That lousy skunk of a monk.'

'No,' said Abbie quickly. Relations had been bad enough for the past thousand years; why make them worse? 'He's never forgiven himself for arguing with you.'

Perdita raised her eyebrows. 'Hasn't he? I don't remember him …' Abbie put a finger to her lips.

'Well pop my peppercorns!' The water bobbed gently. 'Who'd have thought?' The shadow lifted. 'All these years he's been lying there, feeling as bad as I do.' Sunlight capered once more on the lake.

Abbie coughed delicately. 'So. The goblet. Did you find it?'

'Oh, I searched all morning. But the sun was warm and I was tired.' A long, low yawn curled out of the water. 'I lay on the beach and nodded off. Must've rolled in, because next thing I knew I was six foot under water.'

Abbie's mouth went dry. 'So you swam back to shore,' she said hoarsely. How she wished that were true – and how she knew it wasn't.

'Couldn't swim. Couldn't even drown. Just kind of *melted* into the lake. Where Kenneth has hounded me, stirred my waters and churned my mud, for hundreds of years without a minute's rest.'

So *that* was why the lake was never still, why it fretted endlessly beneath a windless sky. 'And the bubbles?' said Abbie. 'The sudden storms?'

'Don't you see?' A sigh tickled the surface. 'His wicked- ness feeds on conflict – jealousy and greed, fighting and rage. Your quarrelling strengthens his power over me. That's why I nearly sucked you down.' The voice was getting softer.

Cold fingers crept up Abbie's spine. All their squabbles and tiffs, all the envy and resentment she'd felt on this trip … she imagined them feeding the cave and fouling the lake like wicked fertiliser. 'Is that what Finbar meant?' She swallowed. 'By friendship being our only hope?'

'It was ours too,' whispered the lake. A brown patch

appeared on the surface, spreading over the blue-green water. 'We could've escaped this, Finbar and I, if only we'd made our peace.'

'You still can,' cried Abbie. 'It's what Finbar wants.'

'It is?' Perdita blinked. 'I never heard him ...'

'Shh!' hissed Abbie. 'I'm just trying to help.'

Muddy clouds were mushrooming all over the lake. The water was turning completely brown. Ripples spread to the shore, licking the pebbles with filthy tongues.

'After all these years – who'd have thought?' The girls craned forwards as a last whispering gasp rose from the water. 'Well I'm sorry ... too ... Brother ... Fin–.'

The voice faded. The ripples calmed. The lake was a still, brown soup.

'Wow,' murmured Perdita. 'Do you think he's found peace at last?'

If only, thought Abbie. *But why the mud? Why the silencing of the lake?* Setting off back to the huts, she tried to ignore the other possibility nibbling the edge of her mind ... that it was anything *but* peace that had shut Brother Oisín up.

***

'What on earth?' Dad ran onto the beach. He'd been searching the undergrowth with Ursula when they'd noticed the lake turning brown. 'For goodness sake, what's going *on* here? And where in Heaven's name could those girls have got–'

'Shh!' Ursula raised a finger. A crunch of pebbles. A murmur of voices. A foot, a leg, and then round the bend came …

'Abbie!' Dad hurtled towards her.

'Perdita!' Ursula scuttled behind him.

***

'It's no good.' Grandma sat on a boulder. 'I've got to 'ave a drink.'

Bacpac bent down. Pulling up a daisy from a patch of grass, he popped it into his mouth. 'Peughh!' he cried – the ancient Quechua word for 'Peughh' – and spat it out. 'In my country,' he said, 'we have flowers that store water. When you thirsty, land provide.'

'Well this isn't your country,' Grandma snapped. 'And if someone doesn't provide pretty soon, I'll be *pushin'* up daisies.'

Chester wriggled down to wipe her face, her neck and – way beyond the call of duty – her armpits. Then he dived into her rucksack, brought out her empty bottle and rolled it a little way down the mountainside.

'Genius!' cried Grandma.

Chunca, who was picking dandelions and blowing the puff, bowed.

'Not you, Peabrain. Chester's offerin' to nip back down through the woods and across to the stream to fill up me bottle.' She lifted the binoculars and peered up the mountain. 'Looks like Klench is diggin'. If 'e stays there a while, we shouldn't fall too far behind.' She picked Chester up and kissed his dusty curls. 'Off you go, chuck. We'll wait 'ere. Quick as you can, now.'

***

Digging Klench was. And digging and digging. And sweating and cussing while Mummy was fussing. 'Hole is too shallow, you pink marshmallow. Give it more velly, you melting jelly.'

His face was indeed pink. His legs did indeed feel like jelly. And he was indeed heading for a meltdown.

23

Abbie's Horrible Hunch

'I think you need to lie down, darling.' Dad leaned over and felt Abbie's forehead with his hand. 'The sun can play the weirdest tricks.'

Abbie pushed him away. 'For goodness sake, Dad. You've got to believe me.'

'It's true,' said Perdita. 'I saw them too.'

They were sitting in Abbie's hut. After their reunion in the undergrowth, Abbie and Perdita had collapsed with exhaustion and promised to tell their story after lunch.

Over a slap-up first course of omelette (made with Kinder eggs) the girls had been updated on who was missing and who was searching. When Perdita learned that Klench was on the island, she almost choked on her Kinder toy.

Over a knockout second course of barley cake and Jungle Jellies, the hut party had been updated on the girls' adventure. When Dad learned that two monks had somehow fused with the landscape, he almost choked on his strawberry anaconda. 'A cave that cracks jokes and a lazy lake? It's a little hard to swallow.' He put his arm round Abbie. 'Though not as hard as you two, by the sound of it.'

Matt hugged Perdita. 'Thank goodness.' The Platts were sitting with their backs to the stone bench. The stretcher lay on top.

'We imagined pretty much everything,' said Coriander, squeezing Perdita's hand. 'Except that.' Her leg was stretched straight in front of her. Henry was massaging her Binkles-wrapped ankle. 'Cave puke,' he said, gazing at the girls with a new respect. 'Awesicks.'

Ursula nibbled a blackcurrant jaguar. 'I don't get it. How can a person turn into landscape?' Everyone looked at Matt.

'Well.' He took off his glasses and rubbed his eyes. 'I guess we're all made of chemicals – carbon and silicon and stuff – just like the land. And when we die, and our bodies decay, they go back into the earth.'

'But Finbar and Oisín didn't die,' said Abbie. 'They're still alive. At least ...' she trailed off, remembering the sealed cave and the muddied lake. 'Who knows what they are?'

Dad jumped up. 'Never mind the science – what about the history? The *living* history!' He paced round the hut. 'Don't you see? This is huge. This is research grants. This is

documentary heaven. I'm seeing academic papers, confer-
ences, a whole new branch of–'

'Dad!' exploded Abbie. 'Don't *you* see? If Finbar merged
with a cave, and Oisín lived on in a lake, then what about
Father Kenneth? They talked about him as if he's still
around. But where?'

The words hung in the air. Dad stopped pacing. Henry
stopped massaging. Ursula stopped nibbling. And three
earwigs stopped discussing who had the biggest bottom.

At last Matt mumbled, 'Where indeed?'

Abbie swallowed. Because suddenly she could guess.
She'd suspected, or rather sensed, it all along. 'The woods.'
It all made sense – or as much sense as anything on this
horrible island. If Kenneth had fallen into that bog at the
edge of the trees, could he somehow have merged with
those woods, just like Finbar had merged with the cave
and Oisín with the lake? It would explain that feeling she'd
had of entering a presence, a living world of watching trees
and breathing earth. Her stomach twisted at the thought
of what they could have disturbed, picking plants and
gathering firewood in that wicked gloom. What the others
might be disturbing right now: Grandma and the Incas, or
Mr Dabbings, Marcus and Terrifica.

Her breath caught in her throat as Oisín's words came
back. *Your quarrelling strengthens his power.* Marcus and
Terrifica would be quarrelling for England.

'We have to find the others,' she said hoarsely. Pressing her hand against the cool, calming stones of the hut wall, she looked round. 'Who's coming with me?'

'Oh no,' said Dad. 'Oh no no no. You've caused enough trouble, my girl. I absolutely forbid you from–'

'Rescuing your mother.'

There was an awkward pause, during which Henry got back to massaging, Ursula resumed her nibbling, and the earwigs found a tape measure to settle things once and for all.

'Oh,' said Dad at last. 'Right. Of course. Off we go then.'

Perdita leapt to her feet.

'No!' cried Coriander, trying to stand up. 'Ow!' She collapsed against the bench.

'You're staying right here.' Matt put a hand on his daughter's shoulder.

'I'll go.' Ursula got up and turned to Perdita. 'You need to look after your mum.'

Perdita shook her head. 'Sorry. But I'm going with the girl who saved my life.'

Coriander clutched a plait. Matt rubbed his teeth. How could they argue with that?

Abbie's heart did a high jump. *Best friends again or what?* She couldn't help a teeny smirk at Ursula.

Who, to her amazement, smiled back. 'OK then,' she said to Perdita, '*I'll* look after your parents.' She patted

Matt's arm. 'You and Henry mind Coriander. I'll stand guard. And if Klench appears, I'll sort him out.'

It was Abbie's turn to smile. A week ago she'd have scoffed to think of this gnat of a girl confronting Klench. Now she almost pitied the hefty horror.

They waited outside while Matt fetched three water bottles from the food tent. 'Good job I filled up the jerrycans this morning,' he said, nodding towards the muddy brown lake.

Everyone agreed and managed not to say what Abbie guessed they must be thinking: *Let's hope the water lasts until we get off this island.*

***

'We haven't seen one wrapper in here.' Marcus peered at the dark soil, littered with leaves and twigs.

'It's hard to see anything in these woods,' said Mr Dabbings. 'Tell you what, why don't I go back to the huts and collect some cand–'

'No,' said Terrifica sternly. 'You're staying right here. We need all the eyes we can get.'

'What's the point?' Marcus kicked a root. 'We've lost the trail. You're right, Sir, we might as well go back.'

Terrifica shook her head. 'A Guide never gives up.'

'Well on you go then.' Marcus shooed her off with his hand. 'And good riddance!'

Terrifica glared at him. 'You're just jealous because I'm better at tracking than you.'

'Why so you are,' Marcus sneered. 'That must be why we're lost.'

Terrifica stormed off between the trees.

'Waity ho!' Mr Dabbings stumbled after her, pushing back branches that interwove ever more thickly. 'Don't wander off, Terrifica. Remember I'm the responsible adult. Besides,' he panted, 'I'll never find the way back alone.'

'I will,' said Marcus behind him. 'Come on, Sir. We're wasting our time.'

'Oh are we?' came Terrifica's triumphant voice.

They stooped under branches that locked together, thick as thatch, and found her grinning and pointing at a footprint. Small and wide, it led to another … and another, between the trees.

Marcus snorted. 'Those could be ours, from when we came in here before.'

'There's only one set. We came in a group.'

'Well so did Grandma.' Mr Dabbings stared at Marcus. Who stared at Terrifica. Who stared through the trees. 'Yikes.'

With a finger on her lips, she crept a few steps beneath dense branches. Beckoning furiously, she crouched down. They joined her at the edge of a clearing. In the middle stood a mint-green tent. The footprints led to the doorway.

The flap had been rolled right up.

'A tent,' Mr Dabbings whispered, rather unnecessarily. 'Grandma had no tent.' His sideburns trembled.

Terrifica peered across into the doorway. 'Empty. Phew.'

'Yeah phew,' muttered Marcus, rolling his eyes. 'Phew that you led us to Klench's hideout.'

Mr Dabbings ducked behind a tree. 'He could be anywhere, waiting to spring on us.'

'Now what, Miss Wonder Woggle?' hissed Marcus. 'Stay here and wait for a deadly criminal to wander home, or leave and risk bumping into him?'

'*I* don't know. *You* think of something for a change.'

'I always do. But you just ignore me and make everyone do what *you* want, like you're the Guide of the Universe. Doesn't she, Sir?'

'Oh belt up!'

The children's mouths fell open. Mr Dabbings had never spoken so harshly. 'To be honest, kids, I've had it with both of you. Nothing but bickering all the way. I'm going back.'

Marcus's eyes went wide. 'But what about Abbie's grandma? You can't leave her to Klench.'

'You just watch me.' Mr Dabbings turned. The others followed the few steps to the spot where Terrifica had found the footprint. The undergrowth seemed thicker and darker than ever.

'Blast!' Mr Dabbings's rucksack caught on a bramble bush. 'Now where?'

Terrifica, who'd followed him pointed to the right.

'No.' Marcus pointed left. 'Remember that holly bush?'

'No,' said Terrifica and, 'Ouch!' as her foot caught in a root.

Marcus frowned at a tree with fungus on the trunk. Had they passed that before?

'Well?' squeaked Mr Dabbings.

Terrifica sat down on a log. 'Let me get my bearings.'

A bramble snagged Marcus's T-shirt. 'Ow!' Unhooking himself, he leaned against a tree. 'Face it, Girl Guide – we're lost.'

***

'Come on Chess, where are you?' muttered Grandma, wiping her forehead with her hanky. Chunca was lying on his back, using Bacpac's backpack as a pillow.

The old servant was looking up the mountain through the binoculars. 'Klench he digging. Klench he stopping. Klench he sitting on rock.'

***

'Vot you doink? Get ups.'

Klench didn't move.

Inner Mummy wagged her finger. 'If you slacken from

251

your duty, how you ever find ze booty?'

Klench folded his arms. 'Zere is no booty here, Muzzer. I'm sure ve are barkink up wronk mountain.'

'How dare you doubt me, lardy cake! You know I never make mistake.'

Despite the confident words, Klench noticed a quiver in her voice that suggested she might just be wondering, for the first time in his life, and possibly hers too, if she had, in fact, made a boo-boo.

Just a quiver, mind. But it was enough to wobble the lid of tyranny that had sat on him all his life. The lid that had suppressed all his rage and rebellion, kept it in check like a simmering stew. The lid that Grandma had loosened.

And that now, at last, blew off.

You don't want to know what words he used. Some were so bad he didn't know them himself. But the gist was clear. There was something about bullying. Something about tormenting. Something about bossing him about while dossing on her butt. Something about abusing him, something about misusing him. Something about a stolen childhood. Something about birthday parties where she ate all his presents, including the Mr Men umbrella. And lots of things about letting rip in lifts and blaming it on him.

When he'd finished, she stared at him, speechless.

He met her inner gaze with cold, triumphant eyes.

Then he stood up, reached for his spade and set off down
the mountain.

24

Out of the Woods

Abbie, Perdita and Dad ran across the moor, jumping over the stream, not stopping till they reached the edge of the woods. Pausing for a quick drink, Abbie plunged inside and led the way between the trees.

Not that she *knew* the way. Grandma, Marcus and the rest could be anywhere in this gloom – if they were here at all. A twig snapped against her shoulder. Catching her breath, she glanced round. Even if they weren't here, *something* was. She could feel it in the stillness and silence, in the shadows that stroked her with weightless fingers. She imagined them stroking Marcus, Terrifica and Mr Dabbings. She pictured brambles snagging, ivy grabbing and soft damp earth sucking them down.

Don't. If there was any hope of rescue, they had to slip calmly and quickly through these woods without awakening more wickedness. Her heart whirring like hummingbird wings, she crept on.

'Aaarrgh!' Everything went dark. She staggered backwards, clutching her face. The darkness wriggled off.

'Chester!' she squealed. 'Oh thank goodness.' He climbed over her head. 'Where's Grandma?' She felt him against her back, rummaging around in her rucksack. 'What are you doing?' He brought out her water bottle and dropped it on the ground. Then he jumped onto her head and stretched up into a cone.

'High?' guessed Perdita. 'Pointy?'

'She's up the mountain,' said Abbie. Chester flew down to the bottle. 'And she wants water.'

They stumbled through the trees trying to keep up with Chester, who darted along the ground or leapt from branch to branch. A squirrel watched him fly between trees and dropped her pine cone to clap.

'Wait!'

Abbie spun round.

'Shh!' Dad had stopped and was standing with his head

cocked and one finger raised. Then she heard it too: a whisper in the undergrowth.

No. She glanced around wildly. *This is it. We've woken Kenneth.*

'Ouch.'

'What?'

'Get off my foot.'

'Terrifica?' Abbie murmured. 'Marcus?'

They followed Chester to the left, towards the voices. Branches scratched Abbie's arms. Her feet sank into spongy earth and caught in tricky roots. The voices grew stronger.

'You trod on it deliberately.'

'There's nothing I'd less rather tread on.'

'Ow. My hair's caught in … *ow!*'

'Sorry Sir. Just trying to pull it out.'

They reached a small clearing. On the right stood a tent. To the left was a cluster of trees and bramble bushes. Sticking up from one was the top of a golden head. 'Mr Dabbings?' Abbie's throat went tight. Had she been right? Were the woods finally devouring them?

The head popped up. 'Abigail! Thank heavens it's only you.' It dived down.

Marcus's head rose. 'We're hiding from Klench.' It ducked again.

Terrifica stood up. 'Not very well. The noise you lot are

making, he'll hear us a mile off. Quick!' She beckoned to Abbie, Dad and Perdita. 'He could be back any minute. We're trying to decide when to make a run for it.'

'Right now,' said Abbie. 'We've got to get out of these woods.'

Mr Dabbings bobbed up again. 'I'm not going anywhere until we know where he is.' He dropped down.

'For goodness' sake.' Abbie crept over to the brambles. 'Klench is the least of our worries. I thought you'd already been … oh never mind. But you've *got* to come. Now.'

Terrifica shot up. 'We haven't *got* to do anything. Stop bossing us about.'

Marcus stood up. 'Says the Empress of boss. Priceless.'

'No,' said Abbie desperately. 'Don't start quarrelling.' She pulled Terrifica's arm.

'Get off!' Terrifica yanked it away. 'I'll come when I'm ready.'

'Well I'm ready now.' Mr Dabbings appeared again. 'Thank goodness you're here, Graham. These two kids refuse to obey me – their teacher!'

'A useless one at that,' snapped Terrifica.

Disaster. They were all at it. Abbie looked at Perdita and Dad. Grabbing arms, T-shirts, rucksacks and hair, they tugged and lugged the squabblers. They had to get out before the woods got them. Chester led them through the dense gloom. At last the trees thinned and stopped, opening out onto the mountainside. Panting and blinking in the sunlight, they flopped down on a patch of grass.

Abbie took her water from her rucksack. Chester wrapped himself round the bottle as she drank. 'Alright, alright,' she said, screwing the lid back on. 'I promise I'll keep the rest for Grandma.'

Terrifica rubbed her arms. 'You didn't have to pull me so hard in there.'

'Oh but I did.' Abbie explained as quickly as she could about the monks and their warning – which was pretty slowly thanks to all the interruptions from Marcus, Terrifica and Mr Dabbings.

'You're kidding.'

'That's incredible.'

'To think we *swam* in that lake.'

It was certainly too slowly for Chester. While they oohed and aahed and you-can't-be-serioused, he squashed himself against the side of the bottle and tried to push it up the slope. But every time he stopped to catch his breath, it rolled back down.

'Give us a sec, Chess,' said Dad. 'Mother's a tough old toaster. She won't mind us resting for a minute.'

Abbie told them her theory: that if Finbar was in the cave and Oisín in the lake, then Kenneth must be in the woods. 'Except,' she frowned. 'How come nothing happened, even when you were quarrelling your heads off?'

Perdita pulled up a clump of grass. 'Maybe we were wrong.' She danced the roots over her lap. 'Maybe Kenneth fell into another bog: not that one by the woods.'

'But I could *feel* something watching us. I've felt it all along.'

Marcus tore a patch of moss from a rock and pressed it between his palms. 'Maybe it wasn't Kenneth you felt, but Klench.'

Of course! Relief surged through Abbie. She wasn't going mad. And even that foul flabster made a more appealing enemy than a tyrannical, landscaped monk.

'So if Kenneth's not in the woods,' said Terrifica, 'where is he?'

'Nowhere.' Dad stood up. 'And I'll tell you why.' He took out a hanky and wiped his forehead theatrically. 'Whatever strange geology is at work here – and I admit it's very strange – the only evidence that Kenneth is still around comes from two witnesses. Assuming – and I admit it's a big assumption – that they are who they *say* they are, how many flaws could there be in their story? Now let's see.' He held up his thumb. 'One. They're a thousand years old. The memory can play tricks. Two,' he waggled a finger, 'they must've felt bad about failing to rescue Kenneth. Guilt can mess up the mind big time. And three,' he raised another finger, 'they're going through some weird rotting process in which they haven't quite died. Who knows how *that's* meddling with their grey matter – or what's left of it? Simple historical detective work.' He bowed. 'I thank you.'

Abbie wanted to believe him, really she did. 'But what about the cave sealing up and the lake going still?'

'Ah.' Dad frowned. 'That's geology, not history. You'll have to ask Matt.'

Abbie hardly felt reassured. But with Chester tickling her like a hysterical duster, it was time to move on.

As they climbed higher, pausing every now and then to admire the view, her anxiety faded. The island spread below them. The treetops and moor, the muddy brown lake and humps of the huts, stood sharp and still as a photograph. Tiny mountain flowers scented the air with vanilla and honey. Insects whirred. Birds cheeped sleepily.

Except for one bird. Its cheep was anything but sleepy. In fact it was more of a bellow. 'We know you're up there!'

Shielding her eyes, Abbie looked up. Ten metres above her stood Grandma and the Incas. Their backs were turned. Grandma was yelling up the mountain.

***

'You can't 'ide from us! We've been watchin' you come down.' Above Grandma rose a slope of loose stones, ending at a rocky outcrop. 'Out you come, you rascal.' She shook her fist at the rocks.

***

260

'Don't you dare! You stay right zere,' hissed Mummy.

Klench gave her a long inner look. Then he sucked in his cheeks defiantly, stuck out his stomach giantly, edged round the rock and emerged at the top of the scree. 'Here I am, Grandma. I am comink to face your musics.'

25

A Rocky Run-in

Abbie gasped at the sight of the man who loomed so large in her nightmares. As usual, he loomed even larger in the flesh – and firmer too, thanks to the last few days of exercise. His biceps curved like courgettes beneath his mint-green shirt. His calves bulged like marrows below his knee-length shorts.

'You,' he snarled, spotting Abbie behind Grandma. 'Alvays you turn up like bad Penelope.'

She swallowed. Now wasn't the time to point out that he'd followed *them* to the island, or that her name was actually Abigail.

Grandma spun round. 'About time too!' she called down the mountain. 'Don't just stand there – chuck us some water.'

Chester had already brought out Abbie's bottle from her rucksack. She threw it up to Grandma who downed it in one. Dad and Mr Dabbings threw their bottles to the Incas who downed them in two. Chester flew up to Grandma's head. The others edged up nervously to join her below the scree. 'Stay where you are,' hissed Dad, nodding up towards Klench. 'He's a dangerous man.' Mr Dabbings dropped only too willingly behind the others.

'Time to go home, Mother.' Dad took Grandma's hand. 'No sudden moves. He's bound to be armed.'

'No!' At the top of the scree, Klench emptied the pockets of his shorts. 'I am veapon-free.'

'And why should we believe you?' barked Grandma. 'When you tricked me and escaped from prison?'

Klench held out his arms beseechingly. 'My head voss turned, Grandma, by You-Know-Who. Ven you mentioned treasure, she bossed me into escapinks.'

Grandma snorted. 'Wild goose chase. There's no treasure 'ere.'

'I know zat now. I have been sveatink my socks off, climbink my feet off and diggink my toes off. And now I have had it viz Her Upstairs. Oh yes, Mums.' He stamped his foot, causing a little landslide down the scree. 'You can stuff it vhere ze sun don't shine. I never bow to you again.' He bowed to Grandma. 'You must believe me, Madams.'

'Pwah!' said Grandma, in a no-I-mustn't sort of way.

'OK,' said Klench desperately. 'See – I am standink above you. I have advantage of higher position. Easily I could smack you down mountainside viz spade. But no.' He picked up the shovel and hurled it away into the rocks, where it landed in the nest of a golden eagle who came home to a rather upsetting dinner of scrambled eggs. 'You see?' Klench hung his head. 'I am truly sorry, Grandma.'

'Sorry?' Grandma put her hands on her hips. 'Sorry never washed the dishes. Sorry never built the Pyramids. It'll take more than sorry to make up for it, my lad. You owe me one.' She winked at the Incas. 'Quick, chaps, now's yer chance.'

Grinning from earhole to earhole, Chunca scrambled up the scree towards Klench. Biting his lip, Bacpac followed. The two old men used their hands to steady themselves on the stones, which rattled and slipped beneath their feet.

Near the top, Chunca turned and shouted down the slope in Ancient Quechua.

'Goodbye Grandma!' Bacpac translated. 'You kind as cocoa and tough as potato.'

Chunca looked up, saluted and shouted something at the burning sun.

'Put kettle on Granddad,' Bacpac translated. 'We there in a jiffy.'

Then Chunca Inca, four hundred and fifty-year-old Son of the Son of the Sun, reached out to take the hand of the stoutest crook.

Who snatched it away. 'Who are zese fruitcakes?'

Chunca reached for his other hand.

'Get offs. You think I help you? I never help anybody in my lifes.'

'Well you'd better start now!' Cupping her hands round her mouth, Grandma shouted up to Klench the Incas' story and prophecy. 'So you can jolly well take their 'ands, you scallywag, or you'll 'ave me to answer to.'

Klench was backing up against the rocks. 'Never!' A look of fear had come into his eyes. 'I do not shake hands viz strangers. Especially foreign vuns.' He shoved his hands in his pockets and shook his head, like a schoolboy refusing to do his homework.

'You do it now,' roared Grandma, 'or I'll 'ave your flabby guts for garters!'

'You do not understand, Grandma – I cannot!'

'Why the poppycock not, you great lummock?'

'Becoss … aaaah!' cried Klench as Chunca reached over and pulled his left hand out of his pocket.

This is it. Abbie caught her breath.

But before the Emp could hold it fast, Klench had snatched his hand free. 'Go avay!' he screamed, thrusting both arms behind his back and kicking at the scree. The Incas slipped down the slope. Chunca yelled. Bacpac yelled. Grandma yelled.

And Klench covered his hands with his ears. 'Shut ups! Shut ups!! Shut UPS!!!' His voice echoed round the rocks.

A stone, perched on a rock, teetered and fell. It rolled down the scree, loosening more stones. They tumbled past Abbie and down the mountainside.

Grandma tried to clamber up the slope. 'Wait till I get my 'ands on you, you mingy great melon!' Her feet loosened more stones.

'No Mother!' Dad tugged her T-shirt. She slid backwards. More rocks fell.

Above them, Klench slipped as the stones gave way beneath him. He slid down the scree on his bottom.

'Run!' roared Dad.

Mr Dabbings, of course, already was. Everyone hurtled after him as stones, rocks and a mint-green boulder that no one fancied being flattened by, tumbled down the slope.

Was she running or falling? It was hard to tell. Abbie's legs seemed to dissolve as they carried her down the

mountain, racing rocks and stones that bit her ankles, clattering and slithering and flinging up dust.

They were saved by the woods. Reaching the trees, more by gravity than leg-power, they plunged into the gloom, leaving the smaller rocks to slow and settle and the bigger ones to crash into the trunks.

After the glare of the mountain, Abbie was blinded by the darkness. But Mr Dabbings was making plenty of noise, snapping and crackling through the trees behind Chester, who seemed to know the way out. Blood thundered in her ears. Her chest was ready to split. But still she stumbled on. No way would she rest until they'd cleared these ghastly woods.

At last light broke through the trees. She staggered out of the undergrowth and flopped onto the moor, gasping for breath.

***

Klench heard the others crashing ahead through the woods. He stopped. Then he turned right and crept between the trees towards his tent.

He sat down on his reinforced air-bed and put his head in his hands. What to do? Wait for them to leave the island then continue his treasure hunt? 'Vot treasure?' he muttered. Grandma was right: there wasn't any.

Phone Brag right now to fly over and fetch him? 'Vot

fetch?' he snorted. Brag would never come if he had no treasure.

Head out of the woods and surrender?

'Vot nonsense!' Mummy shrieked.

There was his answer. If it was bad enough for Mummy, it was good enough for him.

***

'At least the landslide's stopped.' Henry shielded his eyes with his hands and peered up the mountain. Hearing the distant rumble of rocks, they'd all hurried out of Abbie's hut. Or rather Henry had hurried, while Matt and Ursula had made a chair with their arms and carried Coriander. But their view had been blocked by the dust cloud that covered the mountainside.

'I just pray no one was up there,' said Coriander, easing herself down to sit against the wall.

26

Klench's Confession

Grandma and the Incas were the last to emerge from the woods. Hand in hand in hand, they staggered out and collapsed on the heather.

When she'd got her breath back, Abbie turned to Mr Dabbings. 'Where's your phone? Now we know where everyone is, you can call Bundy.'

He needed no encouragement. Fishing the phone from his rucksack, he made the call. 'Bundy's on his way. We'll go to the huts, get the others and head for the beach.'

Everyone jumped up except the Incas. Chunca jabbered and pointed at the woods.

'Master say we cannot leave,' translated Bacpac. 'Not until we find stoutest crook. He run off in trees.'

Grandma snarled. 'That selfish lump. After all I've done for 'im – 'e couldn't even manage one teeny good turn.'

'It's not even a good turn,' said Perdita, 'ending someone's life. You'd think it would be right up his wicked street.'

'No,' squeaked a voice. They looked up. Klench was staggering out of the woods. 'It is up different street entirely.' Keeping his hands firmly behind his back, he blinked round the group. 'Zat is vot I try to explain on mountain. You see ...' he bit his lip. 'In my whole life, I ...' he took a deep breath, 'I never killed no vuns.'

There was a stunned silence. *Of all the biggest, whoppingest* ... Abbie tried to arrange her mouth round the word 'lies.' But it froze.

His crimes raced through her mind. Kidnapping Coriander in the zoo, holding them hostage in the hair museum, running a hotel for supercrooks, smuggling animals, money laundering, robbery, Chinese-burning toddlers and pensioners. Most involved guns, but none actual murder. She'd always thought it was luck that had saved them. But could it possibly have been Klench himself?

She was suddenly back in the Amazon jungle last Christmas. Along with Perdita, Coriander and Grandma, she was staring down the barrel of Klench's gun while he explained his plan to shrink their brains. When Grandma had asked why he didn't just kill them, what had he said? 'Killink is borink.' Had that just been an excuse? Hubris Klench was many things: cruel, spiteful, pompous, greedy, wheedling, creepy, nitpicking. But a killer?

'I cannot do it,' he whimpered. 'I have stomach for many

thinks, but not murder. Plus, I am tired of eefil doinks. My body is free but my mind is broken. I give ups, Grandma. Take me back to jail and teach me to be goods.'

Abbie stared at the dust-streaked, droopy-shouldered, deflated beach ball. Maybe it was exhaustion speaking, maybe despair, but that was the nearest he'd ever come to remorse. Two words flashed across her mind. Words that made as much sense together as 'hot snow' or 'Yippee, maths.'

'Poor' and 'Klench'.

Poor Klench? She gouged her palms with her fingernails. *Don't be crazy. He's fooling us.*

But his face was as grey as a mushroom and his arms were raised in surrender. 'Zere is nothink more for me here. No treasure, no peace. Take me back to prison, Grandma. Only in chains can I be free.'

'With pleasure.' Grandma folded her arms. 'As soon as you've put these fellows out of their misery. Tit for tat.'

'I cannot tat.' Klench shook his head wildly, as if trying to ward off a wasp. 'Shut *up*, Muzzer.' He blinked at Grandma. 'For vunce Mums agree viz you. She tell me to be a man and kill zese fellows. But I cannot.'

'But they *want* to die!' Perdita jumped up. 'Don't you see? You'll be doing them a favour.'

Klench scrunched his lemon peel eyebrows. 'How many times must I tell you – I never do anyvun favours but myself. And if I killed zese chaps, myself vould be vay upset.'

Bacpac was translating rapidly. Chunca jumped up, ran to Klench and tried to grab his arms. But they were clamped firmly behind his back. Klench jerked away. The Emp shook his fists.

'Master say you selfish as snake and piggy as peccary,' said Bacpac. 'He say anyone who disobey Son of Son of Sun will be sorry.'

Klench shrugged. 'Not as sorry as if I obey.'

Bacpac laid a calming hand on his master's arm. But Chunca had torn off his earmuffs. Throwing back his head, he yelled at the sky.

'Uh oh,' said Bacpac in a trembly voice. 'Now he tell Granddad to kick up stink.'

Mr Dabbings clapped a hand to his mouth. 'He can't actually control the sun, can he?'

'Course not, you great flowerpot,' snapped Grandma. ''E just thinks 'e can. 'E can't control anythin' any more. That's the point. 'E's got nothin' to live for.'

Mr Dabbings stood up. 'I'll thank you not to call me a flowerpot, you old battleaxe.'

'Don't you insult my mother,' said Dad.

'But that's exactly what she is.' Terrifica put her hands on her hips.

Marcus nudged Abbie. 'And she's a young one.'

'How dare you compare my grandma to … aagh, what's that?' A shiver rose out of the earth and up Abbie's legs.

Dad strode over to Chunca who was still shouting at the sun. 'Stop it!' He clapped a hand over the Emp's mouth.

Bacpac snatched it away. 'At last Granddad listen. Do not mess with Inca power.'

Abbie blinked up at the sun burning a hole in the sky. Had it really answered the Emperor, shaken the ground at his command? She didn't fancy staying to find out.

They set off towards the huts. Thank goodness there were no more tremors. The moor stretched ahead, still and solid, not a whisper of wind stirring the tiny purple flowers of the heather.

Looking back, Abbie saw Grandma dragging Bacpac by one hand and Chunca by the other. With his free hand the Emp was alternately shouting at the sky and shaking his fist at Klench, who trailed them at a careful distance.

***

'There they are!' shouted Henry. He was standing with Ursula at the top of the ridge squinting across the moor.

'Who?' Coriander called up the slope.

Ursula checked. 'Everyone. Perdita, Mr Dabbings, Abbie's grandma – and the rest.'

'Thank goodness.' Sighing with relief, Coriander sank back against the wall.

'Oh, and there's someone else behind them. A real chunker. Kind of waddling more than walking.'

Coriander shrieked.

'Get down!' yelled Matt, who'd been rewrapping Mr Binkles round her ankle. 'He might have a gun.'

Henry half ran, half fell down the slope. Ursula dived onto her stomach. Peering over the ridge, she called, 'Doesn't look like it. And now he's heading off to the left.'

The Platts looked at each other.

'What's he up to?' said Coriander.

'Who cares? Let's just grab what we can and go.'

***

The engine of the *Fidgety Bridget* juddered to life. 'Wonder what the pwoblem is,' murmured Bundy Pilks, steering the boat out to sea. His hand moved towards his chin. 'Oh poops.' It was at times like this that he most missed his beard. It would have been just the thing to rub thoughtfully. Instead he patted the steering wheel. 'That teacher sounded wowwied on the phone, Bwidgy,' he said to the boat that had become his closest friend in the last six months. 'Ah well. At least it's calm. Come on, old gal. We'll have 'em back by dark.'

27

Wobbles

At last everyone was back at the huts. Well, nearly everyone.

'Where the Butterscotch is 'e?' Grandma looked up at the ridge of the moor. 'I thought 'e said 'e was surrenderin'.'

Everyone had gathered by the wall, where Matt and Ursula had piled the hastily packed rucksacks. They were now taking down the food tent, folding up the poles and canvas. As for the Potted Histories – no one wanted to leave litter but there was no choice. It would be hard enough carrying Coriander without lugging those crates back over the moor.

'I guess Klench has a problem,' said Abbie, leaning against the wall. 'On one side he wants to come with us, which means he has to stay close. On the other side he doesn't want Chunca to hold his hand, which means he has to stay away. And that's what he's doing now.'

Coriander was still sitting with her back to the wall. 'Well away he can stay. I refuse to go on a boat with that

276

monster. He'll find some way to throw me overboard, I know it.' She rubbed her ankle fretfully.

Abbie patted her shoulder. It was true that Coriander shared more horrific history with Klench than anyone. She'd been kidnapped in a zoo, held hostage in a hair museum, holed up in the jungle and threatened with brain shrinkage. You could understand why boarding a boat with him didn't appeal.

But Grandma was having none of it. 'Nonsense. There's bound to be ropes on deck. I'll gladly tie 'im up meself.' She turned to the Incas. 'Then I'll grab 'is chubby paw and you can 'old it as fast as you like.'

Bacpac translated. Chunca blew Grandma a kiss.

'Ropes won't stop him,' cried Coriander. 'Remember the Hair Museum?'

Fair point. Abbie recalled last summer when Klench had been tied up with two others and somehow wriggled free.

'Oh yes they will,' said Grandma. 'Trust me.'

'Why should I?'

Another fair point. Abbie remembered last Christmas when Grandma had persuaded Coriander that Klench was reformable.

'I'll never trust you again where he's concerned,' Coriander shuddered.

'Well too bad, Missus. Coz 'e's comin' with us.'

'No way.' Matt put his arm around Coriander.

'Yes way.' Grandma put her hands on her hips.

Mr Dabbings stepped forward. 'Now look here. As the teacher responsible for these precious children, I can't possibly allow a hardened criminal on board.'

'Bunkum. You can do what I bloomin' well tell you.'

'Bossy boots.' Terrifica glared at Grandma. 'I've got a better plan. We leave him here with the Incas, then they chase him round the island till they catch him.'

Grandma snorted. 'Those old codgers won't get within a mile. 'E may be a porker but he can't 'alf move. And 'e's bound to find some way of escapin'.'

Abbie imagined him breathing in, jumping in and floating away: an inflatable, lemon-haired dinghy.

'Their only chance of death is on the boat.' Grandma folded her arms. 'Klench is comin'. End of story.'

'Oh no it's not.' Matt pushed his glasses up his nose.

'We owe it to the Incas,' snapped Grandma.

'We owe it to ourselves,' said Mr Dabbings.

'Oh shut it, you great wet wipe.' Grandma stamped her foot.

'How dare you … aaagh!' Mr Dabbings staggered backwards as the ground shivered beneath him. Abbie lost her balance and was thrown against the wall. There was a dull thud.

'Look!' cried Ursula. A stone slipped out from the lower part of the wall of the nearest beehive hut. It hit the ground and broke in half. Another stone, loosened by the hole, dropped out.

The ground shuddered again. A slate slid out from another hut. Two more followed.

Those who were standing grabbed each other. Those who were sitting spread their palms on the ground to steady themselves.

The earth went still. Dad couldn't help himself. Walking gingerly across to the nearest hut, he picked up a broken slate. 'Wow.' He shook his head. 'Secure for ten centuries … broken in a second. Unbelievable.'

Abbie stuffed a fist in her mouth as a thought punched through her: terrible, improbable - yet possible. The land-slide on the mountain, the tremble on the moor. It wasn't feet that had loosened the rocks. It wasn't the sun that had shaken the ground. Pressing her hand against her stom-ach, she forced out slow, deep breaths. *Keep calm.* She ran her tongue over her lips and rehearsed what to say. From now on every word counted. 'Listen to me. Take your bags, leave everything else. Go to the beach. Now. No arguing.'

Despite the croak, there was an authority in her voice that made everyone reach for their rucksacks.

Coriander tried to stand. 'Aagh!' She sank against the wall.

Matt turned and crouched in front of her. 'Get on my back.'

'You'll never carry me all the way to the beach.'

'We can take it in turns,' said Ursula. But while she might be strong enough to give a piggy back, she was too small to stop Coriander's foot dragging along the ground.

'Where's the stretcher?' said Abbie.

Matt pointed to the big hut. 'I was going to fetch it when–'

'You carry Coriander up to the ridge.' Abbie turned towards the hut.

'Oh no.' Dad gripped her arm. 'Don't even think of it. It's not safe.'

'It's fine,' said Abbie pulling away as calmly as she could. 'I'll be quick.'

'I said no, Abigail! And this time,' he shouted, 'you'll do what you're jolly well told!' As he lunged towards her, the ground shuddered, throwing him backwards.

'Stop it, Dad,' she said quietly. 'See you in a mo.'

'Come BACK!' he yelled, as she raced towards the biggest hut. Another wave rippled out of the earth. More stones slid out of the walls, leaving gaps that dislodged even more.

As Abbie ducked into the entrance, a stone dropped from above and narrowly missed her head.

At least the ground had stopped shaking. She crept across the floor towards the stone bench, trying not to disturb things further.

'Ow!' A stone stung her head. Her hand flew to her scalp. She pressed her fingertips into the pain. They came down covered in blood. Another stone stung her shoulder. Another and another … now they were tumbling all around. With the base destabilised, the roof must be caving in, like a geological Jenga. Shielding her head with her arms, Abbie fought her way through the razor-shar‑

rain. Oh why were the monks such craftsmen? Why had they honed every stone like a blade?

She reached out to the bench. *Phew.* Her fingers closed round the end of the stretcher. *That's it. Grab and go.*

But she didn't. Because underneath it, something else caught her eye.

A glint of yellow. A wink of red.

She gasped. Stones clattered down around her. Dropping the end of the stretcher, she rubbed her eyes.

For a moment she forgot that the ceiling was falling. For a moment she forgot she could be buried alive or cut to shreds in this vicious air. For a moment she forgot everything except the goblet, standing inside the hollow bench, exposed by the collapsing side, and dripping – yes, dripping – with rubies and diamonds.

Bending forward, she closed a fist round its thick golden stem. It didn't budge. She'd need both hands to lift it.

No! The choice danced before her. *The goblet or the stretcher?* She couldn't carry both. For a second she froze.

Only a second. Because, as she bent over the bench, a stone struck the back of her neck. A dizzying sickness shot through her, blazed into pain and shocked her to her senses. Seizing the end of the stretcher, she staggered across the floor through the falling rubble. By the time she reached the entrance, the archway had collapsed into piles of debris. She heaved the stretcher through and was out, coughing and blinking in the sunlight.

'Abbie!' Dad raced over. He tried to hug her. 'Your head – there's blood!'

'I'm OK.' The cut on her scalp was nothing compared to the pain in the back of her neck. But now wasn't the time to mention it. He was upset enough, trying to hug her and tell her off at the same time.

'That was stupid!'

She pushed him away. *What about brave? What about selfless?*

Over his shoulder the lake lay brown and still.

Your quarrelling strengthens his power.

Swallowing her angry retort, she dragged the stretcher towards the slope. Dad took the other end. Together they carried it up to the ridge where everyone else was waiting.

***

Well, nearly everyone. Grandma and the Incas had already set off for the beach, to give their old legs a head start.

***

And Klench?

If anyone had needed the loo, they'd have been less than relieved on visiting the little brown tent on the moor. He was standing on the seat, watching the escaping group through the air vent.

When they were well ahead, with Coriander sitting on the stretcher and Matt and Ursula carrying either end, he got down, unzipped the tent and crept after them, zigzagging from bush to boulder to bush like a mint-green pinball.

28

Finders Keepers

Abbie told herself it didn't hurt. Her arms and shoulders weren't on fire. The back of her neck didn't throb. She lagged behind the others, clamping her lips over all the pain and panic she mustn't unleash.

Not to mention frustration. The more she tried to forget the goblet, the more brightly it gleamed in her mind. Those rubies the size of Maltesers, the diamonds like glacier mints, winking and mocking from their stone hidey-hole.

It was no good. She had to tell someone or she'd explode. But who could she trust not to blab to the others, which could start a row about whether to go back, which could start … she bit her lip. *Don't go there.*

She fixed her gaze on the horizon. The sea was a grey smudge between moor and sky. The sun was beginning to sink, sprinkling the air with gold dust. A single cloud glowed at the edges like burning paper. Ahead of her Chunca kept looking up and waving.

Perdita hung back. 'He still thinks the sun's behind all this,' she murmured when the others were well ahead.

Abbie stared at her. So she'd worked it out too! 'Let him,' she mumbled, 'and let the others. Let them think anything till we're off this island.'

Except what we think, she added silently. *Because anything's better than that.*

She put a hand on Perdita's arm. 'I found it,' she said softly.

'What? You mean the treas–?' Perdita's yelp was stifled by a hand across her mouth.

'Keep your voice down!' hissed Abbie.

'Sorry.' Perdita's face was all eyes. 'Where?'

When Abbie whispered where she'd found the goblet, Perdita's hands flew to her cheeks. 'So you've been sleeping on it all week. Priceless!'

It certainly was. That was the problem. Regret spilled through Abbie. 'But how could I have carried it?'

'You couldn't. Don't worry, when all this is over, we can send someone back for it. And it's finders keepers.' Perdita lifted Abbie's arm in triumph.

'Shhh!' She pulled it down. But a smile rose through her aching body as she pictured the fame, the fortune, the fuss.

They walked on in silence. Ahead of them the stretcher-bearers were tiring. Matt and Ursula stumbled over mounds and dips in the moor, ever wary of changes in vegetation that could signal boggy land.

What with all the staggering and stopping to rest sore hands and weary legs, progress was slow. But at last the heather gave way to rocks and beach and slapping grey sea. Dad and Ursula lowered the stretcher onto the shingle while the others squinted across the water.

'There!' Terrifica pointed. A dot was bobbing on the horizon. Jumping up, she cupped her hands round her mouth. 'Yoo hoo Bundy!' she yelled, though he was much too far away to hear.

Marcus whooped. 'We're outta here!'

Chunca wagged his finger like a windscreen wiper. Then he turned and pointed back over the moor.

Bacpac followed his gaze. 'Master he say, where Klench?'

'Relax,' said Grandma. ''E'll come soon enough.'

'Master he not believe you.'

'Well Master can stick it in 'is ear'oles, because we're not traipsin' back over that moor again. We'll jolly well wait for 'im 'ere.'

Which is not the way to talk to the Ruler of the Known World and grandson of our nearest star, who's more than six times your age and who, even though he might not understand your words, can pick up your tone no problem. Chunca turned to her and yelled a stream of Inca abuse.

Abbie's hands flew to her ears. 'Be quiet!' she shouted as the ground buckled, then rose beneath her feet, sending her reeling backwards.

'Come back!' Grandma roared. Chunca and Bacpac were staggering back onto the moor. She turned to the others. 'If they run after Klench, 'e'll never come and get on the boat.'

'Thank goodness!' cried Coriander, and, 'Stuff Klench!' shouted Mr Dabbings.

'Stuff you!' bellowed Grandma. She turned to follow the old men.

And fell flat on her bottom. Because the ground was now rising and falling like a trampoline.

'Look!' yelled Henry. Everyone staggered round to follow his pointing finger.

Solid waves were rippling down the beach, rattling the pebbles and punching across the water. In the distance the *Fidgety Bridget* plunged and rose, bounced on a crest and spun away.

'No!' shouted Abbie. 'Bundy's turning back. Call him!'

Mr Dabbings grabbed the satellite phone from his rucksack. 'What do you mean you can't?' he yelled down the phone. 'You've got to come!'

'I'm *twying*!' the phone yelled back.

And failing. The *Fidgety Bridget* twirled like a rubber duck in a Jacuzzi, powerless against the sea's might.

A terrible stillness spread inside Abbie. Over the clatter of pebbles and crashing waves rose a silent scream. *We're stranded.* Slowly and fuzzily, as if in a dream, she turned round. The moor, too, was swelling and dipping: a sea of solid waves beneath a sky that was darkening fast.

Too fast. What was that blocking the sun?

'Look!' She pointed at the black dot in the sky. They watched it grow and judder towards them.

For a second everyone froze. Then all at once Matt and Ursula were stumbling down the beach to grab the stretcher, and everyone else was lurching towards the moor.

Thank you, Bundy, thank you! Abbie seized Grandma's hand. Of course – he'd called air-sea rescue. Hauling Grandma to her feet, she staggered after the others towards the helicopter that hovered over the heaving moor.

***

Klench too was heaving – the heaviest thing he'd ever heaved – over the shuddering earth. Not that he begrudged the weight. Every milligram brought joy to his heart.

And what a fickle heart it was. A heart that had longed to change: to shed its greed and spite and all those other vices that Mummy adored; to learn kindness and love and all those other virtues she abhorred ... until it heard that one little syllable.

Creeping behind the girls over the moor, Klench's sneaky-sharp ears had caught the sound 'Treas–'.

As soon as he'd heard enough, he'd dashed back across the moor to the huts. After fifteen minutes of scrabbling amid the stones he'd unearthed what he wanted. Running from the ruins of the hut, he'd made an urgent call on the phone he'd stuffed in his pocket before leaving his tent.

Now, as he rushed back to the beach to catch his lift, the ground had begun to wob-ble, sending him stumbling forward.

'Clumsy bumsie, do not trip,' shrieked Inner Mum-my. 'Don't you dare let goblet slip!'

If only he could let *her* slip! Hugging the huge cup, he dreamed of leaving her behind on this terrible island while he escaped with his glittering pass-port to wealth, luxury and eternal cream doughnuts.

***

'Cwipes!' squealed Bundy. Another wave curled over the boat and smashed onto the deck like a white-knuckled fist. The *Fidgety Bridget* nosedived, throwing him onto the steering wheel. As the boat bobbed up again, he regained his balance. Steering back towards the island, he stared through the window. Was it all this tossing and turning? Was it the spray blurring the screen? Or was the island really moving up and down?

'Turn awound,' he told his hands.

No, they answered, gripping the wheel. *Those kids are in twouble.*

'And we're in double twouble. We've got to go back.'

But whether from stubbornness or stupidity, Bundy's hands did the bravest thing of their lives. They wefused.

29

Gloop

Everyone stumbled towards the helicopter. It hovered ten metres above the quaking moor, the downdraught from the rotors flattening the heather. *Even if it can't land,* thought Abbie, *it'll send down ropes.*

'What's it doing?' screamed Terrifica, waving her arms above her head. 'Hey – we're over here!' But the helicopter was now veering to the left where a blob had appeared on the moor, silhouetted against the glowing sunset.

At the front of the group, Chunca let out a cry. Grabbing Bacpac's hand, he turned and lumbered towards the blob that took shape as a familiar fat figure, front-heavy with a load that sparkled in the fading sunlight.

'The *GOBLET!*' Marcus stopped dead. Matt crashed into him. Ursula dropped the back end of the stretcher, tipping Coriander onto the quivering ground. While they bundled her back on, Abbie staggered towards the helicopter. What was it doing? Why had it turned away? And who was that in the cockpit?

Reaching Klench, the helicopter swung round to face her. And now she understood. A claw gripped her heart as she recognised the grinning face beneath the wide-brimmed hat. That cowboy from the Amazon jungle! The villain who'd teamed up with Klench and tried to shoot her ... who'd been arrested then released because his fingerprints didn't match those of Brag Swaggenham, notorious oil baron and one of the crookedest crooks in the book.

'No!' she wailed as a single rope dropped through the sky from the helicopter. 'You've *got* to take us!' She blundered on, knowing it was useless: that he'd scoop Klench up and scarper.

Klench staggered towards the rope that swayed drunkenly in the propeller draught. He let go of the goblet with one hand and reached for the rope. But the cup was too heavy, even for him. It fell from his grasp and rolled away. Lunging forward, Klench cried out.

'What's 'e sayin'?' yelled Grandma behind Abbie.

'I can't hear. But it looks like his foot's stuck in a bog.'

Klench flailed his arms, trying simultaneously to pull out his leg and retrieve the goblet. But it was just beyond his reach, sinking slowly into the bog.

'Well don't just stand there. ''Elp 'im!'

Help? Abbie stared at the struggling blob. *Him?* The man who'd filled her nightmares and dogged her daydreams for nearly a year. The man who'd tried to remove her memory and ruin her life.

The man who couldn't kill.

She found herself moving towards him. Was it for Grandma, who was already pushing past her? Was it for the goblet that he'd managed to grasp with one hand? Or was it for Klench himself: that black-hearted, lemon-haired postman of cruelty, who'd brought her twice to the letterbox of death but never quite popped her in?

Before she knew it, Abbie had scrambled over the shaking earth and reached out to grab Klench's free hand.

'You!' he gasped, twisting round. His piggy eyes were a battleground of amazement, confusion and terror.

'Leave the goblet!' she yelled. 'I need to grab both your hands to pull you out!'

But now greed joined the struggle in his eyes. Instead of reaching for Abbie, he leaned out further, his fingers tightening round the rim of the cup.

'I'm losing my grip!' screamed Abbie. 'Drop it!'

Grandma grabbed her waist from behind. 'I gotcha!'

'It's no good. He won't let go. I can't ... *ooofff.* Something yanked Abbie backwards. She fell yelling and sprawling on top of Grandma. They looked up to see Bacpac standing over them.

A shriek split the air. Released from Abbie's grip, Klench

had lost his balance. Stumbling forward, his other foot had landed in the bog. He stood in the goo, waving one hand wildly as he began to sink. The other still clutched the goblet.

Abbie and Grandma lurched to their feet. Strong hands pushed them down.

'Leave us.' Bacpac's eyes were calm. 'Our time has come. Now he will hold our hands.' The old servant joined his master at the edge of the bog.

'Save me!' Klench was knee-deep in gloop.

Chunca reached out a hand.

The stoutest crook seized it. 'Get me outs!' he screamed.

The emperor looked up at the darkening sky. The dying sun danced in each shining eye. Then Chunca Inca, Ruler of the Known World and Pencil Case of the Unknown, jumped.

Bacpac leapt in after him.

'No!' screamed Klench.

'Yes!' sang Chunca, his feet plopping into the bog. Bacpac landed beside him. The Incas both seized Klench's free hand and held on for dear death.

Abbie crawled on all fours to the edge of the bog. The ground was bowing and rising more vigorously. While Grandma bobbed like a toddler on a bouncy castle, Abbie lay down on her stomach. She reached out both arms as far as she could towards Klench's other hand. It was still clasped round the top of the cup, now nothing but a golden ring in green goo. 'You have to let go!'

His knuckles whitened round the rim. He fixed her with glittering eyes. Then – Abbie couldn't tell if he lost his grip or gave up on the cup – he was reaching for her. She clutched his hand and tugged with every atom of strength.

It was a bucketload of atoms. But not enough. Klench was sinking faster by the second as if the bog, on tasting this vast profiterole, couldn't gobble it fast enough. Swamp slid up his thighs. His mouth gaped in silent anguish. Tears streamed down his face.

Chunca was grinning and shouting at him.

'Master say you hero,' said the sinking Bacpac. 'You have rescued us from the jaws of life. Do not cry.'

Klench cried.

Abbie was losing strength. Klench's weight was dragging her towards the bog. Her stomach sang with pain. She clawed at the ground with her free hand, cramming soil under her fingernails, uprooting clumps of heather. Her eyes blurred with sweat. Tasting earth and salt and the sour tang of terror, she slid uncontrollably towards the bog.

And stopped. She twisted her head round. Grandma had crawled behind and grabbed her ankles.

With Grandma pulling one end and Klench the other,

she felt like a Christmas cracker – without the joke inside. Something had to give.

The maths was simple.

$$O + O \neq \textbf{O}$$

Abbie plus Grandma does not equal Klench.

'Scchhhnnniiiikkkkkk!'

Klench's hand lost Abbie's. It smacked down, sending green blobs flying. He fixed her with tiny, bewildered eyes, up to his chest in swamp.

The Incas, too, were sinking fast. Chunca waved his free arm and shouted at the sky.

Faithful to the end, Bacpac translated. 'Milk and two sugars, Granddad. We comiiiing!' With a whoop and a gloop, the two old men sank into bright green silence.

And Klench? His head jerking backwards, he screamed his last word. Was it 'Money' or 'Mummy'?

***

'So long, suckers.' Brag Swaggenham pressed a button. The rescue rope reeled up into the helicopter.

When the jewelled goblet had sunk into the bog, Brag had let out a word that his mother never taught him. But he couldn't tear himself away from the drama. The death of The Flabmeister (as Klench was un-fondly known among his criminal un-friends) was not to be missed. So he'd hovered above the bog, enjoying the shrinkage of his former partner into a circle of lemon hair, a few bubbles and bright green oblivion.

Now he tipped his hat to the losers below, kids and adults, wriggling like weevils over the quaking moor. He smiled. Too bad about the treasure. But hey, this was fun. Why not hang around a while, watch those fools suffer, before abandoning them for Monaco and a good night's sleep?

***

Bundy's phone flew from the dashboard and smashed on the floor of the cabin. 'No!' Out of touch, out of reach, out of options … 'It's you and me now, Bwidgy!' he yelled, steering for his life towards the shore.

30

Wescue

Abbie stared at the bog. No Klench. No Incas. Just bright green soup, churning and slopping as the moor pulsed up and down.

She pressed her face into the heather and breathed its sweet, woody smell. For a moment she relaxed, let her body ride the rippling muscle of the earth.

Just for a moment. Because now she was slipping. She shrieked as the ground dropped behind her. Sliding backwards on her stomach, she crashed into Grandma. They rolled and slithered unstoppably towards the beach. The others, too, were tumbling uncontrollably. Coriander had long since lost the stretcher and was sliding on her bottom, with Matt one side and Ursula the other. Perdita, Marcus and Terrifica were still on their feet, half-running, half-falling. Dad and Mr Dabbings held onto each other, reeling and colliding like rubbish barn dancers.

Abbie clawed at tufts of heather, but they just came away in her hands. Clasping her head, she closed her eyes and surrendered to gravity. Oh the pain! Oh the sting and ache as the moor gave way to rocks that stabbed her already-smarting arms. Oh the dizzying sickness as she clattered down the beach, her brain break-dancing round her skull.

The ground was levelling beneath her. Rolling to a stop, she opened her eyes. Spray stung her face from the waves breaking over the beach … and over something else too.

'Quick!' she screamed, pointing. There was the *Bridget*, fidgeting away in the raging shallows. And there was Bundy, shouting and beckoning from the cabin.

Matt hoisted Coriander onto his back and led the way, splashing through the water to the rock'n'rolling boat, clambering up the ladder and falling onto the deck, the others close behind.

And then they were off, though in what direction was anyone's guess. They plunged and rose in the furious sea.

Lurching across the deck, Abbie looked up. The helicopter was still circling in the ink-blue sky peppered with the first stars. No doubt that horrible cowboy was waiting to enjoy the final spectacle of the boat smashing up in the waves. Crazy with rage, she threw her head back and yelled. Perdita lunged over and pulled her towards the cabin.

They didn't make it. A wave smashed over the stern, knocking them over and shooting the boat forward.

Not a moment too soon. Struggling onto her knees, Abbie looked up.

And screamed.

There are many kinds of scream. There's the spider-in-the-bath scream, the brother-in-your-bedroom scream, the caught-with-hand-in-sweet-tin scream and falling-in-cold-water scream. The I scream, you scream, we all scream for …

This was a new scream. Because no one in the history of screams had ever screamed at what Abbie was screaming at.

An island standing up.

The beach had tilted vertically and curved into a hollow, as if breathing in. The rest of the island was rising above it in a monstrous wall. The helicopter danced in front like a drunken insect, trapped in who knows what wild currents of air?

The sea was all at sea. Waves fought in all directions, clashing and cancelling or doubling in height. A breaker smashed over the side of the boat, punching a hole in the cabin wall. The *Bridget* listed to the right. Everyone tumbled through the hole onto the deck. More waves blitzed the boat. Abbie rolled and clung to whatever she could: ropes, iron posts, a ladder.

Bundy was still in the cabin clinging grimly to the wheel. But if he was trying to steer, he was wasting his time. No rudder or motor could fight the fury unleashed by the rising rock.

Catching hold of a rail on the side of the boat, Abbie pulled herself up. She clung on and stared in wordless horror as rocks fell from the climbing wall, crashed into the water and churned up the waves even more.

The island heaved upright, a colossal tower that blocked out the night. Stars came and went as it rocked forward and backward, ever more rickety.

The boat twirled wildly round the teetering pile. The mountains came into view, one above the other, two great triangles sticking out into the night.

Abbie's mouth fell open. Salt spray burned her tongue. But she didn't close it.

Because, just for a second, silhouetted against the sky, the island was a massive, monstrous **K**.

And then it was falling.

Everything faded – the roar of the sea, the bone-chilling cling of her clothes, the ache in her fingers from gripping the rail. She watched in a dream as the island curled over. Slowly at first, from the top – like a giant bowing its head – it toppled unstoppably, picking up speed as it fell.

She closed her eyes, unable to look.

She opened them, unable not to.

With a terror so complete it was calm, Abbie watched the island bear down on the helicopter, like a hand on a fly, smacking it into the sea.

The last thing she heard before the world exploded was Dad. '**Ho-ho-hold … o-ho-hon!**'

Everything went silent, fizzy and whizzy. Silent because the world exploding is enough to deafen the strongest ears. Fizzy because of the foam splattering her face. And whizzy because she was whizzing. At least her legs were, shooting out behind while her hands squeezed the rail as if her life depended on it – which, she discovered, it did. Because the *Fidgety Bridget* was flying.

Hitting the water, the end of the island had whipped up the wildest waves of all. One rising swell had caught the boat, carried it up and tossed it into the air. Now it was sailing through the sky. Through the spray she saw the others clinging on with their front ends while their back ends hovered above the deck – all except Chester who'd been flung off Grandma's head and was flying alongside.

Screwing up her face, Abbie braced herself for the landing, or rather sea-ing. The boat smacked on the water, sending her teeth into her brain and the deck into her stomach. Waves towered above the boat: skyscrapers in a liquid New York that roared louder than all the traffic in the world. The *Bridget* soared and dipped, hitting the stars and plunging into the troughs of waves.

Abbie's insides gave way to the ride. Her heart said hello to her mouth. Her stomach popped into her feet. Her lungs jiggled, her kidneys wiggled. A strange peace spread as she surrendered to the might of the sea.

Little by little the waves subsided. Every peak lowered, every trough rose. The rollercoaster levelled. And then they were bobbing in a great bathtub beneath a silent wide-eyed moon.

31

Best Friends

It was Grandma who broke the silence. 'We'd 'ave paid a fortune for that at Butlins.' She was sitting on Abbie's right, leaning against the railing. One of the lenses of her glasses had shattered. Squinting round, with Chester on her shoulder, she looked like a pirate with a hairy parrot.

A light rain began to fall. Abbie tilted her head back and opened her mouth. Oh the soft cold comfort on her salt-parched tongue! Oh the freshness of rain – the first on this trip – from a sky with the lid taken off.

Her hands were killing her. She looked down. They were still gripping the boat rail. Letting go, she wriggled her fingers and looked round. Miraculously the cabin lights were still working, bathing the boat in a dim halo. The other campers sat in a daze round the edge of the boat, bedraggled and shiny as seaweed.

Through the cabin window Abbie saw Bundy slumped over the wheel. The *Bridget* fidgeted left then right, nudged off course by the gentle waves. Chester scuttled into the cabin, crawled up and over Bundy's head and took the wheel.

Leaving Chester to steer, the little Cap'n staggered out to the deck. He sank down, dropping his head onto his knees. As if on cue, everyone shuffled over on their bottoms, still too nervous to stand.

'Well done.' Dad patted Bundy's oilskin back.

'Thank you,' said Coriander, laying a hand on his arm.

The chinless hero looked up. 'It was nothing,' he mumbled.

'It most certainly wasn't,' said Grandma. 'But what the bilberry *was* it?'

Bundy shook his head. Matt rubbed his temples. Coriander shrugged. Dad pressed his lips together. Mr Dabbings raised a teacherly finger … and dropped it.

'Not what,' murmured Abbie, 'who.' She gazed round the baffled faces. 'We were looking for Kenneth in the woods. But he was all over the island. He *was* the island. His jealousy and selfishness and greed had seeped into everything: the earth, the water, the trees. He even had the weather in his stifling grip. He infected Finbar and Oisín, sucked them into the island itself. And when we came along he infected us too, fuelled our jealousy and selfishness and greed.'

Perdita nodded. 'And we fuelled him with all our

arguing. The island got hotter and stickier as he got stronger and stronger, until that final dose.'

'Overdose, you mean.' Abbie shivered. 'Maybe Klench fell into the same bog as Kenneth did a thousand years ago. Maybe there was such a focus of wickedness there that Klench, with all *his* greed and selfishness, was too much to absorb – and the island finally flipped.'

Dad gave a low whistle.

Bundy looked utterly baffled. 'Sowwy guys. Wun that by me again.'

But just as Abbie was about to tell him all about the monks and the goblet, the curse, the cave and the lake, she heard a funny little snort. Then a sniff, then a grunt, then a soggy kind of snuffle.

She reached out her hand. 'It's OK, Grandma. Don't cry.'

'I'm not! It's me sinuses … the rain … me specs … the government … oh alright.'

For the first time in her life Abbie saw tears roll down the old lady's cheeks. 'I could've 'elped 'im, I know it. All 'e needed was another chance.'

Abbie patted Grandma's shoulder. 'He had plenty of chances. But he made his choice – to hold onto the goblet until it was too late.'

No one knew what to say. So they sat in silence and listened to little waves tick against the boat like the hands of a sluggish clock.

At last Matt got up and went into the cabin. While he took over the steering, Chester scampered out and dabbed Grandma's face.

'I'm all right, chuck,' she sniffed. 'Why don't you make yourself useful?' She nodded at Bundy. Chester wriggled over and wrapped himself round the actor's mini chin. 'Just a loan, mind,' she said, as Bundy stroked his living beard in wonder. 'I want 'im back when we get to the mainland. But I promise we'll find you a proper new beard.'

Bundy tickled Chester. 'That's vewy kind,' he said thoughtfully, 'but I'm not sure I'll need it. What we've just been thwough is enough to put bwistles on anyone's chin.'

Abbie, Terrifica and Ursula clutched their jaws in alarm.

'Not litewally.' Bundy giggled. 'I just mean, when you've seen an island cwash into the sea, audiences don't seem quite so scawy.' He grinned. 'So what if they laugh at my chin?' He clapped his hands. 'Who cares if they scoff at my jaw?' He stood up. 'They can widicule my voice.' He paced the deck. 'They can pooh pooh my jokes.' He punched the air. 'They can whistle and tease and thwow wotten tomatoes.' His voice was getting louder, his back straighter. 'They can mock my Macbeth, they can pan my Hamlet. But guess what?' He threw back his head and blew a raspberry at the moon. 'I don't give a hoot!'

It was a stirring performance. Everyone clapped. Bundy

bowed. Then he peeled Chester off and gave him back to Grandma. 'I'm weady to bwave the stage again.'

And that's exactly what he did. The critics raved at his new confidence. Within a few months the roles were pouring in. Sherlock Holmes, Robin Hood – even a stint as Tracy Beaker – you name it, he played it, never once with a beard.

Except at Easter. Every April he returned to the west coast of Ireland and stepped into the huge beard (tied firmly round his head) of Cap'n Winkymalarkey O'Rourkemelads. His fame drew boatloads of fans. With his trusty crew of Grandma and Chester, he ferried them in the *Fidgety Bridget* to a funny little whirlpool in the otherwise-calm sea: all that remained of Remote Ken. With 'Ahars' and 'Ahoos' – not to mention a few 'Cloot me rumscutters' – he told a tale of ancient monks and Irish treasure, of world-weary Incas and the stoutest crook, of two brave schoolgirls and the friendship that sank an island. When anybody doubted the story (and somebody always did) Grandma simply put a finger to her lips and pointed to the strange little eddies that smacked and fussed with an unmistakable 'Schnik' sound. Then the doubters apologised and everyone threw a ceremonial doughnut into the water.

Dad went home and made a BBC documentary called 'Sunken Monks: a Living Legend', narrated, of course, by

Bundy. When a Cambridge University historian wrote a letter to *The Sunday Times* accusing him of Hystoria, Dad wrote back and said, 'Believe what you like, Dr Nurdapples, the viewing figures speak for themselves.'

The children came home to find the rest of the class rehearsing a Zoosical. On the last day of the Easter holidays the whole school sat in front of the African savannah area and watched Bradleigh Zoo's ballet of the Lion King. It wasn't the easiest choice, considering there were no lions at the zoo. But Mum and Wendy had been working so hard at costumes that you'd never guess Simba was played by a tapir (dancing did wonders for his shyness) or that Scar the wicked lion was actually

Silvio the tiger. For an orang-utan, young Minnie did a wonderful job as the meerkat Timon. Her dad Vinnie made a less convincing Pumba. Despite the traffic cones sticking out of his mouth, the lazy orang lumbered far too slowly for a warthog. All in all, though, it was a splendid show, especially as it distracted Abbie from the difficulty she faced going back to school.

As the problem was mathematical, the obvious person to consult was Perdita. But Abbie came into the classroom next morning to find her best friend telling Claire Bristles breathlessly about their island adventure.

Or rather *one* of her best friends. When Perdita didn't even look up, Abbie turned to another one.

'Well,' said Marcus. 'You've got one seat next to you, and five days of the week. Why not sit by a different best friend each day?' Twenty minutes later he'd helped her draw up a timetable.

Day of the week	Who to sit next to	What this friend is best for
Monday	Marcus	• Being cool • Making fun of teachers in a (mostly) nice way

Tuesday	Ursula	• Comparing notes on embarrassing parents • Lifting stones when it's my turn to dust the classroom rockery
Wednesday	Terrifica	• Organising my homework timetable • Making hooks for crab-fishing in the class pond
Thursday	Henry	• Shouting out the wrong answer before Mr Dabbings asks me • Being generous with small pieces of fabric*
Friday	Perdita	• Being generous with all sizes of fabric, and people too • Being the best fun • Helping with maths • Not caring what people think (in a good way) but • Caring about the actual people (in a *very* good way)

*In an act of true heroism, Henry had donated Mr Binkles to cover Wendy's tum and keep the growing baby company.

Weekends, of course, were kept free for the zoo. Which is where she was on the second Sunday of term, helping to build a waterpark. Over the week, Matt had dug a ring-shaped channel at one end of the zoo pond, cutting off a little island. When it was finished, children would be able to cross over the walkway he'd built and explore the cave he'd constructed on the island. A hidden wind machine would whoosh them through a hole in the cave wall into an artificial lake that bubbled and churned.

Abbie looked up from the fibreglass cave she was painting with the rest of the class – or rather most of them.

'Where are Perdita and Urse?' Abbie put the finishing red touches round the mouth of the cave.

Matt shrugged. 'Maybe they've got something better to do.'

Abbie felt a sting in her chest. Why hadn't they invited her? *It's OK.* She took a deep breath. *They can do what they like. They're still my friends.*

'I was thinking, maybe I could make the cave and the lake talk,' said Matt. 'Then you could write a script and Bundy could voice it.'

'What? Oh, sure.' Abbie swallowed. *They don't have to invite me to everything. It's fine. Really.*

'Do you remember how Brother Finbar spoke?' said Matt. 'How he introduced himself?'

'Um.' She thought back to her conversation with the

cave. 'Something like, "In nomine Patris …"' she trailed off miserably.

'Et Filii, et Spiritus Sancti,' chanted a voice.

'Yes indeedie,' said another. 'Brother Finbar, pleased to meet you, top o' the morning, Amen.'

Abbie gasped as two monks in brown robes glided across the walkway. Reaching the island they stopped and threw back their hoods.

'For you.' Ursula (who was wearing her new Guide uniform underneath) put down the golden, jewel-studded goblet she was carrying. It was as tall as she was. On closer inspection, the gold turned out to be Ferrero Rocher wrappers, the rubies Wine Gums and the diamonds Glacier Mints. The inside was dripping with Kit Kats and Yorkies, Fruit Gums and Crunchie bars.

'Wow,' is what Abbie would have said if she'd been able to speak. Instead she stood and stared while Perdita explained.

'You found the treasure. And you never got to keep it. So the whole class chipped in and organised some real treasure – a year's supply of chocolate bars.'

And even when Abbie did get her voice back there really wasn't time to talk, what with all the eating and sharing – because, if there was one thing she knew, it was that there's always enough chocolate and friendship to go round.

Have you read the first two books in the series?

Welcome to the Hair Museum, where history has hairdos and fish have beards ...

When Squashy Grandma's teeth get stuck behind the radiator, Abbie meets the Very Odd Job Man, Matt Platt, and his daughter, Perdita. Drawn into a hair-raising hunt for Perdita's missing mum, Coriander, Abbie is helped along the way by Fernando, the heartbroken shrunken head of a Spanish conquistador, and Chester, a helpful patch of chest hair.

But waddling in the shadows is the white-suited, burger-shaped Hubris Klench. Abbie soon discovers that finding Coriander is one thing, but saving the world from Klench's 'eefil doinks' quite another.

www.mercierpress.ie

Illustrated by
Stella Macdonald

DEAD
HAIRY

Debbie Thomas

Welcome to the Amazon, where heads shrink and villains slink.

Abbie Hartley can't wait to join her friend Perdita Platt on the trip of a lifetime. Their destination? The Amazon jungle. Their mission? To find the wife of their friend Fernando.

There's only one problem. Fernando and his wife are shrunken heads and the Amazon jungle is huge.

Oh, and another one. Squashy Grandma insists on coming with her shopping bag on wheels and pet wig.

And just one more. Abbie's arch-enemy Dr Hubris Klench is lurking in the undergrowth with some very wicked tricks up his very wide sleeve.

www.mercierpress.ie

Jungle Tangle
Debbie Thomas
illustrated by
Stella Macdonald

MERCIER PRESS

IRISH PUBLISHER - IRISH STORY

We hope you enjoyed this book.

Since 1944, Mercier Press has published books that have been critically important to Irish life and culture.

Our website is the best place to find out more information about Mercier, our books, authors, news and the best deals on a wide variety of books. Mercier tracks the best prices for our books online and we seek to offer the best value to our customers, offering free delivery within Ireland.

A large selection of Mercier's new releases and backlist are also available as ebooks. We have an ebook for everyone, with titles available for the Amazon Kindle, Sony Reader, Kobo Reader, Apple products and many more. Visit our website to find and buy our ebooks.

Sign up on our website or complete and return the form below to receive updates and special offers.

www.mercierpress.ie
www.facebook.com/mercier.press
www.twitter.com/irishpublisher

Name: _____

Email: _____

Address: _____

Mobile No.: _____

Mercier Press, Unit 3b, Oak House, Bessboro Rd, Blackrock, Cork, Ireland